STREETS OF
BLOOD

Other books in the AMERICAN VAMPIRE SERIES

THE AMERICAN VAMPIRE SERIES

STREETS of BLOOD

VAMPIRE
STORIES
FROM
NEW YORK CITY

LAWRENCE SCHIMEL AND MARTIN H. GREENBERG

CUMBERLAND HOUSE
NASHVILLE, TENNESSEE

For Charles Ardai,

a fine writer,
a fellow anthologist and New Yorker,
and a friend.

—L. S.

Published by Cumberland House Publishing, Inc., 431 Harding Industrial Park Drive, Nashville, TN 37211.

Cover and interior design by Joel Wright.

Library of Congress Cataloging-in-Publication Data
Streets of blood : vampire stories from New York City / [edited by] Lawrence Schimel and Martin H. Greenberg.
   p. cm. — (The American vampire series)
  ISBN 1-888952-78-4 (alk. paper)
  1. Vampires—New York (State)—New York—Fiction. 2. Horror tales, American—New York (State)—New York. I. Schimel, Lawrence. II. Greenberg, Martin Harry. III. Series.
PS648.V35S77 1998
813'.0873808375'097471—dc21   98-5223
                                              CIP

Printed in the United States of America
1 2 3 4 5 6 7—04 03 02 01 00 99 98

Contents

Introduction

People come from all over the world to live in, work in, or visit New York City. And with them they bring their superstitions—and their monsters.

The city that never sleeps makes the perfect home for a vampire. At all hours, there's a pulse of life on the streets, ready and waiting to be tapped into. With more than eight million inhabitants crammed into such a small space, it's easy to maintain anonymity within the crowds—especially since New Yorkers are so inured to violence and danger. They keep their eyes on the ground in front of them. They don't look up, don't get involved. It's easy to lose oneself in the hustle and bustle, in the perpetual shadows cast by the tall skyscrapers.

At the same time, New York is famous for its many celebrities, and for the fact that one can run into some incredibly well-known people—actresses and sports stars and many others—on a street corner or in a favorite local eatery. There is a certain vampiric nature to fame, where ones fans and audience draws sustenance from a star, draining them of energy. Sometimes this relationship works the other way, as well. And sometimes . . . sometimes it is not merely a vampiric *nature* to the relationship, but a vampire indeed!

The city itself often seems to act as a vampire, draining energy through its relentless and unforgiving pace. Yet although New York has a reputation for eating people alive, still many are attracted by the allure of possibility that the city holds out to them—of fame, of fortune, of success. They flock to these streets to visit, to live, and sometimes to die.

The vampires in *Streets of Blood* are a cosmopolitan lot—they may arrive by airplane from some distant shore or leave by train to escape for a while the scene of their blood crimes. Some of these stories may visit other locales, for New Yorkers are always going someplace, even it it's just climbing the ladder of success. And in this city of skyscrapers, there's almost no end to the number of high vantage points one can find. If one is a vampire, these make perfect places from which to survey the night; but if one is a mere mortal, one had better watch the skies. . . .

The vampires in these stories have lived in the old world and have adapted to the new. You'll find stories about the underbelly of society and about its elite. You'll find stories with settings and characters that have made New York famous, elements that define the city—taxicab drivers and Central Park and Broadway, among many others.

But throughout all these stories there is one element that remains the same: that creature of darkness who prowls the streets of this city that never sleeps, looking for victims to feed its insatiable hunger.

—Lawrence Schimel

Acknowledgments

This book would not exist without the assistance of Stefan Dziemianowicz, which is greatly appreciated by both editors.

John Helfers also provided invaluable help in compiling and processing this project.

Thanks are also due to many others for suggestions and help in tracking down some of the stories included, but especially to: Keith Kahla, Greg Cox and The Transylvanian Library, Ellen Datlow, and Margaret L. Carter.

Sometimes one needs help that only the dead can give.

Nightside

BY MERCEDES LACKEY

t was early spring, but the wind held no hint of verdancy, not even the promise of it—it was chill and odorless, and there were ghosts of dead leaves skittering before it. A few of them jittered into the pool of weak yellow light cast by an aging streetlamp—a converted gaslight that was a relic of the previous century. It was old and tired, its pea-green paint flaking away; as weary as this neighborhood, which was older still. Across the street loomed an ancient church, whose congregation had dwindled over the years to a handful of little old women and men who appeared, like scrawny blackbirds, every Sunday and then scattered back to the shabby houses that stood to either side until Sunday should come again. On the side of the street that the lamp tried (and failed) to illuminate was the cemetery.

Like the neighborhood, it was very old—fifty years shy of being classified as "Colonial." There were few empty gravesites now, and most of those belonged to the same little old ladies and men that had lived and would die here. It was protected from vandals by a thorny hedge as well as a ten-foot wrought-iron fence. Within its confines, as seen through the leafless branches of the hedge, granite cenotaphs and enormous Victorian monuments bulked shapelessly against the bare sliver of a waning moon.

The church across the street was dark and silent; the houses up and down the block showed few lights, if any. There was no reason for anyone of this neighborhood to be out in the night.

So the young woman waiting beneath the lamp-post seemed that much more out-of-place.

Nor could she be considered a typical resident of this neighborhood by any stretch of the imagination—for one thing, she was young; perhaps in her mid-twenties, but no more. Her clothing, was neat but casual, too casual for anyone visiting an elderly relative. She wore dark, knee-high boots, old, soft jeans tucked into their tops, and a thin windbreaker open at the front to show a leotard beneath. Her attire was far too light to be any real protection against the bite of the wind, yet she seemed unaware of the cold. Her hair was long, down to her waist, and straight—in the uncertain light of the lamp it was an indeterminate shadow, and it fell down her back like a waterfall. Her eyes were large and oddly slanted, but not Oriental; catlike, rather. Even the way she held herself was feline; poised, expectant—a graceful tension like a dancer's or a hunting predator's. She was not watching for something—no, her eyes were unfocused with concentration. She was *listening*.

A soft whistle, barely audible, carried down the street on the chill wind. The tune was of a piece with the neighborhood—old and timeworn.

Many of the residents would have smiled in recollection to hear "Lili Marlene" again.

The tension left the girl as she swung around the lamp-post by one hand to face the direction of the whistle. She waved, and a welcoming smile warmed her eyes.

The whistler stepped into the edge of the circle of light. He, too, was dusky of eye and hair—and heartbreakingly handsome. He wore only dark jeans and a black turtleneck, no coat at all—but, like the young woman, he didn't seem to notice the cold. There was an impish glint in his eyes as he finished the tune with a flourish.

"A flair for the dramatic, Diana, *ma cherie?*" he said mockingly.

STREETS OF BLOOD

"Would that you were here for the same purpose as the lovely Lili! Alas, I fear my luck cannot be so good . . ."

She laughed. His eyes warmed at the throaty chuckle. "Andre," she chided, "don't you ever think of anything else?"

"Am I not a son of the City of Light? I must uphold her reputation, *mais non?*"

The young woman raised an ironic brow. He shrugged. "Ah well—since it is you who seek me. I fear I must be all business. A pity. Well, what lures you to my side of this unseasonable night? What horror has *Mademoiselle* Tregarde unearthed this time?"

Diana Tregarde sobered instantly, the laughter fleeing her eyes. "I'm afraid you picked the right word this time, Andre. It is a horror. The trouble is, I don't know what kind."

"Say on. I wait in breathless anticipation." His expression was mocking as he leaned against the lamp-post, and he feigned a yawn.

Diana scowled at him and her eyes darkened with anger. He raised an eyebrow of his own. "If this weren't so serious," she threatened, "I'd be tempted to pop you one—Andre, people are dying out there. There's a 'Ripper' loose in New York."

He shrugged, and shifted restlessly from one foot to the other. "So? This is new? Tell me when there is *not!* That sort of criminal is as common to the city as a rat. Let your police earn their salaries and capture him."

Her expression hardened. She folded her arms tightly across the thin nylon of her windbreaker; her lips tightened a little. "Use your head, Andre! If this were an ordinary slasher-killer, would I be involved?"

He examined his fingernails with care. "And what is it that makes it *extraordinary*, eh?"

"The victims had no souls."

"I was not aware," he replied drily, "that the dead possessed such things anymore."

She growled under her breath, and tossed her head impatiently, and the wind caught her hair and whipped it across her throat. "You are *deliberately* being difficult! I have half a mind—"

It finally seemed to penetrate his mind that she was truly angry—and truly frightened, though she was doing her best to conceal the fact; his expression became contrite.

"Forgive me, *cherie*. I *am* being recalcitrant."

"You're being a pain in the neck," she replied acidly. "Would I have come to you if I weren't already out of my depth?'

"Well—" he admitted. "No. But—this business of souls, *cherie*. How can you determine such a thing? I find it most difficult to believe."

She shivered, and her eyes went brooding. "So did I. Trust me, my friend, I know what I'm talking about. There isn't a shred of doubt in my mind. There are at least six victims who no longer exist in *any* fashion anymore."

The young man finally evidenced alarm. "But—how?" he said, bewildered. "How is such a thing possible?"

She shook her head violently, clenching her hands on the arms of her jacket as if by doing so she could protect herself from an unseen—but not unfelt—danger. "I don't know, I don't know! It seems incredible even now—I keep thinking that it's a nightmare, but—Andre, it's real, it's not my imagination—" Her voice rose a little with each word, and Andre's sharp eyes rested for a moment on her trembling hands.

"*Eh bien*," he sighed. "I believe you. So there is something about that devours souls—and mutilates bodies as well, since you mentioned a 'Ripper' persona?"

She nodded.

"Was the devouring before or after the mutilation?"

"Before, I think—it's not easy to judge." She shivered in a way that had nothing to do with the cold.

"And you came into this how?"

"Whatever it is, it took the friend of a friend; I—happened to be there to see the body afterwards, and I knew immediately there was something wrong. When I unshielded and used the Sight—"

"Bad." He made it a statement.

"Worse. I—I can't describe what it felt like. There were still residual emotions, things left behind when—" Her jaw clenched. "Then when I started checking further I found out about the other five victims—that what I had discovered was no fluke. Andre, whatever it is, it has to be stopped." She laughed again, but this time there was no humor in it. "After all, you could say

STREETS OF BLOOD

stopping it is in my job description."

He nodded soberly. "And so you became involved. Well enough, if you must hunt this thing, so must I." He became all business. "Tell me of the history. When, and where, and whom does it take?"

She bit her lip. "'Where'—there's no pattern. 'Who' seems to be mostly a matter of opportunity; the only clue is that the victims were always out on the street and entirely alone, there were no witnesses whatsoever, so the thing needs total privacy and apparently can't strike where it will. And 'when'—is moon-dark."

"Bad." He shook his head. "I have no clue at the moment. The *loup garou* I can recognize, and others, but I know nothing that hunts beneath the dark moon."

She grimaced. "You think I do? That's why I need your help; you're sensitive enough to feel something out of the ordinary, and you can watch and hunt undetected. I can't. And I'm not sure I *want* to go trolling for this thing alone—without knowing what it is. I could end up as a late-night snack for it. But if that's what I have to do, I will."

Anger blazed up in his face as if from a cold fire. "You go hunting alone for this creature over my dead body!"

"That's a little redundant, isn't it?" Her smile was weak, but genuine.

"Pah!" He dismissed her attempt at humor with a wave of his hand. "Tomorrow is the first night of moon-dark; *I* shall go a-hunting. Do *you* remain at home, else I shall be most wroth with you. I know where to find you, should I learn anything of note."

"You ought to—" Diana began, but she spoke to the empty air.

The next night was warmer, and Diana had gone to bed with her windows open to drive out some of the stale odors the long winter had left in her apartment. Not that the air of New York City was exactly fresh—but it was better than what the heating system kept recycling through the building. She didn't particularly like leaving her defenses open while she slept, but the lingering memory of Katy Rourk's fish wafting through the halls as she came in from shopping had decided her. Better exhaust fumes than burned haddock.

She hadn't had an easy time falling asleep; and, when she finally managed to do so, tossed restlessly, her dreams uneasy and readily broken—as by the sound of someone in the room.

Before the intruder crossed even half the distance between the window and her bed, she was wide awake, and moving. She threw herself out of bed, somersaulted across her bedroom, and wound up crouched beside the door, one hand on the light-switch, the other holding a polished dagger she'd taken from beneath her pillow.

As the lights came on, she saw Andre standing in the center of the bedroom, blinking in surprise, wearing a sheepish grin.

Relief made her knees go weak. "Andre, you *idiot!*" She tried to control her tone, but her voice was shrill and cracked a little. "You could have been *killed!*"

He spread his hands wide in a placating gesture. "Now, Diana—"

"'Now Diana' my eye!" she growled. "Even *you* would have a hard time getting around with a severed spine!" She stood up slowly, shaking from head to toe with released tension.

"I didn't wish to wake you," he said, crestfallen.

She closed her eyes and took several long, deep, calming breaths; focusing on a mantra, moving herself back into stillness until she knew she would be able to reply without screaming at him.

"Don't," she said carefully, "Ever. Do. That. Again." She punctuated the last word by driving the dagger she held into the door frame.

"*Certainement, ma petite,*" he replied, his eyes widening a little as he began to calculate how fast she'd moved. "The next time I come in your window when you sleep, I shall blow a trumpet first."

"You'd be a *lot* safer. *I'd* be a lot happier," she said crossly, pulling the dagger loose with a twist of her wrist. She palmed the light-switch and dimmed the lamps down to where they would be comfortable to his light-sensitive eyes, then crossed the room, the plush brown carpet warm and soft under her bare feet. She put the silver-plated dagger back under her pillow. Then with a sigh she folded her long legs beneath her to sit on her rumpled bed. This was the first time Andre had ever caught her asleep, and she was irritated far beyond what her disturbed dreams warranted. She was somewhat obsessed with her privacy and with keeping her night-boundaries unbreached—she and Andre were off-and-on lovers, but she'd never let him stay any length of time.

He approached the antique wooden bed slowly. "*Cherie,* this was no idle visit—"

"I should bloody well hope not!" she interrupted, trying to soothe her jangled nerves by combing the tangles out of her hair with her fingers.

"—I have seen your killer."

She froze.

"It is nothing I have ever seen or heard of before."

She clenched her hands on the strand of hair they held, ignoring the pull. "Go on—"

"It—no, *he*—I could not detect until he made his first kill tonight. I found him then, found him just before he took his hunting-shape, or I would never have discovered him at all; for when he is in that shape there is nothing about him that *I* could sense that marked him as different. So ordinary—a man, I think, and like many others—not young, not old; not fat, not thin. So unremarkable as to be invisible. I followed him—he was so normal I found it difficult to believe what my own eyes had seen a moment before; then, not ten minutes later, he found yet another victim and—fed again."

He closed his eyes, his face thoughtful. "As I said, I have never seen or heard of his like, yet—yet there was something familiar about him. I cannot even tell you what it was, and yet it was familiar."

"You said you saw him attack—*how,* Andre?" She leaned forward, her face tight with urgency as the bed creaked a little beneath her.

"The second quarry was—the—is it 'bag lady' you say?" At her nod he continued. "He smiled at her—just smiled, that was all. She froze like a frightened rabbit. Then he—changed—into dark, dark smoke; only smoke, nothing more. The smoke enveloped the old woman until I could see her no longer. Then—he fed. I—I can understand your feelings now, *cherie.* It was—nothing to the eye, but—what I felt *within*—"

"Now you see," she said gravely.

"*Mais oui*, and you have no more argument from me. This thing is abomination, and must be ended."

"The question is—" she grimaced.

"How? I have given some thought to this. One cannot fight smoke. But in his hunting form—I think perhaps he is vulnerable to physical measures. As you say, even *I* would have difficulty in dealing with a severed spine or crushed brain. I think maybe it would be the same for him. Have you the courage to play the wounded bird, *ma petite*?" He sat beside her on the edge of the bed and regarded her with solemn and worried eyes.

She considered that for a moment. "Play bait while you wait for him to move in? It sounds like the best plan to me—it wouldn't be the first time I've done that, and I'm not exactly helpless, you know," she replied, twisting a strand of hair around her fingers.

"I think you have finally proven that to me tonight!" There was a hint of laughter in his eyes again, as well as chagrin. "I shall never again make the mistake of thinking you to be a fragile flower. *Bien*. Is tomorrow night too soon for you?"

"Tonight wouldn't be too soon," she stated flatly.

"Except that he has already gone to lair, having fed twice." He took one of her hands, freeing it from the lock of hair she had twisted about it. "No, we rest—I know where he is to be found, and tomorrow night we face him at full strength." Abruptly he grinned. "*Cherie*, I have read one of your books—"

She winced, and closed her eyes in a grimace. "Oh Lord—I was afraid you'd ferret out one of my pseudonyms. You're as bad as the Elephant's Child when it comes to 'satiable curiosity.'"

"It was hardly difficult to guess the author when she used one of my favorite expressions for the title—and described me so very intimately not three pages from the beginning."

Her expression was woeful. "Oh *no*! Not *that* one!"

He shook an admonishing finger at her. "I do not think it kind, to make me the villain, and all because I told you I spent a good deal of the Regency in London."

"But—but—Andre, these things follow *formulas,* I didn't really have a choice—anybody French in a Regency romance has to be either an expatriate aristocrat or a villain—" She bit her lip and looked pleadingly at him. "—I needed a villain *and* I didn't have a clue—I was in the middle of that phony medium thing and I had a deadline—and—" Her words thinned down to a whisper, "—to tell you the truth, I didn't think you'd ever find out. You—you aren't angry, are you?"

He lifted the hair away from her shoulder, cupped his hand beneath her chin and moved close beside her. "I *think* I may possibly be induced to forgive you—"

The near-chuckle in his voice told her she hadn't offended him. Reassured by that, she looked up at him, slyly. "Oh?"

"You could—" He slid her gown off her shoulder a little, and ran an inquisitive finger from the tip of her shoulder blade to just behind her ear, "—write another, and let me play the hero—"

"Have you any—suggestions?" she replied, finding it difficult to reply when his mouth followed where his finger had been.

"In that 'Burning Passions' series, perhaps?"

She pushed him away, laughing. "Andre, you can't be serious!"

"Never more." He pulled her back. "Think of how enjoyable the research would be—"

She grabbed his hand again before it could resume its explorations. "Aren't we supposed to be resting?"

He stopped for a moment, and his face and eyes were deadly serious. "*Cherie*, we must face this thing at strength. You need to sleep—and to relax. Can you think of any better way to relax—"

"No," she admitted.

"Well then?"

She briefly contemplated getting up long enough to take care of the lights—then decided a little waste of energy was worth it, and extinguished them with a thought. "C'mere you—let's do some research."

He laughed deep in his throat as they reached for one another.

She woke late the next morning—so late that in a half hour it would have been 'afternoon'—and lay quietly for a long, contented moment before wriggling out of the tumble of bedclothes and Andre. No fear of waking him—he wouldn't rouse until the sun went down. She arranged him a bit more comfortably and tucked him in, thinking that he looked absurdly young with his hair all rumpled and those long, dark lashes lying against his cheek—he looked much better this morning, now that she was in a position to pay attention. Last night he'd been pretty pale and hungry-thin. She shook her head over him. Someday his gallantry was going to get him into trouble. "Idiot—" she whispered, touching his forehead, "—all you ever have to do is *ask*—"

But there were other things to take care of—and to think about. A fight to get ready for; and she had a premonition it wasn't going to be an easy one.

So she showered and changed into a leotard, and took herself into her barren studio at the back of the apartment to run through her *katas* three times—once slow, twice at full speed— and then into some *Tai Chi* exercises to rebalance everything. She followed that with a half hour of meditation, then cast a circle and charged herself with all of the Power she thought she could safely carry.

Without knowing what she was to face, it was all she could to, really—that, and have a good dinner.

She showered and changed again into a bright red sweatsuit and was just finishing that dinner when the sun set and Andre strolled into the white-painted kitchen, shirtless, and blinking sleepily.

She gulped the last bite of her liver and waggled her fingers at him. "If you want a shower, you'd better get a fast one—I want to get in place before he comes out for the night."

He sighed happily over the prospect of a hot shower. "The perfect way to start one's—day. *Petite*, you may have difficulty in dislodging me now that you have let me stay overnight—"

She showed her teeth. "Don't count your chickens, kiddo. I can be very nasty!"

"*Ma petite*–I–" He suddenly sobered, and looked at her with haunted eyes.

She saw his expression and abruptly stopped teasing. "Andre— please don't say it—I can't give you any better answer now than I could when you first asked—"

He sighed again, less happily. "Then I will say no more, because you wish it—but—what of this notion—would you permit me to stay with you? No more than that. I could be of some

STREETS OF BLOOD

use to you, I think, and I would take nothing from you that you did not offer first. I do not like it that you are so much alone. It did not matter when we first met, but you are collecting powerful enemies, *cherie*."

"I—" She wouldn't look at him, but only at her hands, clenched white-knuckled on the table.

"Unless there are others—" he prompted, hesitantly.

"No—no, there isn't anyone but you." She sat in silence for a moment, then glanced back up at him with one eyebrow lifted sardonically. "You *do* rather spoil a girl for anyone else's attentions."

He was genuinely startled. "*Mille pardons, cherie,*" he stuttered, "I—I did not know—"

She managed a feeble chuckle. "Oh Andre, you idiot—I *like* being spoiled! I don't get many things that are just for me—" she sighed, then gave in to his pleading eyes. "All right then, move in if you want—"

"It is what *you* want that concerns me."

"I want," she said, very softly. "Just—the commitment—don't ask for it. I've got responsibilities as well as Power, you know that; I—can't see how to balance them with what you offered before—"

"Enough," he silenced her with a wave of his hand. "The words are unsaid, we will speak of this no more unless you wish it. I seek the embrace of warm water."

She turned her mind to the dangers ahead, resolutely pushing the dangers *he* represented into the back of her mind. "And I will go bail the car out of the garage."

He waited until he was belted in on the passenger's side of the car to comment on her outfit. "I did not know you planned to race him, Diana," he said with a quirk of one corner of his mouth.

"Urban camouflage," she replied, dodging two taxis and a kamikaze panel truck. "Joggers are everywhere, and they run at night a lot in deserted neighborhoods. Cops won't wonder about me or try to stop me, and our boy won't be surprised to see me alone. One of his other victims was out running. His boyfriend thought he'd had a heart attack. Poor thing. He wasn't one of us, so I didn't enlighten him. There are some things it's better the survivors don't know."

"*Oui.* Drive left here, *cherie.*"

The traffic thinned down to a trickle, then to nothing. There are odd little islands in New York at night; places as deserted as the loneliest country road. The area where Andre directed her was one such; by day it was small warehouses, one-floor factories, an odd store or two. None of them had enough business to warrant running second or third shifts, and the neighborhood had not been gentrified yet; no one actually lived here. There were a handful of night-watchmen, perhaps, but most of these placed depended on locks, burglar-alarms, and dogs that were released at night to keep out intruders.

"There—" Andre pointed at a building that appeared to be home to several small factories. "He took the smoke-form and went to roost in the elevator control house at the top. That is why I did not advise going against him by day."

"Is he there now?" Diana peered up through the glare of sodium-vapor lights, but couldn't make out the top of the building.

Andre closed his eyes, a frown of concentration creasing his forehead. "No," he said after a moment. "I think he has gone hunting."

She repressed a shiver. "Then it's time to play bait."

Diana found a parking space marked dimly with the legend "President"—she thought it unlikely it would be wanted within the next few hours. It was deep in the shadow of the building Andre had pointed out, and her car was dead-black; with any luck, cops coming by wouldn't even notice it was there and start to wonder.

She hopped out, locking her door behind her, looking now exactly like the lone jogger she was pretending to be, and set off at an easy pace. She did not look back.

If absolutely necessary, she knew she'd be able to keep this up for hours. She decided to take all the north-south streets first, then weave back along the east-west. Before the first hour was up she was wishing she'd dared bring a 'walk-thing'—every street was like every other street; black brick walls broken by dusty, barred windows and metal doors, alleys with only the occasional dumpster visible, refuse blowing along the gutters. She was bored; her nervousness had worn off, and she was lonely. She ran from light to darkness, from darkness to light, and saw and heard nothing but the occasional rat.

Then he struck, just when she was beginning to get a little careless. Careless enough not to see him arrive.

One moment there was nothing, the next, he was before her, waiting halfway down the block. She knew it was him—he was exactly as Andre had described him, a nondescript man in a dark windbreaker and slacks. He was tall—taller than she by several inches. His appearance nearly startled her into stopping—then she remembered that she was supposed to be an innocent jogger and resumed her steady trot.

She knew he meant her to see him, he was standing directly beneath the streetlight and right in the middle of the sidewalk. She would have to swerve out of her path to avoid him.

She started to do just that, ignoring him as any real jogger would have—when he raised his head and smiled at her.

She was stopped dead in her tracks by the purest terror she had ever felt in her life. She froze, as all of his other victims must have—unable to think, unable to cry out, unable to run. Her legs had gone numb, and nothing existed for her but that terrible smile and those hard, black eyes that had no bottom—

Then the smile vanished, and the eyes flinched away. Diana could move again, and staggered back against the brick wall of the building behind her, her breath coming in harsh gasps, the brick rough and comforting in its reality beneath her hands.

"Diana?" It was Andre's voice behind her.

"I'm—all right—" she said, not at all sure that she really was. Andre strode silently past her, face grim and purposeful. The man seemed to sense his purpose, and smiled again—

But Andre never faltered for even the barest moment.

The smile wavered and faded; the man fell back a step or two, surprised that his weapon had failed him—

Then he scowled, and pulled something out of the sleeve of his windbreaker; and, to Diana's surprise, charged straight for Andre, his sneakered feet scuffing on the cement—

And something suddenly blurring about his right hand. As it connected with Andre's upraised arm, Diana realized what it was—almost too late.

"Andre—he has nunchuks—they're *wood*," she cried out urgently as Andre grunted in unexpected pain. "He can *kill* you with them! Get out of here!"

Andre needed no second warning. In the blink of an eye, he was gone.

Leaving Diana to face the creature alone.

She dropped into guard-stance as he regarded her thoughtfully, still making no sound, not even of heavy breathing. In a moment he seemed to make up his mind, and came at her.

At least he didn't smile again in that terrible way—perhaps the weapon was only effective once.

She hoped fervently he wouldn't try again—as an empath, she was doubly-vulnerable to a weapon forged of fear.

They circled each other warily, like two cats preparing to fight—then Diana thought she saw an opening—and took it.

And quickly came to the conclusion that she was overmatched, as he sent her tumbling with a badly bruised shin. The next few moments reinforced that conclusion—he continued scatheless while she picked up injury after painful injury.

She was a brown-belt in karate—but he was a black-belt in kung-fu, and the contest was a pathetically uneven match. She knew before very long that he was toying with her—and while he still swung the wooden nunchuks, Andre did not dare move in close enough to help.

She realized (as fear dried her mouth, she grew more and more winded, and she searched frantically for a means of escape) that she was as good as dead.

If only she could get those damn 'chuks away from him!

And as she ducked and stumbled against the curb, narrowly avoiding his strike, an idea came to her. He knew from her moves—as she knew from his—that she was no amateur. He would never expect an amateur's move from her—something truly stupid and suicidal—

So the next time he swung at her, she stood her ground. As the 'chuks came at her she took one step forward, smashing his nose with the heel of her right hand and lifting her left to intercept the flying batons.

As it connected with her left hand with a sickening crunch, she whirled and folded her entire body around hand and weapon, and went limp, carrying it away from him.

She collapsed in a heap at his feet, hand afire with pain, eyes blurring, and waited for either death or salvation.

And salvation in the form of Andre rose behind her attacker. With one *savate* kick he broke the mans back; Diana could hear it crack like a twig—and, before her assailant could collapse, a second double-handed blow sent him crashing into the brick wall, head crushed like an eggshell.

Diana struggled to her feet and watched for some arcane transformation.

Nothing.

She staggered to the corpse, her face flat and expressionless—a sign she was suppressing pain and shock with implacable iron will. Andre began to move forward as if to stop her, then backed off again.

She bent slightly, just enough to touch the shoulder of the body with her good hand—and released the Power.

Andre pulled her back to safety as the corpse exploded into flame, burning as if it had been soaked in oil. She watched the flames for one moment, wooden-faced, then abruptly collapsed.

Andre caught her easily before she could hurt herself further, lifting her in his arms as if she weighed no more than a kitten. "*Ma pauvre petite,*" he murmured, heading back toward the car at a swift but silent run. "It is the hospital for you, I think—"

"Saint—Francis—" she gasped, every step jarring her hand and bringing tears of pain to her eyes, "One of us—is on the night staff—Dr. Crane—"

"*Bien,*" he replied. "Now be silent—"

"But—how are you—"

"In your car, foolish one."

"But—"

"I can drive."

"But—"

"*And* I have a license. Now, will you be silent?"

"How?" she said, disobeying him.

"Night school," he replied succinctly, reaching the car, putting her briefly on her feet to unlock the passenger-side door, then lifting her into it. "You are not the only one who knows of urban camouflage."

This time she did not reply—because she had fainted from pain.

The emergency room was empty—for which Andre was very grateful. His invocation of Dr. Crane brought a thin, bearded young man around to the tiny examining cubicle in record time.

"Godalmighty! What did you tangle with, a bus?" he exclaimed, when stripping her sweatsuit jacket and pants revealed that there was little of Diana that was not battered and black-and-blue.

Andre wrinkled his nose at the acrid antiseptic odors around them, and replied shortly. "No, your 'Ripper.'"

The startled gaze the doctor fastened on him revealed that Andre had scored. "Who—won?"

"We did. I do not think he will prey upon anyone again."

The doctor's eyes closed briefly; Andre read prayerful thankfulness on his face as he sighed with relief. Then he returned to business. "You must be Andre, right? Anything I can supply?"

Andre laughed at the hesitation in his voice. "Fear not, your blood supply is quite safe, and I am unharmed. It is Diana who needs you."

The relief on the doctor's face made Andre laugh again.

Dr. Crane ignored him. "Right," he said, turning to the work *he* knew best.

She was lightheaded and groggy with the Demerol Dr. Crane had

STREETS OF BLOOD

given her as Andre deftly tucked her into her bed; she'd dozed all the way home in the car.

"I just wish I knew *what* that thing was—" she said inconsequentially, as he arranged her arm in its Fiberglas cast a little more comfortably. "—I won't be happy until I *know*—"

"Then you are about to be happy, *cherie*, for I have had the brainstorm—" Andre ducked into the living room and emerged with a dusty leather-bound book. "Remember I said there was something familiar about it? Now I think I know what it was." He consulted the index, and turned pages rapidly—found the place he sought, and read for a few moments. "As I thought—listen. 'The *gaki* also knows as the Japanese vampire—takes its nourishment only from the living. There are many kinds of *gaki*, extracting their sustenance from a wide variety of sources. The most harmless are the 'perfume' and 'music' *gaki*—and they are by far the most common. Far deadlier are those that require blood, flesh—or souls.'"

"Souls?"

"Just so. To feed, or when at rest, they take their normal form of a dense cloud of dark smoke. At other times, like the *kitsune*, they take on the form of a human being. Unlike the *kitsune*, however, there is no way to distinguish them in this form from any other human. In the smoke form, they are invulnerable—in human form, however, they can be killed; but to destroy them permanently, the body must be burned—preferably in conjunction with or solely by Power.' I said there was something familiar about it—it seems to have been a kind of distant cousin." Andre's mouth smiled, but his eyes reflected only a long-abiding bitterness.

"There is *no way* you have any relationship with that—thing!" she said forcefully. "It had no more honor, heart or soul than a rabid beast!"

"I—I thank you, *cherie*," he said, slowly, the warmth returning to his eyes. "There are not many who would think as you do."

"Their own closed-minded stupidity."

"To change the subject—what made you burn it as you did? I would have abandoned it. It seemed dead enough."

"I don't know—it just seemed the thing to do," she yawned.

"Sometimes my instincts just work . . . right . . ."

Suddenly her eyes seemed too leaden to keep open.

She fought against exhaustion and the drug, trying to keep both at bay without success. Sleep claimed her for its own.

He watched her for the rest of the night, until the lethargy of his own limbs told him dawn was near. He had already decided not to share her bed, lest any movement on his part cause her pain—instead, he made up a pallet on the floor beside her.

He stood over her broodingly while he in his turn fought slumber, and touched her face gently. "Well—" he whispered, holding off torpor far deeper and heavier than hers could ever be—while she was mortal. "You are not aware to hear, so I may say what I will and you cannot forbid. Dream; sleep and dream—I shall see you safe—my only love."

And he took his place beside her, to lie motionless until night should come again.

Mercedes Lackey is the author of many best-selling novels, including a handful featuring Diana Tregarde: *Burning Water, Children of the Night, Sacred Ground,* and *High Jinx.* Her most popular works, however, are the Valdemar series, which include *Magic's Price, Arrows for the Queen,* and *The Oathbound,* among others.

Sometimes the underbelly of society shows its scales—and its fangs!

Lowlifes

BY ESTHER M. FRIESNER

urray and I are sitting up late at the G&C Luncheonette down near the river when Jimmy Delancey comes in looking like he has lost his best friend. This is impossible, of course. Any stiff with an ounce of what the uptown crowd calls gray mattress between the ears can tell you, Jimmy Delancey's best and only friend in this town is one Mister James Delancey.

Still, Murray is a soft touch, especially since the ponies have been cooperative to him today (there being no mudders; Murray can not pick a mudder to save his soul), so he asks, "Whassamarrer, Jimmy? Your boy go down?" Jimmy is a fight manager who always has a boy in the bouts somewhere. His boys also always seem to be losing these bouts, so Murray's question is a safe bet.

"Maybe he got a letter from Pres'dent Roozfelt tellin' him that W.P.A. don't do nothin' for punk fighters," says one of the local G&C wags.

"Pipe down," says Ernestine from behind the counter.

Jimmy just shakes his head and says, "It's no good, boys. I am finished. It's that bloodsucking leech. It's that no good stinking vampire what's been my downfall."

Here is where Murray remarks, "It looks to my untrained ear

like congratulations are in order. I was unaware that you was so much as stepping out with a lady of the fair sex, let alone had committed matrimony."

Jimmy looks up from the glass of tea that Ernestine puts in front of him and his eyes are cold. (Ernestine is the best and only waitress at the G&C, on account she is also the proprietress. There is just her and Billy the cook who she got off a Norwegian freighter when it maroons him without pay by the Brooklyn Navy Yard. But this is another story. She knows us and what we like to drink and what we eat on Tuesday lunch as opposition to Wednesday dinner and how deep in the hole we are to the G&C Luncheonette. She will forgive a man for bouncing a check off her like she was a handball court, but God alone help you if you tell her "I would prefer a cuppa coffee insteada tea today, just for a change." Ernestine does not like changes.)

(Oh yeah: Billy the cook's name is not Billy. It is something more in keeping with him being Norwegian or Swede or one of them. Ernestine calls him Billy because her other cook was named Billy only he died from drinking grain alcohol in the wrong company and a knife in the belly after. But like I am saying, this is also another story likewise.)

So like I am saying already, Jimmy looks up, and he has got a face on him that looks like a hank of Atlantic City saltwater taffy, the green pulled on the machine. "I see you boys are not above making light of another man's troubles," he says.

Now here you have got to understand that Murray and I are separated from Jimmy Delancey by religious differences: We are strictly betting with the horses but Jimmy does the fight game. There is no facet of the manly art as she is played in New York than Jimmy does not have a finger in at one time or another.

Back when he was not Jimmy Delancey but plain Hymie Leibovitz of a modest Delancey Street *pied a terrapin,* like the Frenchies would have it, he even went a few rounds at some local clubs. That was when he changed his name. (He figured if a Delancey hits the canvas it is not so bad, but if a Leibovitz takes a pounding out in public it is just giving the goys what they want to see and ticket prices do not repay this with sufficient liberality.) He did pretty good, too. It did not take him long, however, to discover that it was possible to make a good dollar in the fights without getting someone else's fist through your teeth.

Now when you have got your usual run of sporting men in this town, you will find most of them spread their losses around to a number of entertainments. Only once in a while you will encounter people like Murray and I and Jimmy who are afictionados of one game and no other. This makes our devotion all the more fierce. Also this accounts for a certain amount of good-natured jibery among us at the expense of the other fella's chosen manner of losing money.

But what Jimmy says about Murray and I making fun of a mug in a jam is an insult! Murray gets all red the way he does, so you could see these white patches stand out on top of his head where there is no hair worth mentioning. When he gets good and mad, they look like the map of Europe. I was compelled to terminate my association with P.S. 26 before we made any great study of geography, but even I could pick out a clear France on Murray's bald spot, so you can imagine his feelings.

"Delancey, you oughta be shamed!" Murray thunders.

"Shaddup," says Ernestine. She brigs us a nice apple pie.

"Shaddup, you want?" Murray sits up straighter on his stool, one hand pressed to the bosom of his shirt. "I should shaddup when a man accuses me of hitting him when he's down? Phil, you ever know me I hit a man when he's down?"

"Never," I say. This is good enough for Murray. He snorts at Jimmy and gets down to business with the pie. (Ernestine's pie is truly sublime; a wise man does not treat it in a cavalier manner.) This would have been the end of the discussion, only Jimmy opens up his yap again.

"A quarter a million dollars," he says like the words are acid. He drinks his tea. There is not much custom in the G&C Luncheonette during our usual hours of patronage, but what there is shuts up and sits up tall and pays a whole lot of attention to Jimmy Delancey all of a sudden.

Murray is the first one to ask, "This a quarter a million bucks of which you speak, Jimmy . . . you know someone which has got it?"

"Had it." Jimmy finishes his tea. Ernestine brings him a fresh glass and a nice meatloaf sandwich because she knows. "It is I and no other of which I speak in connection with the previously mentioned sum of cash. And I could have it again, if . . ." His voice sort of trails off.

Murray hops down from his stool and scurries over to jump onto the one next to Jimmy. "If—?" he says, smiling and making encouraging moves with his hands.

But all Jimmy does is throw his head back and tell the ceiling fan, "Oh, that rotten, lowdown, lousy, stinking *bitch!*"

It is shortly thereafter that I step out of the G&C Luncheonette to see whether Jimmy and Murray could use a hand climbing out of the gutter. This is where Ernestine has tossed the two of them, being as she went to Catholic school and has a strict sensibility about indelicate language in her establishment. Ernestine stands in a hairnet shy of six feet tall and weighs in like a Packard sedan, so it is a wise man who respects her little foibles.

Murray picks himself up and brushes off the suit. "This is what I get for associating with pugs," he says bitterly.

Jimmy is truly shamed. He knows how Murray was only subjected to Ernestine's rough treatment because of where he was sitting. When Ernestine hears a word she does not like, she ejects everyone in the general vicinity of that word, just to make sure she got the right party.

"I'm sorry, Murray," Jimmy says. "You got to understand, I am a desperate man. I was not lying when I spoke of a quarter a million dollars, which is even as we speak dangling inches from my palm." He sighs. "It might as well be dangling on the moon."

"How would a mug like you come even within smelling distance of that kind of dough?" Murray asks. All the old pony-player's contempt for pugilistic people comes right to the top, even if it is not polite. Murray's dignity has been wounded, which makes him forget his manners.

"Come with me to Sherry's and I'll tell you," Jimmy says. "I'll treat." This is acceptable to Murray's dignity, so we go.

Sherry's is a little after-hours club that used to be a speak before Repeal. The whole West Side was crawling with places like that in the old days—nothing fancy, just a bunch of little hideaways where a man could go forget his troubles or look up some promising new ones. Now most of them got liquor licenses and went legitimate or broke, but Sherry's stayed the same. Sherry herself always said that her mama back in Arkansas must of named her after a drink for a reason. She never had use for any other license than her birth certificate. It saw her through Prohibition and three marriages and let her earn enough to put her kid through the Gunnery and into Yale and she was damned if she was gonna monkey with success.

(I realize that Sherry's aversion to licenses does not quite jibe with her matrimonial history. Suffice it to say, the lady herself has been known to refer to her partners, present and previous, as husbands-without-portfolio, and that is official enough for her. Besides, two of them from the Boom years became unavoidably shot by their business competitors and Sherry was herself personally constrained to ventilate the third as a discouragement to his continued socializing with a Keith circuit contortionist named Ginger, so it hardly paid to take out a license on them. She is what the Frenchies term an *espree libra* and the cops never did make the charges stick.)

There is no sign to tell you where to find Sherry's. If you do not already have this information then it is none of your business. Sherry's fourth husband, Salvatore, hangs around the establishment's front door to help those poor souls who do not have the native smarts to know what is and is not their business. He smiles when he sees us, though, and even yells back to Sherry to come out and see what the cat dragged in.

Sherry is a beautiful woman of what the Frenchies call *dune certain domage*. She comes soaring out of the back room in a cloud of egret feathers and *My Sin* and hugs us, spending most of her time on Jimmy. Sherry is a good businesswoman of whom I have often heard expressed that she has a nose for money. It is a very cute nose, which is not to detract from its accuracy, so I figure if she is hanging onto Jimmy like that there must be something in what he says about this a quarter a million.

"Where have you been?" she squeals, giving him one more squeeze. She has left a big pink splotch of face powder over his blue stubble. It is kind of like a Belasco stage lighting effect. "The last I hear, you finally got your mitts on a fighter who could do something besides waltz with the turnbuckle."

"You heard right," Jimmy tells her. "Nicolino Battista has got the fists and the moves and the smarts to take him and me both all the way to the top. Unfortunately, this will not happen. If you will be kind enough to serve me and my associates, I will tell you the whole sorry tale."

Sherry plops us down at a good table and brings us what to drink, then she joins us. Her face is hard as my mother-in-law's kugel. In the circles in which I move, there is only one thing worse than having no prospects and that is to poor mouth good prospects. Anyone can be flat—those are the breaks—but it takes a real bum to say he's got a sure thing that isn't gonna work. It is bad for the rest of our morale.

The story which Jimmy now unfolded under the hard eye of Sherry and the compassionate ear of Murray and I was simple and plain and old as hard luck. Jimmy often checked out the local churches and the Y for talent. He found a kid named Nicolino Battista in a church basement in Little Italy where the priest gave boxing lessons so that later on the parish kids could pound each other blind on the street in a more sportsmanlike manner.

It didn't take Jimmy long to see that Nicolino had what it takes. It didn't take Nicolino long to see that Jimmy was his ticket off Mulberry Street and into the highlife. It was not such a frequent occurrence that Jimmy ran into a fighter whose plans for the future went beyond laying out his next opponent, but Nicolino was that man. Only nineteen and already he had his whole life figured. He would fight, he would win, he would make it to the top, and then he would take his winnings and buy a nice chunk of land out in California, maybe in the San Fernando Valley where he had an uncle and some grapes.

With Jimmy training and managing him, Nicolino soon made short work of the minor talents along the way. Murray and I do not follow the fight game, but Sherry nods her head and says, "I think I recall reading something in the *Trib* about a rising young middleweight named Little Nicky Battista."

"That would be he." Jimmy taps his nose so as to indicate *bingo*.

"Then that would also be the same Little Nicky who is presently looking at the championship?" Sherry asks.

Again Jimmy makes with the nose. "Now you see where I have

been for so long. What with the gymnasium training and the Jersey camps and the out-of-town fights and all, I have been looking after business. I am also making a nice dollar on the side, laying wagers on my boy. Nicolino was a pleasure to manage. When we was out of town in a hotel I would never have to keep an eye on the maid to make sure he didn't bribe her to smuggle him in any liquor or nothing. I told him a thing was bad for a boy in training, he listened. He was smart enough to value my experience in the fight game and I was smart enough to smell gold in his fists. It was a marriage made in heaven."

Jimmy sighs. "The only trouble with a marriage is you need a woman for at least some of it."

Here Jimmy lays his cards on the table and they are all coming up female. Even Sherry shakes her head the way you do while viewing the guest of honor at a good Irish wake. She knows that for a fighter in training, women are spelled N-O.

"I don't know where he met her," Jimmy says. "It happens in town, this I do know, but where he found an item like her—!"

"Maybe she found him," Sherry says. She is wise to the ways of her fellow women. "Lots of ladies find young fighters very congenial company."

"There, there, Jimmy," Murray says, patting him on the shoulder. "So your boy has made a little stumble on his way to the finish line. This happens. It don't mean he's outa the race. If he has the smarts you claim he does, he will put aside the lady behind him and think of his future once more."

"No, he won't." Jimmy looks about as optimistic as a turkey the day before Thanksgiving. "Not this doll."

This surprises us. Jimmy is not one to be impressed by the allurements of the opposite sex, being as he is a businessman first. Indeed, all of his commerce with the fairer section of the populace is conducted on a strictly cash basis. The word from the sporting girls on Broadway is that he is a good, steady customer who does not make trouble. His trade is therefore very welcome among the, as the Frenchies call them, *fees de jaw.*

Jimmy drinks his drink and Sherry pours him another. "A quarter a million dollars," he says into the glass. "What with the purses this kid could win and the friendly wagers an honest man could lay on the side and the interested parties who might be willing to buy a piece of a headliner, let alone a champeen, a quarter a million dollars is a modest estimation of what this woman has leeched out from under me. This is a fact." He drinks the drink and takes the bottle from Sherry, to spare her the trouble of the next few several refills.

Sherry gets this look on her. In the old days I saw her look like that when some rich Midwest wheat king got a few too many under his belt and started acting like he owned the place. He would wake up the next morning in police custody and not remember anything much except the very clear notion that he did not own Sherry's.

"Jimmy," she says, "I'm going to help you with this one. Little Nicky's gotta be set straight. You may not be my friend, but you're a good, clean fight manager. I respect this about you. The fights've been my especial weakness for a long time and it pains me to see a promising new talent like Little Nicky about to go down for the count just because there's some rich harpy out there sucking him dry."

"How do you know she is rich?" I ask.

Sherry gives me a look like I was just hatched. "They're always rich. This gives them too much time on their hands and not enough brains to know what to do with it." She stands up from the table like she's the Queen of Sheba about to give orders and says, "Take me to the bitch."

She is so magnificent when she says this that I believe in all sincerity not even Ernestine would be able to lay a glove on her for using that kinda language. For one thing, Salvatore is always right there to back up Sherry and he can whip Ernestine three out of five in a fair fight.

"Awright," Jimmy agrees, pushing his chair back and getting up slow. "Awright, I can do that. She's got an apartment at the Plaza which is probably right where Little Nicky is right now. I been there enough times, yelling for him to get the hell out and rest up, so I can take you right there. But it won't do a damn bit of good."

"We'll see about that," says Sherry, and the smell I catch off her isn't *My Sin,* it's gunpowder, dry.

By the time Salvatore gets the last customers encouraged out of

Sherry's and the place is locked up, it is pushing dawn. Sherry has used the time well, going upstairs to there apartment and changing into battle clothes and warpaint. When Murray and I see her, we can not help but whistle and utter other sundry expressions of appreciation. Not every woman can wear that many diamonds at once to some advantage. She is also wearing a dress of blue satin and a quantity of white minks that causes her *onsumbul* to remind me of a *Winter in Connecticut* postcard which my lovely wife Sylvia once sent me as a sentimental keepsake prior to our nuptials.

Salvatore gets us a cab and we motor over to the Plaza. You can just see the first rays of sun laying themselves down over Fifth from the crosstown streets like yellow Board of Ed. pencils outa the East River. The doorman is half asleep, and the other half's breathing out something Canadian, so when he catches an eyeful of Sherry's minks and diamonds he doesn't even try to stop us. This is despite of the fact that while Salvatore's still got a tux on, Jimmy and Murray and I are as usual.

Jimmy does not lie when he says he knows where the lady is rooming. He takes us to it like a bird dog. She has a suite not too far down from the top floor and he pounds on the door good and loud. From inside we hear a deep voice expressing a few sharp thoughts in Eyetalian, then a softer purr bubbling up and soothing the savage breast.

The latch clicks and the door opens slow. I am starting to get second thoughts about all this. If the lady is as rich as Jimmy says, what is she most likely to do when she finds a crowd like us on her doormat at this hour of the morning? I will give any odds she hollers for the cops. I step around behind Salvatore so as to anticipate a hasty departure, should this prove necessary. My Sylvia is a very understanding woman when it comes to the hours I keep but she draws the line at bailing me out of penal facilities.

"Greetings," says a voice that's like sliding into a nice hot bath after a hard day. "I am Irene Kerapalios."

I peek out from around behind Salvatore. My jaw hits the carpet. Now I see what they mean about there is no sure thing in this world except leaving it on the horizontal. (Except for Sylvia's uncle Pinchas, who was caught in a fireworks factory blowup down south. But that does not significate.) All my bets about the lady taking one gawk at us and screaming are so much also-rans.

She is standing there in the doorway, cool like ice, wearing a little silk nothing from maybe Scrapperelli that trickles all the way down so it covers her feet. It is the same deep green like her eyes; which remind me of the ocean off Coney Island. Her hair is black and falls all over her shoulders, which are so white and soft-looking they are giving Sherry's minks a run for the money.

"May I help you gentlemen?" she asks. We just stand there. Even Salvatore is knocked for a loop. I am hearing this drip-drip-drip from his general direction and when I look to see what is amiss I worry that maybe the Plaza, being a classy joint, will object to a man which is drooling on their carpet.

Only Jimmy is not stunned by the lady's looks. (Neither, it should go without saying, is Sherry, but she is doing the slow burn and is therefore as speechless as the rest of us.) He lunges forward, wagging a finger in Miss Kerapalios' face, and bawls, "Where's Little Nicky? I know you got him in there and I'm here to get him the hell out!"

"I see," she says. The lady smiles like Jimmy has just got off a good Marx Brothers line. I never see lips that red unless it comes out of a tube, only somehow I get the hunch that with this doll it is strictly Mother Nature working overtime. "And I see you have also brought some—how do you say it?—muscle." Her eye-lashes are maybe an inch thick and she bats them at Salvatore. He takes a couple clumsy steps forward like he's a doped-up dog someone's yanking on a leash until Sherry steps in and gives him one in the belly with the elbow.

Miss Kerapalios laughs. She steps aside and bows her head a little like she's the men's washroom attendant at Radio City. "Come in by all means," she says.

These are some fancy digs which Miss Kerapalios has at the Plaza. The draperies are drawn over the windows, but she has got enough lamps going for a man to see that the appointments here are strictly first-rate. Most of the stuff is *Ompeer* style—which I know because that is my Sylvia's favorite. (She says it is my great knowledge of Frenchie scholarship which has influenced her taste in this direction.) There are also some assorted gewgaws and knickknacks scattered about in a casual manner which a lesser man than myself would pocket if not for the fact that most of it is too big to fit without stretching the material all out of shape bad.

It is also like Jimmy says: Little Nicky is here. He does not look Ompeer in the slightest. He is sprawled out on Miss Kerapalios's sofa wearing a pair of blue satin pajama bottoms. He sits there and he smiles when he sees us. For a kid nineteen, he has got a deal of meat on the bone, not to mention stubble on the face and hair on the chest. I am thinking up a theory which I may sent to Perfesser Einstein down in Jersey (after I test it out on Murray) about how spaghetti grows hair on a party. When I was nineteen, I did not in any way resemble this specimen. The only hair I had on my chest belonged to whatever Eyetalian kid was presently pinning me to the sidewalk.

When Jimmy gets an eyeful of his boy, he hits the ceiling. Right away he is jumping up and down, shaking his fists and calling Little Nicky ten kinds of stupid wop. Little Nicky does not appear to take offense at whatever Jimmy says. I am at this time keeping my eye on Salvatore, in case that gentleman should take it into his noggin to resent Jimmy's choice of vocabulary as applied to a fellow Eyetalian *landsman* and clobber him one, *dapray le steal de Ernestine,* as the Frenchies would say. But Salvatore is still ogling Miss Kerapalios, so that is all right.

It is Sherry who steps in. She must figure that Little Nicky is so accustomed to Jimmy's lectures that they are to him like water off a duck's ass, so she grabs Jimmy by the collar and hauls him back so she can take on the kid. She jams her hands on her hips and leans forward so he cannot help but get a good look at what her diamonds and her minks and her dress are not covering. Sherry is still a dish by any standard, but she is no competition for the goods what Miss Kerapalios is selling. Still, she had got it, and she is smart enough to use it to get the kid's attention.

"Little Nicky," she says, "quit fooling around. You're breaking training and you know it. You tired of the fight game? Then be honest and cut poor Jimmy loose once and for all, clean, instead of taking him down with you by inches."

"Save it, baby." Little Nicky laughs. "I'll be all right," he says, waving Sherry off. "I'm gonna be the Friday night headliner at the Garden. You'll see. Irene, she says I'm one of the gods."

"In a pig's eye!" Sherry kind of spits back. "Unless now the stumblebums and canvasbacks got into the god business."

Little Nicky goes stiff, but Sherry changes her approach without him getting the chance to say nothing. It is like watching Joan Crawford turn into Shirley Temple, like Lon Chaney. "Look, maybe this is really all you're good for," she tells him. "Maybe this is what you want. But Jimmy doesn't get a cut of all the gold cigarette cases and satin underwear this cooch gives you 'cause you made her day. A man's gotta earn a dollar in this town. All the time he wastes on you, Jimmy could be managing some other fighter who's serious about making it to the top. How you're going, the only way you'll see the inside of the Garden on a Friday night is from behind a broom."

This does it. Little Nicky stops smiling. He jumps up, both fists open for business. I do not think he intends to clobber Sherry, but that is something that will have to remain what we call one of the mysteries of the universe because before he can take a swing or anything he goes white in the face and cross-eyed. Next we know, he is falling forward and lands right on his puss on a very nice rug indeed.

Jimmy lets out a wail like he's a mother lion which has lost her pups. Murray and I do not know the fight game, like I say, but we do know that all Jimmy's caterwauling is not going to do Little Nicky a lot of good. We get down on the carpet and turn the boy over like he was a flapjack. He is still smiling with his eyes open and for a very unsettling minute or two or less I think he is maybe dead.

"He is not dead," says Miss Kerapalios. She has chosen to seat herself on what the Frenchies in the furniture trade would call your *maury chase lounge* and is toying with the affections of a box of bonbons on a side table. Her long silk gown trails off the end of the chair, still covering up her feet, and through the flimsy cloth you can observe some mighty fine action on the part of her haunches. Salvatore is doing this observing.

"Then what's the matter with him?" Jimmy howls. "Lookit! Just lookit!" He makes this big gesture with his hand which is generally reserved for movie heroines showing off their starving babies in the weepies. "If you got him on dope, lady, I don't care if you own the stinking Plaza, I'm gonna get the bulls on you so fast—"

"He should not have exerted himself so soon afterward, that is all. I did not take enough blood for him to die." *Blood?* She says it like this is nothing. She picks out a chocklit, she opens her mouth, and there are these two very unsettling fangs where your usual run of doll has got the pearlies. She jabs the candy with one of these, sucks out the center, and tosses away the empty. "Ugh. Coconut," she says, making a face.

In view of developments, Murray and I give little Nicky the once over. Sure enough, on his neck there are these two puncture marks. Salvatore falls to his knees, big lug that he is, and starts fumbling with the front of his shirt until he manages to yank up this gold crucifix on a chain. He commences to pray very loud, totally indifferent to the allure of Miss Kerapalios's silk-upholstered haunches. Miss Kerapalios ignores him, once more rifling the candy box.

"Aha!" Sherry yells. It escapes me why she should look so happy to learn that there is this new wrinkle to Miss Kerapalios's personality. Then she strides across the room and yanks the draperies wide open. Sunshine comes pouring in over everything in sight. This includes our hostess.

Miss Kerapalios looks up and makes like Mona Lisa. "I saw that movie seven times," she tells Sherry. "I read the book twice, I adore Bela Lugosi, don't you?" She gets her another chocklit and sucks the daylights out of it. "I am not a vampire," she says, licking her fangs. "I am *lamia.*"

"I don't care if you're Eleanor Roosevelt!" Sherry hollers. "In this town we don't go around drinking middleweights!"

"I beg your pardon," Miss Kerapalios replies, very smooth and *cheek.* "I was unaware of the local customs."

She sashays over to this big mirror in a gilt-edged frame and we can see her image the same as if she was normal. "There," she says, showing us what we already see. "The undead cast no reflection. To them, sunshine is anathema, and the stake through the heart brings death. But not to me." She goes back to the *chase* and winks at Sherry, who is sizing up the chair legs with maybe that bit about the stake in mind. "Don't bother," she says.

Jimmy is besides himself, pacing up and down, wringing his hands. "A leech I called her!" he tells the ceiling. "A vampire, even! Was I right? Was I right?"

Murray and I tell him he was right. This does not assuage Jimmy Delancey. "*Now* she stands there and says she drinks my boy's blood but she's *not* no vampire! So what else is left she should be? A landlord, maybe? Is this a system?"

Miss Kerapalios clicks her tongue, only it sounds different, probably on account of the fangs. "I tell you, I am not any sort of what you would call vampire; I am *lamia. Lamia!*"

Sherry sighs and tears her eyes off the chair legs real reluctant. "Well, honey, whatever you call yourself, it's all Greek to me."

"Yes! Yes, that is it exactly!" Miss Kerapalios leaps from the *chase* and is across the room kissing Sherry on both cheeks before anyone can blink, like maybe she is fixing to aware her the *craw dugair* (of the which Frenchie medal for military progress I was sorely cheated out of during the late war, but I am not bitter). "It is Greek!" Miss Kerapalios exclaims. "I am Greek! I am also unlike the northern vampire who must pawn his soul to hell in exchange for his unnatural life. I have no soul to pawn. I am by my very nature immortal."

"Aw, lady," Murray protests, still chafing Little Nicky's wrists. "Please, lady, don't be so hard on yourself. So you made a mistake—he's a good looker, the kid—but you can turn it around. We won't say anything if you won't." Murray is very *galawnt.*

"Not *immoral,* you dope," Sherry says. She gives Miss Kerapalios one of these looks like *Men!* All of a sudden the dolls are very buddy-buddy, but I have never laid any odds to understanding them so I let it pass.

"The *lamiae* are an ancient race," Miss Kerapalios says. Now Murray and I are paying some attention. If there is one thing we know it is races. "We delight in the society of mortals, for without the bright achievements of your evanescent lives our own eternity would be one unending tedium. Poets especially charm us, as do all creative souls. From time to time we sample your blood, believing that through its unique bouquet we may someday discover what it is that separates the artist from the clod. Yet we do not require your blood to sustain us. No, in truth we prefer to feast on rarer fare."

Murray is looking at me and I at him. "Do you get it, Phil?" he asks.

"All I am getting from this is that she is a society dame who likes a nice bouquet of flowers once in awhile, as what doll don't?"

"Also champagne," Murray indicates. "On account of it is, like she says, evanescent. Unless she means Moxie."

Miss Kerapalios looks us over, one by one. She is not smiling so much. "What an age!" she says at the ceiling. Between her and Jimmy the ceiling is having all the good conversations. "What a leaden age of animate clay! I shall perish for lack of decent fare, I know it!"

"Again with the fare? Lady, I don't know what's your beef," Murray tells her. "You don't like what the hacks charge, you can always take the El like the rest of us."

Miss Kerapalios yowls so loud I am afraid maybe the hotel dick will show up to ask where she is keeping the cats. Salvatore is still praying pretty strong into the stretch and Murray and I are starting to get a little color back into Little Nicky's cheeks, so it is left to Jimmy and Sherry to pound the lady on the back and try to make her shut up some.

"Look," Jimmy tells her, "I think I getcha. What I don't get is how come you pick on my boy? He's a fighter, not a poet."

"So you *do* understand." I could maybe be wrong, but I think I see something flare up in Miss Kerapalios's eyes like someone struck a pair of green matches on their trouser seat. She grabs Jimmy's wrists and pulls him close. "Yes, I read it in your soul that you are not like these earthworms." She gives Murray and I the fish eye.

"Hey!" Murray objects. "I resent that!" He does. On his bald spot, France is showing up loud and clear.

Jimmy shrugs. "Well, you gotta make allowances for them, on account they are mere railbirds." This remark lets me pinpoint Paris on Murray's dome.

"But surely you must understand, then," she says, lacing her arm around Jimmy's a coupla times like it's a potted ivy from The Five and Dime. "The art of pugilism is precisely that: an art! It was recognized as such in my native Greece, and as such it must likewise claim its artists. He is one, your young Mr. Battista. I can scent these things. I am never mistaken. The first time I saw him fight, the passion for complete and utter possession of his gifts welled up so hotly within me that I lost consciousness of all else." By the time she unloads all this, her eyes are heating up the room like a three-alarmer.

"Lady, I don't know from art," Jimmy says. "All I know is if you don't put a lid on it, Little Nicky's gonna be so outa condition he couldn't lick the ref."

"But what am I do to?" Miss Kerapalios whimpers. "The blood, the sex, they are only poor substitutes for what I truly desire, yet he will not grant it to me. Feeding this way I hunger, but at least I do not starve!"

"*Sex?*" Sherry is livid. She has got these two little red dots on her cheeks that are standing out like stoplights. "You've got the gall to talk like that in mixed company, with a *kid* here?" She waves at Little Nicky. It is obviously immaterial to Sherry that the boy is presently out cold and has not heard a thing, nor that he had been the frequent recipient of the item which Miss Kerapalios has so improperly mentioned out loud. What counts by her is that he is not yet twenty-one and has got a mother somewhere on Mulberry Street. "The kind of mouth you've got, honey, isn't fit for a decent woman to listen to. If my mama was here, she'd wash it out for you but good! You know, I wouldn't go bellyaching about how hungry you are if I were you. From where I stand, I'd say you could do with shedding a few off those hips, sister."

All the fire in Miss Kerapalios's eyes goes off to join Peary at the Pole. She reaches for these skinny little straps holding up her gown, yanks them both off the shoulder and makes with a wiggle. The whole *megillah* falls to the floor in a puddle of green silk at her feet.

Which feet she has not got. We are looking at a sample of very handsome naked female woman from the waist up, and a couple five dozen pounds of naked boa constrictor from the waist down.

"Might you suggest the proper diet for me then, Madame?" she asks Sherry, smiling so the fangs show up good.

Sherry screams. Salvatore faints. Murray and I both check the door but she is between us and it. I am trying to remember

34   STREETS OF BLOOD

whether Sylvia knows where I hide the life insurance policy until I remember we cashed it in last summer so we could go to Saratoga.

Only Jimmy is not acting at all perturbed by this reptilish turn of events. Maybe he is going to the Bronx Zoo more often than Murray and I, who knows? Maybe he is just falling back on the cold-blooded way a lot of ex-fighters get when they find themselves in a tight spot. However, I would say that Miss Kerapalios looks to have wrote the book on cold-blooded.

Miss Kerapalios stops smiling. She looks at Jimmy like she is the one on the receiving end of seeing a freak. "I do not frighten you?" she asks.

"I seen worse," he says, very cool. "No offense."

Now she is smiling again. These ripples run from her belly button down to the tip of her tail and the scales melt away until she is standing there on a set of very attractive pins looking all female, only still buck naked. "And now?" she asks sweetly.

Jimmy sucks in his lower lip and says, "I have got to admit, I have not seen much better. I assume you got a reason for choosing to look like a sidewinder in front of guests?"

She shrugs. "Looking fully human all the time is for me like wearing a tuxedo is for you. It is fine to behold from the outside, but it is not comfortable from the in."

"Okay," Jimmy says. "It's your digs. Make yourself to home."

Miss Kerapalios gives these shivers again and whammo, she's back to being half a snake. She slithers over to the *chase* and leans back on the cushions. "Chocolate?" she says, offering the box to Sherry.

This is, as they say, an empty gesture. Sherry has stopped screaming and is presently taking five down on the floor with Murray and I and Little Nicky and Salvatore, which leaves Jimmy the only fighter still on his feet. By him I am guessing this is as good as a win, even if it is only a judgment call. He decides to go for the purse.

"Awright, so it's not the blood and it's not the—" he checks Sherry, who is still peacefully folded up on the carpet, before he says "—sex. So what is it? You want something Little Nicky's not giving you, maybe we can make a deal. You leave my boy alone, I find you someone who can give you what you're after. Okay?"

Miss Kerapalios gets this funny look on her, like my old second grade teacher Miss O'Brien used to get when I explained how come I wasn't in class for a couple few weeks on account I was attending my gramma's funeral out at Belmont. "You are a unique man, sir," she says. "If I so desired, I could wrap my tail around your neck—around all of your necks—and snap them like a bundle of dried straws. Yet you have the audacity to offer me *deals?*"

Jimmy makes with the shoulders. "We deal, everyone's happy. You got something against happy? But we don't deal, we both lose. It's like Sherry said: I can Let Little Nicky go. Word gets out he's washed up; he don't get no more fights, he's a bum, you're out a cheap lunch. Also, like you say, you're out a ring artist. Me, I gotta start at the bottom again with another boy. That's no picnic, but I'll live. I been on the bottom enough times so I know the neighborhood. Look, you want artists? I'll get you artists. I got a cousin Benny down In Greenwich Village who does things with paint. Just say the word and he's yours. But you gotta tell me what you want or—"

"Souls," she says. "I want human souls."

"Oh." Jimmy scratches his head. "Sorry, you can't have Benny, then. Aunt Rifka would kill me."

Miss Kerapalios commences to cry. It is a very moving spectacle, not unlike some scene which happened in *Ben Hur* the details of which elude me. "Alas, they were right, my people!" she wails. "They warned me not to emigrate. They said that America was a wasteland where I would perish of hunger. Can you know how long I seek a true artist? Only to learn, on finding him, that he will deny me that which I most crave."

"Well, honey, when you waltz up to a guy and ask for his soul—" Jimmy has at his disposal a very much Frenchie *kay voolay voo* sort of gesture, which he now employs. "Mulberry Street is no picnic, but it beats the hell out of—well, hell."

The tears which have been clouding Miss Kerapalios's pretty kisser now dry up. "Ai!" she is heard to exclaim. "You Americans. If you do not confuse me first with the Balkan vampire you confound me with your devils. I am no such fiend. I devour the artist's soul, but fill him at the same time with a searing, immortal fire which pours itself back into his art until all dross is burned

STREETS OF BLOOD

away, leaving only the light. His body may perish in the conflagration, yet his art is hardened in the flame. It endures forever."

"How about them apples," says Jimmy, duly impressed. He scratches his chin, then crooks a finger Miss Kerapalios should slither over to him so they can have a private conversation. She does this.

Murray and I are watching them for some time until Miss Kerapalios lifts her chin and stares at Jimmy. She lays a red fingernail to her lips and says, "In your own way, Mr. Delancey, in your own chosen medium, I believe that you too must be an artist."

(Murray remarks to me *DeSoto vochi* that what Jimmy Delancey is an artist in is what you generally find decorating improperly maintained stalls at Belmont.)

"Call me Hymie," Jimmy says, and slips one arm around Miss Kerapalios's scaly yet svelte midsection.

It is several weeks since Murray and I have seen Jimmy Delancey over to the G&C Luncheonette. We are not rendered too dejected by his absence, as our last social contact with this individual was him encouraging Miss Kerapalios to ring up the hotel dick and give the rest of us the bum's rush out of her suite.

It being Friday night, Ernestine has just bestowed on us an order of codfish balls with mashed potatoes and peas, when all of a sudden the door opens and in comes Sherry. This does not merely take Murray and I aback, it completely stupefies us, as Friday night is a heavy traffic time over to Sherry's place of business. Murray, always the gent, gets up and offers her both his stool and his codfish, the both of which the lady accepts graciously.

"So, Sherry," Murray says, taking the seat beside her and signaling for Ernestine to fetch him another order of victuals. "What brings you here? Is Salvatore minding the shop?"

"Salvatore is in a seminary upstate," Sherry replies. She sounds quite philosophical.

"What were the charges, if that is not too indiscreet a question?" I ask.

"I'm not talking Sing-Sing," Sherry tells me, stabbing a codfish ball with cruel violence. "I'm talking a real seminary, like they go to to become priests. Ever since we came back from the Plaza, that time we went with Jimmy Delancey, my Sally's been talking nothing except saving his soul, finding his vocation. He thinks that Greek bimbo was some sort of heavenly sign about how all dames are poison. I tried to tell him she was just a monster—I mean, he's seen enough Karloff movies—but he wouldn't listen." She chomps the codfish ball, but there is something in the way her jaws are working that tells me she is thinking about chewing up another sort of similarly shaped apparatus entirely.

This is perhaps not the best of moments to be posing such a question, but Murray knows nothing of timing so he asks, "And do you hear anything from either Jimmy Delancey or the reptilian doll lately?"

Sherry's hand slams down on the lunch counter. When she lifts it it has laid down two pair of ringside tickets for the Garden tonight. "Not a peep outa them," she says, "but you can bet your life they are gonna plenty hear from me."

So we go. Ernestine locks up and comes along because by the time she sees the tickets and says how she means to attend the middleweight championship bout, it is too late to tell her otherwise, not that we would dare try. On the way over to the Garden Sherry tells us how she got the tickets in the mail from Little Nicky Battista.

"He said he owed us the saving of his soul," Sherry says. "I was the only one who he could find an address." Her mouth gets small. "Somebody owes me something, that's for sure, and it's not just some lousy boxing tickets."

There are long stories and there are short stories and that about covers all bets. To make one into the other, when we get to the Garden, there is Jimmy Delancey in Little Nicky's corner and there in the shadow of the turnbuckle is Miss Kerapalios. She is wearing again the very *cheek cootoor,* only since her sable coat goes all the way to the floor it is my bet she is scales and not gams underneath. She sees us and smiles and waves. Sherry does something back, only it is not a wave and it is not friendly and I am glad Ernestine does not catch a glimmer of it or she might get her foibles in an uproar and attempt to bust that finger right off Sherry's hand.

I am no expert, but even to me it looks like a good bout. Little

Nicky fights the good fight, and for a time it is anybody's match. Even though Murray and I are not followers of the manly art, there is a certain fascination which overtakes one when seated so close to the action. Pretty soon Murray is jumping up and down and shouting and even hugging Ernestine when Little Nicky lands a good one. I, however, become distracted by the sudden departure of Sherry, who is seated to my left.

I see where she is going and I am trepidated. She is circling around to get to where Jimmy and Miss Kerapalios are holding down the fort for Little Nicky. I follow her, since I feel that the doll has been given the fuzzy end of the lollipop insofar as the tragic loss of Salvatore to the religious life. Sherry has already got a rep for being a smidgen too hot-blooded in matters *doo coor,* as the Frenchies so aptly put it, and deserves better out of life than an attempted murder charge with Jimmy Delancey in the supporting role. That, or becoming the murder victim herself should Miss Kerapalios forestall her with that little trick she said she can do with her tail.

So I am there, two steps behind, when Sherry is closing in on the guilty parties. Miss Kerapalios is not aware of Sherry's presence, being as how she is yelling and cheering and in general egging on Little Nicky in a number of foreign tongues including English, Greek, and Brooklynese. From the look in Sherry's eye things are about to get very ugly indeed.

Now here is the funny part: I am not watching Sherry and Miss Kerapalios any more. Something seems to lay hold of my eyes and drag them over to where Jimmy Delancey is standing. He is shouting instructions to his boy, directing Little Nicky's strategy like a good manager is supposed to do. I have never seen Jimmy at work before. He is not the same schmuck I know. He is a different schmuck altogether. There is a fire in his eyes which makes Miss Kerapalios's personal brand of headlamp sparks look like a firefly next to Krakatoa. Everything he's got, he's got focused on Little Nicky. I get the feeling that if I was to hold my hand out in his general direction he would melt my wristwatch, and such items do not come cheap.

Miss Kerapalios is leaning close to him, but she is not melting. She has got her fingers dug into his shoulders while she is yelling at the fighters for blood. From out the corner of my eye, I see Sherry open up her purse and reach her hand in. I am wondering what she is going after, whether a lipstick or something of a somewhat higher caliber. But I can not spare her more than a wink because of what is happening with Jimmy.

The fight is getting more intense. Little Nicky has got the moves, but he is the challenger and the champ did not get where he is without knowing a few moves of his own. The crowd is roaring. The fighters are hammering each other good. This is not going to be a decision bout, this much even I know.

Jimmy is shouting louder, with Miss Kerapalios almost climbing his back. He is shining like someone mashed all the lights of Coney Island into one little man and turned on the juice. Miss Kerapalios has got her claws deeper into him, and I look down in time to see that I win the bet because here comes her snake tail wrapping itself around his legs while the light coming off him flows back into her. I know what I am seeing here, even if no one believes me after. It does not always take a tout to pick a winner, and it does not always take a religious man to know when he has seen a soul.

Then Sherry yanks her hand out of her purse and points something shiny at the two of them. I yell for her to stop, but there is too much yelling going on. Jimmy yells for Little Nicky to jab for the champ's ribs. Miss Kerapalios yells whatever she damn well feels like in Greek. Sherry is yelling too, but so is everyone else ringside, so no one hears my yell for beans.

Only someone sees. Little Nicky is in a clinch with the champ, who has got him turned so that he is looking right at his corner. What he sees there makes his eyes go wide. He pushes the champ off, gives him one wild punch right in the kisser that lays him out sweet and pretty, then runs straight for the turnbuckle. Jimmy is livid. He is screaming louder and louder for his boy to pull back, stop, what the hell is he doing, knock it off, like that. The light around him is glowing hotter and brighter. I see Miss Kerapalios latched onto him and never in my life do I see a dame more happy. The brightness is wrapped around them both and she is swelling up with it like she is a cross between a tick and a lightbulb, her mouth open, her tongue hanging out like she is laying it all down in the home stretch. Jimmy shakes his fists at Little

STREETS OF BLOOD

Nicky and Miss Kerapalios's sables are starting to singe, but she does not seem to care.

Neither does Little Nicky. He leapfrogs over the turnbuckle like it's a hydrant on Mulberry Street and he lands on top of Sherry just as there's this big bang and this explosion of light and this smell like fried chicken everywhere and the ref is going nuts and I look around just in time to see Murray kissing Ernestine.

No one ever manages to see Jimmy Delancey or Miss Kerapalios again after that night, not even the Fights Commissioner, which is okay by me as I consider some marriages are made in heaven, but this one was strictly a fire hazard.

Little Nicky loses the championship for leaving the ring without permission, but he is able to earn quite a nice dollar indeed as the manager at Sherry's, without portfolio. I hear rumors as how once he turns twenty-one, Sherry is even going to give him the portfolio, with maybe Father Salvatore there to officialate. Maybe later they will move out to California, but for now Little Nicky is happy enough even though the closest he comes to grapes is in bottles.

Ernestine renames the G&C Luncheonette the E&M in honor of her and Murray becoming nuptialized. This is fine by her, on account she never knew what G&C were when she bought the place and it is finally time for a change.

I go there a lot and Murray and I rehash old times. The pie is still good and Murray still cannot pick a mudder.

Ploosa shanj, as the Frenchies would put it. And so would I.

Esther Friesner is the editor of the anthology *Blood Muse,* a collection of vampire stories about the arts, and is the author of numerous fantasy novels, including *Blood of Mary, Psalms of Herod, The Sherwood Game,* and *Druid's Blood.* She also has stories in both *Southern Blood* and *Blood Lines,* as well as many other anthologies.

A portrait of the artist as a young vampire . . .

Exposure

BY LAURA ANNE GILMAN

he timer clicked, a cicada in the dark. Lifting the tongs off their rest, he swirled the paper gently; watching, deeming Good to go by the rules, better to work by instinct. Finally deeming it complete, he lifted the sheet out of its bath, placing it in another shallow tub and turning the water on, cold, over it.

The music played, one CD after another, continuous shuffle so that he never knew what would come up next: Melissa Etheridge, Vivaldi, the exotic noises of a rain forest. It suited his mood, prepped him for the evening's work. For now the lilting strains of *The Four Seasons* kept him company. Tugging at his ear where it itched, he studied the image floating face-up at him. Satisfied, he lifted it between two fingertips, shaking some of the wetness off. Turning off the water, he transferred the print to his right hand and reached out to flick the toggle switch on the wall next to the room's exit. Stepping into the revolving door, he pushed the heavy plastic with one shoulder and emerged from the darkroom.

Blinking in the sudden fluorescent lighting, he cast a glance over his shoulder to make sure that the warning light had gone off, then carried the print over to the line strung across the far end of the studio. Clipping it to the line, he stepped back to examine the other prints already there. Several, most notably the three shots of the hookers talking over coffee, leaning intently across the table to get in each others' faces, pleased him. Others were less successful, but overall he was satisfied. Checking his watch once again, he took off the stained apron he wore, hung it on a hook beside the door, shut off the stereo, and went to take a shower. Time to go to work.

◊◊◊

"Hey, Westin!"

He slung the bag more comfortably over his shoulder, and stopped to wait for the overweight Latino cop who chugged up alongside him. "Going out again tonight, huh?"

"As I've done every night this week," Westin replied. "And the week before that."

"But not the week before that," the cop said.

"But the entire month before that I didn't miss a single night. So why are you asking now?"

The cop ignored the slight edge to Westin's voice. "There's some weirdo out there, past few nights. Scared the hell out of a couple slits Tuesday, cut into their business too. Guy's wearing Pampers and some kinda bonnet, according to reports. If you happen to run into him . . ."

"I should take his picture for your album?"

"The brass'd be thankful. And ya gotta know the *Post*'d pay for that picture. Anyway, keep your eyes out."

"I always do," Westin said, holding up his camera. He watched with detached affection as the cop loped back to his post, holding up a wall in the upper hall of the Port Authority. Swaddling and a bonnet. That was a new one. He could certainly understand johns keeping away, but why were the hookers afraid of him? Westin thought briefly about following up on it, then put those thoughts away. If he came into the viewfinder, then would be the time to wonder. For now, there was the rent to pay. He stepped into the men's room to moisten his contact lenses, darkened to protect his hypersensitive eyes. Another thing to bless technology for. Even he couldn't take photographs through sunglasses.

Leaving the bustling noise of the terminal, he exited into the sharp cold night of Eighth Avenue and paused. Where to go? Where were the pictures, the images waiting for him to capture? He turned in a slow half-circle, ignoring the line of dinner-hour cabs waiting in front of him, letting his instinct pick a direction. There. The hot white lights were calling him.

Walking briskly, he cut crosstown, one hand on his camera, the other hanging loosely by his side. The sidewalk hustlers and gutter sharks watched him pass, recognizing a stronger predator. But the hookers, ah, the hookers were another story. They swarmed to him, offered him deals, enticements. He did love women so, their softness hiding such strong, willful blood. But he was not feeding tonight. At least, not of that. Tonight was for a different passion. Bypassing Times Square itself, he wandered the side streets, catching the occasional sideways stare from well-dressed theatergoers on their way from dinner to their entertainment. Only the expensive Konica hanging by his side kept them from assuming he was a panhandler. The long trench had seen better decades, and not even the Salvation Army had been able to find anything nice to say about his boots except for the fact that they had once been sturdy. And the less said about his once-white turtleneck, the better. But he preferred these clothes, using them the same way wildlife photographers hid within camouflaged blinds. He was stalking wildlife as well, a form that was more easily spooked than any herd of gazelles or a solitary fox.

For the next seven hours he took shot after shot of the ebb and flow of humanity around him, occasionally moving to a new spot when people became too aware of him or, more accurately, of the camera. His choices satisfied him. The elderly woman in rags stepping over a crack in the sidewalk with graceful poise. The businesswoman striding along, topcoat open to the bracing wind. Two too-young figures doing a deal with brazen indifference to the mounted policeman just yards away, and the cop's equal indifference to their infractions. The hooker holding a Styrofoam cup in her hands, allowing the steam to rise to her face, taking delicate sips. He loved them all, carefully, surreptitiously, with each click of the shutter, every zoom of the lens to catch their expressions, the curve of their hands, the play of neon across their skin. He could feel the beat of their blood, pulling him all unwilling, and he blessed the cold which kept their scents from him. He couldn't afford the distractions.

Stopping in a Dunkin' Donuts to pick up a cup of coffee, he dug in his trench pocket for a crumpled dollar bill to pay for it. "Why can't you carry a wallet?' he could hear Sasha complain. "That way when someone finally puts you out of your misery I'll know to collect the body." Lovely, longsuffering Sasha. But she forgot her complaints when he had a show ready for her pale white walls, secure in her status as Michael Westin's only gallery. For three long, hungry years she had supported him, and for the last eleven he had returned the favor. He understood obligation, and needing, and the paying of debts.

Finally he came to the last roll of film he had prepared for the night. He took it out of the pouch hanging from his belt and looked at it, black plastic against the black of his thin leather gloves. High-speed black and white, perfect for catching moments silhouetted against the darkness, sudden bursts of light and action. His trademark. One roll left. He still had time to shoot this roll before heading home, still subjects to capture.

Or he could try again, a little voice whispered inside his head. There was time.

Shaking his head to silence the unwanted voice, he removed the used film from the camera, marked it with the date, location, and an identifying number, then replaced it in the pouch. Still the unused film sat in his palm. He could reload the camera, finish the evening out. Or he could save it for the next trip, cutting the session short and going home. At the thought his lips curled in a faint smile. Home to where Danielle slept in their bed, her hair fanned out against the flannel sheets. She would be surprised to see him, surprised and pleased, if he knew his Dani.

Or you could try again.

"Damnit, enough!" He would be a fool to listen to that voice, a fool to even consider it. Hadn't the three attempts been enough to teach him that? If the third time wasn't a charm, then certainly the fourth was for fools. And his kind didn't survive by being fools.

But still the thought lingered, caressing his ego, his artist's conceit. He could picture the shot, frame it perfectly in his mind. The conditions were ideal tonight, the location tailor-made. It would be the perfect finish to this show, the final page of the book he knew Sasha would want to do.

Stuffing the thought back into the darkness of his mind, he deftly inserted the black cartridge, advancing the shutter until the camera was primed. He cast one practiced eye skyward. Four A.M., give or take fifteen minutes. He had another hour, at most, before he would have to head home, wrap his head under a pillow, and get the few hours of sleep he still required before locking himself in the darkroom to develop this night's work. Then dinner with Dani, and perhaps he would take tomorrow night off. Fridays were too busy to get really good photos. Better to spend it at home, in front of a roaring fire, and his smooth-necked, sweet-smelling wife and a bottle of her favorite wine.

You work too hard, she had fussed at him just last month, rubbing a minty-smelling oil into his aching muscles after a particularly grueling night hunched over the lightboard, choosing negatives. *Always pushing, always proving. You don't have anything to prove.* But he did. Had to take better photos, find the most haunting expressions, the perfect lighting. All to prove to himself that he was the photographer his press made him out to be, and not just some freak from a family of freaks, that his work was the result of talent and dedication, not some genetic mutation, a parasite on human existence.

Shh, my love, he could hear Dani whisper. *I'm here, and I love you.* She would whisper that, baring her neck so that he might graze along that smooth dark column, feel the pulsing of her blood . . .

He swore, cutting off those thoughts before his body reacted to the thought of her strength, her warmth. Jamming his hands into the pockets of his trench, he watched the street theater, looking for something that would finish the evening on a positive note, leave him anxious to see the proof page. But the street was empty for the moment, leaving him with the little voice, which had crept back the moment his attention was distracted. *The perfect photograph*, it coaxed him. *Something so heartbreakingly perfect that only you could create. Otherwise this exhibit is going to end on a downer, and there's enough of that in this world, isn't there?*

Cursing under his breath, he scared off a ragged teen who had sidled up next to him. Westin watched the kid's disappearing backside with wry amusement. It had been a long time since anyone had tried to mug him, and he would have given the boy the twenty or so bucks he had in his pocket, just to reward such *chutzpa*.

Checking the street one last time, he sighed and gave up. Time to call it a good haul, and head on home. *To bed, perchance to screw, and then to sleep.* Hanging the camera strap around his shoulder, he adjusted the nylon webbing until the shoulder patch fit snugly against his coat. *There's still film left*, the little voice said, sliding and seducing like a televangelist. *Can't go home with film left.*

"I'll take shots of some of New York's Finest," he told himself. Fragile humans, holding back the night. It would be a good image, and it would please Miguel to be included. And Tonio, his partner. Kid was so green his uniform squeaked when he walked. Veteran and rook, side by side, against the squalor of the bus terminal. Maybe he'd catch them in an argument. He could see that, frame it in his head. The possibilities grew, flicking across the screen in his head fast enough to wipe all thoughts of That Shot out of his head. By the time he reached the corner of Seventh Avenue, he had it all planned out. Stopping to look up at the still-dark sky, he thought he could see just the faintest hint of light creeping skyward from the east. False dawn. At home, he would be watching the deer come down from the wooded area to eat his bushes. He had done an essay on them for National Wildlife which paid well enough to replace the rosebushes the hoofed terrorists had devoured the spring before.

Waiting at the light on the corner of Forty-first and Eighth, something made him tilt his head to the right. There. By the chain-link fence protecting an empty lot. A shadow that wasn't a shadow. His soothing thoughts broke like mirror shards, and he turned his head to stare straight across the street. Live and let live. The fact that he chose not to hunt—did not, in fact, have to—did not mean others might not. Only once had he made it his concern, when a kinswoman had gotten messy, leaving corpses over the city—*his city*. His mouth tightened as he remembered the confrontation that had followed. He hadn't wanted to destroy her—but he wasn't ready to end his existence yet either. And letting her continue was out of the question. Only fools saw humans as fodder. They were kin, higher in some ways, lesser in others, but in the balance of time, equal. He believed that, as his father had believed that, raising his children to live alongside the daylight-driven world as best they could, encouraging them to build support groups, humans—companions—that would offer so that they need not take. It was possible, his father had lectured them, to exist without violence. And so they had. And the daylight world had given him good friends, a loving wife—and the means to express the visions which only his eyes could see.

With that thought in mind, he turned slowly, looking up at the sky behind him. False dawn. It was almost upon him.

The perfect photograph. It would only take one shot. One exposure, and then it's done.

A scrap of memory came over him. "If 't were done, 't were best done quickly . . ." *Damn. Damn damn damn damn.*

It seemed almost as though another person took control; moved his body across the street, dodged the overanxious cabs turning corners to pick up the last fare of the night. Someone else walked across the bare floor of the terminal that even at this hour still hosted a number of grubby souls wandering, some slumped over knapsacks, asleep, some reading newspapers or staring down into their coffee as though it held some terrible answer. His hand powered by someone else reached for the camera, holding it like a talisman, a fetish. Standing on the escalator, he watched out of habit, his mind already on what he was going to do. He could feel it pulling him, a siren's song, and he cursed himself. But he couldn't stop, no more than the first three times he had tried. Tried, and failed.

Crossing over to the next level of escalators, he paused at the first step, willing his body to stop, turn around, get on the bus that would take him home. Only a fool would continue, only a madman. Looking down, he saw first one boot, then the other, move on to the metal steps, his left hand grasping the railing. With his right hand he fingered the camera's casing, stroking his thumb over the shutter button.

At the end of this escalator he stopped, hitting his free hand against the sign that thanked him in Spanish and English for not giving money to panhandlers. The pain made him wince. At least in that they were equal, humans and he. Pain was a bitch. He hit his hand again, then gave up. The siren call, as strong as blood, had him again, and he had no choice but to give in. If it was to be done, it had to be done fast. Get in, get out, go home. Punching the up button, he waited for the elevator that would take him to the rooftop parking lot.

He adjusted the camera in his hand, barely aware of the sweat that ran down the back of his neck and down the front of his shirt. Shifting closer to the roof edge, he leaned against the ornate masonry, bracing himself. A glint of light caught his attention and he squinted, the hair along his arm rising in protest. "One minute more," he told himself. "Just one damn more minute, you bitch, and I'll have you. Come on, come on, do it for me!" He swallowed with difficulty, wishing for the water bottle at arms' reach, as impossible as if it were on another planet.

Another flicker of light caught the first building, fracturing against the wall of windows. "Come on," he said under his breath, unaware of anything except the oncoming moment. He could feel it, a sexual thrill waiting to shoot through his body, better than anything, even the flush of the first draw of blood. This was why he was alive. This was it, this was the perfect moment . . . He drew the camera to his face, focusing on primal instinct. The light rose a fraction higher, and he was dropping the camera, running for the maintenance door, aware only of the screaming animal need to hide, survive, get away from that damn mocking bitch. The camera lay where it fell: abandoned, broken.

"Goddamn," Westin swore, shaking himself free of the memory. "Go home, Westin. It's a fucking picture. Not worth dying for." The woman exiting the elevator glanced at him, pulling her coat closer around her body as she swept past him, eyes forward in a ten-point exhibition of New York street sense. The first rule: never let them see you seeing them. He moved past her on instinct, not realizing until the doors had closed that he passed the Rubicon. "Well goddamn," he said again, but he was grinning. A predator's flash of too-white teeth, a grin of hungry anticipation. His fangs tingled, the veins underneath them widening in response to the

STREETS OF BLOOD

rush of adrenaline coursing through his body.

The parking lot was mostly deserted—the late-night partiers having headed home, and the Jersey commuters not yet in. There were a handful of cars parked in the back for monthly storage, and one beat-up blue Dart pulled in as he stood there. He waited in the shadows until the driver, a heavy-set man wearing workboots and carrying a leather briefcase, passed by him into the elevator.

Going to the edge of the lot, he sat on the cold metal railing, hooking one foot under the longest rung to keep himself from slipping five stories to the pavement waiting below. The air was noticeably colder here, the wind coming at him without buffer. Dawn was coming, damn her. He could feel it in every sinew of his body, every instinct-driven muscle screaming for him to find a dark cave in which to wait the daylight hours out.

Forcing himself to breathe evenly, he took control of those instincts, forcing them back under the layers of civilization and experience. There would be plenty of time to find a bolthole somewhere in the massive bulk of the Port Authority. He had done it before, here and elsewhere. It was all timing. Timing, he reminded himself, and not panicking.

Squinting against the wind, he swung his body into better position, facing eastward, toward the East River. Toward the rising sun.

Idiot, a new, more rational voice said in tones of foreboding. *Do the words crispy critter mean anything to you?* He shrugged off the voice, lifting the camera to his eye. There was only the moment, and the shot. His entire universe narrowed down to that one instant, his entire existence nothing more than the diameter of the lens. His fingers moved with a sure steadiness, adjusting the focus minutely, his body tense.

A particularly aggressive gust of wind shook the rooftop, making him lose the frame. Swearing, he fought to regain it, all the while conscious of seconds ticking by, each moment more deadly than the last. A taloned claw clenched in his gut, and sweat ran along his hairline and down under his collar. "Damn, damn, damn," he chanted under his breath, a mantra. The muscles in his back tightened, his legs spasming. But his arms, his hands, remained still, the muscles cording from the strain.

The first ray of light touched the rooftops, glinting deadly against empty windows. He swore again, his finger hovering over the shutter button.

"Come on, baby," he coaxed it, a tentative lover. "Come here. That's it, you're so perfect."

Another ray joined the first, the faintest hint of yellow in the pure light. The hairs along his arms stirred underneath the turtleneck, his heart agitating with the screaming in his head to *get out get away you dumb fuck get OUT*. His hands remained steady, his eyes frozen, unblinking: waiting, just waiting. He could smell it now, that perfect moment, with more certainty than he'd ever known. Everything slowed, his breathing louder that the wind still pushing the building beneath him, his body quivering under the need for release.

A third ray sprang across the sky, then a fourth and fifth too fast to discern. Suddenly the rooftops were lit by a glorious burst of prism-scattered light, heart-stopping, agonizing, indelible. A ray flashed toward him, reflected by a wall of glass, and glanced off the brick barely a foot to the left. His forefinger oh so slowly pressed toward the shutter button while every muscle twisted in imagined agony. "Come on come on come on . . ." he whispered, holding himself back for the perfect second.

The smooth metal was underneath his fingertip when the first light caught him, slashing against his cheek, his chest, reaching through the skin into his vital organs.

He screamed, falling backwards in a desperate attempt to keep the deadly light from him, slamming to the cold cement floor even as his finger pushed, even as his ears heard the click of the shutter closing underneath the sound of his own primal voice.

His skin was burning, the blood seeping from the pores of his face and arms. The pain was everywhere, searing him, branding him. Tears tinctured with red washed a track down his narrow nose.

Crawling to his feet, Westin barely retained the presence of mind to shove the camera back into its padded carry-bag before dragging himself to the elevator and slamming his fist against the Down button. Blood dripped down his arm and onto the fabric.

The elevator opened in front of him. Westin pushed himself into the empty space, shaking. He leaned against the back wall and drew a deep breath, knowledge of his own stupidity battling with the sheer exhilaration of a different sort of hunt.

All too soon, the rush was over, and he was himself again, drenched in sweat and drying blood. In his memory, the sun rose like some killer angel, and he knew his actions for what they were–vanity.

But he would do it again.

Laura Anne Gilman is the editor, with Keith R. A. DeCandido, of an anthology of shapechanger stories titled *Otherwere*. Her stories have appeared in various anthologies, including *The Day the Magic Stopped, Highwaymen: Robbers and Rogues,* and *Lammas Night,* among others. She works as an editor in New York City, and lives in New Jersey.

*Three are some who will do anything to get into the spotlight . . .
and some who prey upon those desires.*

To Feel Another's Woe

BY CHET WILLIAMSON

had to admit she looked like a vampire when Kevin described her as such. Her face, at least, with those high model's cheekbones and absolutely huge, wet-looking eyes. The jet of her hair set off her pale skin strikingly, and that skin was perfect, nearly luminous. To the best of my knowledge, however, vampires didn't wear Danskin tops and Annie Hall flop-slacks, nor did they audition for Broadway shows.

There must have been two hundred of us jammed into the less than immaculate halls of the Ansonia Hotel that morning, with photo/résumés clutched in one hand, scripts of *A Streetcar Named Desire* in the other. John Weidner was directing a revival at Circle in the Square, and every New York actor with an Equity card and a halfway intelligible Brooklyn dialect under his collar was there to try out. Stanley Kowalski had already been spoken for by a new Italian-American film star with more *chutzpah* than talent, but the rest of the roles were open. I was hoping for Steve or Mitch, or maybe even a standby, just something to pay the rent.

I found myself in line next to Kevin McQuinn, a gay song-and-dance man I'd done Jones Beach with two years before. A nice guy, not at all flouncy. "Didn't know this was a musical," I smiled at him.

"Sure. You never heard of the Stella aria?" And he sang softly, "I'll never stop saying Steh-el-*la* . . .*"

"Seriously. You going dramatic?"

He shrugged. "No choice. Musicals these days are all rock or opera or rock opera. No soft shoes in *Sweeney Todd*."

"*Sweeney Todd* closed ages ago."

"That's 'cause they didn't have no soft shoes."

Then she walked in holding her P/R and script, and sat on the floor with her back to the wall as gracefully as if she owned the place. I was, to Kevin's amusement, instantly smitten.

"Forget it," he said. "She'd eat you alive."

"I wish. Who is she?"

"Name's Sheila Remarque."

"Shitty stage name."

"She was born with it, so she says. Me, I believe her. Nobody'd *pick* that."

"She any good?"

Kevin smiled, a bit less broadly than his usually mobile face allowed. "Let's just say that I've got twenty bucks that says she'll get whatever part she's after."

"Serious?"

"The girl's phenomenal. You catch *Lear* in the park this summer?" I nodded. "She played Goneril."

"Oh *yeah*." I was amazed that I hadn't recalled the name. "She *was* good."

"You said good, I said phenomenal. Along with the critics."

As I thought back, I remembered the performance vividly. Generally Cordelia stole the show from Lear's two nasty daughters, but all eyes had been on Goneril at the matinee I'd seen. It wasn't that the actress had been upstaging, or doing anything to excess. It was simply (or complexly, if you're an actor) that she was so damned *believable*. There'd been no trace of *acting*, no indication shared between actress and audience, as even the finest performers will do, no self-consciousness whatsoever, only utterly true emotion. As I remembered, the one word I had associated with it was *awesome*. How stupid, I thought, to have forgotten her name. "What else do you know about her?" I asked Kevin.

"Not much. A mild reputation with the boys. Love 'em and leave 'em. A Theda Bara vampire type."

"Ever work with her?"

"Three years ago. *Oklahoma* at Allenberry. I did Will Parker, and she was in the chorus. Fair voice, danced a little, but lousy presence. A real poser, you know? I don't know what the hell happened."

I started to ask Kevin if he knew where she studied, when he suddenly tensed. I followed his gaze, and saw a man coming down the hall carrying a dance bag. He was tall and thin, with light-brown hair and a nondescript face. It's hard to describe features on which not the slightest bit of emotion is displayed. Instead of sitting on the floor like the rest of us, he remained standing, a few yards away from Sheila Remarque, whom he looked at steadily, yet apparently without interest. She looked up, saw him, gave a brief smile, and returned to her script.

Kevin leaned closer and whispered. "You want to know about *Ms.* Remarque, *there's* the man you should ask, not me."

"Why? Who is he?" The man hadn't taken his eyes from the girl, but I couldn't tell whether he watched her in lust or anger. At any rate, I admired her self-control. Save for that first glance, she didn't acknowledge him at all.

"Name's Guy Taylor."

"The one who was in *Annie?*"

Kevin nodded. "Three years here. One on the road. Same company I went out with. Used to drink together. He was hilarious, even when he was sober. But put the drinks in him and he'd make Eddie Murphy look like David Merrick. Bars would fall apart laughing."

"He went with this girl?"

"Lived with her for three, maybe four months, just this past year."

"They split up, I take it."

"Mmm-hmm. Don't know much about it, though." He shook his head. "I ran into Guy a week or so ago at the *Circle of Three* auditions. I was really happy to see him, but he acted like he barely knew me. Asked him how his lady was—I'd never met her, but the word had spread—and he told me he was living alone now, so I didn't press it. Asked a couple people and found out she'd walked out on him. Damn near crushed him. He must've had it hard."

"That's love for you."

"Yeah. Ain't I glad I don't mess with women."

Kevin and I started talking about other things then, but I couldn't keep my eyes off Sheila Remarque's haunting face, nor off the vacuous features of Guy Taylor, who watched the girl with the look of a stolid, stupid guard dog. I wondered if he'd bite anybody who dared to talk to her.

At ten o'clock, as scheduled, the line started to move. When I got to the table, the assistant casting director, or whatever flunky was using that name, looked at my P/R and at me, evidently approved of what he saw, and told me to come back at two o'clock for a reading. Kevin, right beside me, received only a shake of the head and a "thank you for coming."

"Dammit," Kevin said as we walked out. "I shouldn't have stood behind you in line, then I wouldn't've looked so un-macho. I mean, didn't they *know* about Tennessee Williams, for crissake?"

When I went back to the Ansonia at two, there were over thirty people already waiting, twice as many men as women. Among the dozen or so femmes was Sheila Remarque, her nose still stuck in her script, oblivious to those around her. Guy Taylor was also there, standing against a wall as before. He had a script open in front of him, and from time to time would look down at it, but most of the time he stared at Sheila Remarque, who, I honestly believe, was totally indifferent to, and perhaps even ignorant of, his perusal.

As I sat watching the two of them, I thought that the girl would make a stunning Blanche, visually at least. She seemed to have that elusive, fragile quality that Vivien Leigh exemplified so well in the film. I'd only seen Jessica Tandy, who'd originated the role, in still photos, but she always seemed too horsey-looking for my tastes. By no stretch of the imagination could Sheila Remarque be called horsey. She was exquisite porcelain, and I guess I must have become transfixed by her for a moment, for the next time I looked away from her toward Guy Taylor, he was staring at me with that same damned expressionless stare. I was irritated by the proprietary emotion I placed on his face, but found it so disquieting that I couldn't glare back. So I looked at my script again.

After a few minutes, a fiftyish man I didn't recognize came out and spoke to us. "Okay, Mr. Weidner will eliminate some of you without hearing you read. Those of you who make the final cut, be prepared to do one of two scenes. We'll have the ladies who are reading for Blanche and you men reading for Mitch first. As you were told this morning, ladies, scene ten, guys six. Use your scripts if you want to. Not's okay too. Let's go."

Seven women and fifteen men, me and Guy Taylor among them, followed the man into what used to be a ballroom. At one end of the high-ceilinged room was a series of raised platforms with a few wooden chairs on them. Ten yards back from this makeshift stage were four folding director's chairs. Another five yards in back of these were four rows of ten each of the same rickety wooden chairs there were on the stage. We sat on these while Weidner, the director, watched us file in. "I'm sorry we can't be in the theater," he said, "but the set there now can't be struck for auditions. We'll have to make do here. Let's start with the gentlemen for a change."

He looked at the stage manager, who read from his clipboard, "Adams."

That was me. I stood up, script in hand. Given a choice, I always held book in auditions. It gives you self-confidence, and if you try to go without and go up on the lines, you look like summer stock. Besides, that's why they call them readings.

"Would someone be kind enough to read Blanche in scene six with Mr. Adams?" Weidner asked. A few girls were rash enough to raise their hands and volunteer for a scene they hadn't prepared, but Weidner's eyes fell instantly on Sheila Remarque. "Miss Remarque, isn't it?" She nodded. "My congratulations on your Goneril. Would you be kind enough to read six? I promise I won't let it color my impressions of your scene ten."

Bullshit, I thought, but she nodded graciously, and together we ascended the squeaking platform.

Have you ever played a scene opposite an animal or a really cute little kid? If you have, you know how utterly impossible it is to get the audience to pay any attention to you whatsoever. That was exactly how I felt doing a scene with Sheila Remarque. Not that my reading wasn't good, because it was, better by far than I would have done reading with a prompter or an ASM, because she gave me something I could react to. She made Blanche so real that I had to be real too, and I was good.

But not as good as her. No way.

She used no book, had all the moves and lines down pat. But like I said of her Goneril, there was no *indication* of acting at all. She spoke and moved on that cheapjack stage as if she were and had always been Blanche DuBois, formerly of Belle Rêve, presently of Elysian Fields, New Orleans in the year 1947. Weidner didn't interrupt after a few lines, a few pages, the way directors usually do, but let the scene glide on effortlessly to its end, when, still holding my script, I kissed Blanche DuBois on "her forehead and her yes and finally her lips," and she sobbed out her line, "'Sometimes—there's God—so quickly!'" and it was over and Blanche DuBois vanished, leaving Sheila Remarque and me on that platform with them all looking up at us soundlessly. Weidner's smile was suffused with wonder. But not for me. I'd been good, but she'd been great.

"Thank you, Mr. Adams. Thank you very much. Nice reading. We have your résumé, yes. Thank you," and he nodded in a gesture of dismissal that took me off the platform. "Thank you too, Miss Remarque. Well done. While you're already up there, would you care to do scene ten for us?"

She nodded, and I stopped at the exit. Ten was a hell of a scene, the one where Stanley and the drunken Blanche are alone in the flat, and I had to see her do it. I whispered a request to stay to the fiftyish man who'd brought us in, and he nodded an okay, as if speaking would break whatever spell was on the room. I remained there beside him.

"Our Stanley Kowalski was to be here today to read with the Blanches and Stellas, but a TV commitment prevented him," Weidner said somewhat bitchily. "So if one of you gentlemen would be willing to read with Miss Remarque . . ."

There were no idiots among the men. Not one volunteered. "Ah, Mr. Taylor," I heard Weidner say. My stomach tightened. I didn't know whether he'd chosen Taylor to read with her out of sheer malevolence, or whether he was ignorant of their relationship, and it was coincidence—merely his spotting Taylor's familiar face. Either way, I thought, the results could be unpleasant. And from the way several of the gypsies' shoulders stiffened, I could tell they were thinking the same thing. "Would you please?"

Taylor got up slowly, and joined the girl on the platform. As far as I could see, there was no irritation in his face, nor was there any sign of dismay in Sheila Remarque's deep, wet eyes. She smiled at him as though he were a stranger, and took a seat facing the "audience."

"Anytime," said Weidner. He sounded anxious. Not impatient, just anxious.

Sheila Remarque became drunk. Just like that, in the space of a heartbeat. Her whole body fell into the posture of a long-developed alcoholism. Her eyes blurred, her mouth opened, a careless slash across the ruin of her face, lined and bagged with booze. She spoke the lines as if no one had ever said them before, so any onlooker would swear that it was Blanche DuBois's liquor-dulled brain that was creating them, and in no way were they merely words that had existed on a printed page for forty years, words filtered through the voice of a performer.

She finished speaking into the unseen mirror, and Guy Taylor walked toward her as Stanley Kowalski. Blanche saw him, spoke to him. But though she spoke to Stanley Kowalski, it was Guy Taylor who answered, only Guy Taylor reading lines, without a trace of emotion. Oh, the *expression* was there, the nuances, the rhythm of the lines and their meaning was clear. But it was like watching La Duse play a scene with an electronic synthesizer. She destroyed him, and I thought back, hoping she hadn't done the same to me.

This time Weidner didn't let the scene play out to the end. I had to give him credit. As awful as Taylor was, I couldn't have brought myself to deny the reality of Sheila Remarque's performance by interrupting, but Weidner did, during one of Stanley's longer speeches about his cousin who opened beer bottles with his teeth. "Okay, fine," Weidner called out. "Good enough. Thank you, Mr. Taylor. I think that's all we need see of you today." Weidner looked away from him. "Miss Remarque, if you wouldn't mind, I'd like to hear that one more time. Let's see . . . Mr. Carver, would you read Stanley, please." Carver, a chorus gypsy who had no business doing heavy work, staggered to the platform, his face pale, but I didn't wait to see if he'd survive. I'd seen enough wings pulled off flies for one day, and was out the door, heading to the elevator even before Taylor had come off the platform.

I had just pushed the button when I saw Taylor, his dance bag over his shoulder, come out of the ballroom. He walked slowly down the hall toward me, and I prayed the car would arrive quickly enough that I wouldn't have to ride with him. But the Ansonia's lifts have seen better days, and by the time I stepped into the car he was a scant ten yards away. I held the door for him. He stepped in, the doors closed, and we were alone.

Taylor looked at me for a moment. "You'll get Mitch," he said flatly.

I shrugged self-consciously and smiled. "There's a lot of people to read."

"But they won't read Mitch with *her*. And your reading *was* good."

I nodded agreement. "She helped."

"May I," he said after a pause, "give you some advice?" I nodded. "If they give you Mitch," he said, "turn them down."

"Why?" I asked, laughing.

"She's sure to be Blanche. Don't you think?"

"So?"

"Have you seen me work?"

"I saw you in *Annie*. And in *Bus Stop* at ELT."

"And?"

"You were good. Real good."

"And what about today?"

I looked at the floor.

"Tell me." I looked at him, my lips pinched. "Shitty," he said. "Nothing there, right?"

"Not much," I said.

"She did that. Took it from me." He shook his head. "Stay away from her. She can do it to you too."

The first thing you learn in professional theater is that actors are children. I say that, knowing full well that I'm one myself. Our egos are huge, yet our feelings area as delicate as orchids. In a way, it stems from the fact that in other trades, rejections are impersonal. Writers aren't rejected—it's one particular story or novel that is. For factory workers, or white-collars, it's lack of knowledge or experience that loses jobs. But for an actor, it's the way he looks, the way he talks, the way he moves that make the heads nod yes or no, and that's rejection on the most deeply personal scale, like kids calling each other Nickel-nose or Fatso. And often that childish hurt extends to other relationships as well. Superstitious? Imaginative? Ballplayers have nothing on us. So when Taylor started blaming Sheila Remarque for his thespian rockslide, I knew it was only because he couldn't bear to admit that it was *he* who had let his craft slip away, not the girl who had taken it from him.

The elevator doors opened, and I stepped off. "Wait," he said, coming after me. "You don't believe me."

"Look, man," I said, turning in exasperation, "I don't know what went on between you and her and I don't care, okay? If she messed you over, I'm sorry, but I'm an actor and I need a job and if I get it I'll *take* it!"

His face remained placid. "Let me buy you a drink," he said.

"Oh Jesus . . ."

"You don't have to be afraid. I won't get violent." He forced a smile. "Do you think I've *been* violent? Have I even raised my voice?"

"No."

"Then please. I just want to talk to you."

I had to admit to myself that I *was* curious. Most actors would have shown more fire over things that meant so much to them, but Taylor was strangely zombielike, as if life were just a walk-through. "All right," I said, "all right."

We walked silently down Broadway. By the time we got to Charlie's it was three thirty, a slow time for the bar. I perched on a stool, but Taylor shook his head. "Table," he said, and we took one and ordered. It turned out we were both bourbon drinkers. "Jesus," he said after a long sip. "It's cold."

It was. Manhattan winters are never balmy, and the winds that belly through the streets cut through anything short of steel.

"All right," I said. "We're here. You're buying me a drink. Now. You have a story for me?"

"I do. And after I tell it you can go out and do what you like."

"I intend to."

"I won't try to stop you," he went on, not hearing me. "I don't think I could even if I wanted to. It's your life, your career."

"Get to the point."

"I met her last summer. June. I know Joe Papp, and he invited me to the party after the Lear opening, so I went. Sheila was there with a guy, and I walked up and introduced myself to them, and told her how much I enjoyed her performance. She thanked me, very gracious, very friendly, and told me she'd seen me several times and liked my work as well. I thought it odd at the time, the way she came on to me. Very strong, with those big, wet, bedroom eyes of hers eating me up. But her date didn't seem to care. He didn't seem to care about much of anything. Just stood there and drank while she talked, then sat down and drank some more. She told me later, when we were together, that he was a poet. Unpublished, of course, she said. She told me that his work wasn't very good technically, but that it was very emotional. 'Rich with feeling,' were the words she used.

"I went to see her in Lear again, several times really, and was more impressed with each performance. The poet was waiting for her the second time I went, but the third, she left alone. I finessed her into a drink, we talked, got along beautifully. She told me it was all over between her and the poet, and that night she ended up in my bed. It was good, and she seemed friendly, passionate, yet undemanding. After a few more dates, a few more nights and mornings, I suggested living together, no commitments. She agreed, and the next weekend she moved in with me.

"I want you to understand one thing, though. I never loved her. I never told her I loved her or even suggested it. For me, it was companionship and sex, and that was all. Though she was good to be with, nice to kiss, to hold, to share things with, I never loved her. And I know she never loved me." He signaled the waiter and another drink came. Mine was still half full. "So I'm not a . . . a victim of unrequited love, all right? I just want you to be sure of that." I nodded and he went on.

"It started a few weeks after we were living together. She'd want to play games with me, she said. Theater games. You know, pretend she was doing something or say something to get a certain emotion out of me. Most of the time she didn't let me know right away what she was doing. She'd see if she could get me jealous, or mad, or sullen. Happy too. And then she'd laugh and say she was just kidding, that she'd just wanted to see my reactions. Well, I thought that was bullshit. I put it down as a technique exercise rather than any method crap, and in a way I could understand it—wanting to be face-to-face with emotions to examine them—but I still thought it was an imposition on me, an invasion of my privacy. She didn't do it often, maybe once or twice a week. I tried it on her occasionally, but she never bit, just looked at me as if I were a kid trying to play a man's game.

"Somewhere along the line it started getting kinky. While we were having sex, she'd call me by another name, or tell me about something sad she'd remembered, anything to get different reactions, different rises out of me. Sometimes . . ." He looked down, drained his drink. "Sometimes I'd . . . come and I'd cry at the same time."

The waiter was nearby, and I signaled for another round. "Why did you stay with her?"

"It wasn't . . . she didn't do this all the time, like I said. And I *liked* her. It got so I didn't even mind it when she'd pull this stuff on me, and she knew it. Once she even got me when I was stoned, and a couple of times after I'd had too much to drink. I didn't care. Until winter came.

"I hadn't been doing much after the summer. A few industrials here in town, some voice-over stuff. Good money, but just straight song and dance, flat narration, and no reviews. So the beginning of December Harv Piersall calls me to try out for *Ahab*. The musical that closed in previews? He wanted me to read for Starbuck, a scene where Starbuck is planning to shoot Ahab to save Pequod. It was a good scene, a strong scene, and I got up there and I couldn't do a thing with it. Not a goddamned thing. I was utterly flat, just like in my narration and my singing around a Pontiac. But there it hadn't mattered—I hadn't had to put out any emotion—just sell the product, that was all. But *now,* when I had to feel something, had to express something, I couldn't. Harv asked me if anything was wrong, and I babbled some excuse about not feeling well, and when he invited me to come back and read again I did, a day later, and it was the same.

"That weekend I went down to St. Mark's to see Sheila in an OOB production—it was a new translation of *Medea* by some grad student at NYU—and she'd gotten the title role. They'd been rehearsing off and on for a month, no pay to speak of, but she was enthusiastic about it. It was the largest and most important part she'd done. Papp was there that night, someone got Prince to come too. The translation was garbage. No set, tunics for costumes, nothing lighting. But Sheila . . ."

He finished his latest drink, spat the ice back into the glass. "She was . . . superb. Every emotion was real. They should have been. She'd taken them from me.

"Don't look at me like that. I thought what you're thinking too, at first. That I was paranoid, jealous of her talents. But once I started to think things through, I knew it was the only answer.

"She was so loving to me afterward, smiled at me and held my arm and introduced me to her friends, and I felt as dull and lifeless as that poet I'd seen her with. Even then I suspected what she'd done, but I didn't say anything to her about it. That next week when I tried to get in touch with the poet, I found out he'd left the city, gone home to wherever it was he'd come from. I went over to Lincoln Center, to their videotape collection, and watched *King Lear.* I wanted to see if I could find anything that didn't jell, that wasn't quite *right.* Hell, I didn't know what I was looking for, just that I'd know when I saw it."

He shook his head. "It was . . . incredible. On the tape there was no sign of the performance I'd seen her give. Instead I saw a flat, lifeless, amateurish performance, dreadfully bad in contrast to the others. I couldn't believe it, watched it again. The same thing. Then I knew why she never auditioned for commercials, or for film. It didn't . . . *show up* on camera. She could fool people, but not a camera.

"I went back to the apartment then, and told her what I'd found out. It wasn't guessing on my part, not a theory, because

I *knew* by then. You see, I *knew*.

Taylor stopped talking and looked down into his empty glass. I thought perhaps I'd made a huge mistake in going to the bar with him, for he was most certainly paranoid, and could conceivably become violent as well, in spite of his assurances to the contrary. "So what . . ." My "so" came out too much like "sho," but I pushed on with my question while he flagged the waiter, who raised an eyebrow, but brought more drinks. "So what did she say? When you told her?"

"She . . . verified it. Told me that I was right. 'In a way,' she said. In a way."

"Well . . ." I shook my head to clear it. ". . . didn't she probably mean that she was just studying you? That's hardly, hardly *stealing* your emotions, is it?"

"No. She stole them."

"That's silly. That's still silly. You've still got them."

"No. I wanted . . . when I knew for sure, I wanted to kill her. The way she smiled at me, as though I were powerless to take anything back, as though she had planned it all from the moment we met—that made me want to kill her." He turned his empty eyes on me. "But I didn't. Couldn't. I couldn't get angry enough."

He sighed. "She moved out. That didn't bother me. I was glad. As glad as I could feel after what she'd done. I don't know *how* she did it. I think it was something she learned, or learned she had. I don't know whether I'll ever get them back or not, either. Oh, not from *her*. Never from her. But on my own. Build them up inside me somehow. The emotions. The feelings. Maybe someday."

He reached across the table and touched my hand, his fingers surprisingly warm. "So much I don't know. But one thing I do. She'll do it again, find someone else, *you* if you let her. I saw how you were looking at her today." I pulled my hand away from his, bumping my drink. He grabbed it before it spilled, set it upright. "Don't," he cautioned. "Don't have anything to do with her."

"It's absurd," I said, half stuttering. "Ridiculous. You still . . . show emotions."

"Maybe. Maybe a few. But they're only outward signs. Inside

it's hollow." His head went to one side. "You don't believe me."

"N—no . . ." And I didn't, not then.

"You should have known me before."

Suddenly I remembered Kevin at the audition, and his telling me how funny and wild Guy Taylor had gotten on a few drinks. My own churning stomach reminded me of how many we had had sitting here for less than an hour, and my churning mind showed me Sheila Remarque's drunk, drunk, perfectly drunk Blanche DuBois earlier that afternoon. "You've had . . ." I babbled, ". . . how many drinks have you had?"

He shrugged.

"But . . . you're not . . . showing any *signs* . . ."

"Yes. That's right," he said in a clear, steady, sober voice. "That's right."

He crossed his forearms on the table, lowered his head onto them, and wept. The sobs were loud, prolonged, shaking his whole body.

He wept.

"There!" I cried, staggering to my feet. "There, see? See? You're *crying*, you're *crying!* See?"

He raised his head and looked at me, still weeping, still weeping, with not one tear to be seen.

◊◊◊

When the call came offering me Mitch, I took the part. I didn't even consider turning it down. Sheila Remarque had, as Kevin, Guy Taylor, and I had anticipated, been cast as Blanche DuBois, and she smiled warmly at me when I entered the studio for the first reading, as though she remembered our audition with fondness. I was pleasant, but somewhat aloof at first, not wanting the others to see, to suspect what I was going to do.

I thought it might be difficult to get her alone, but it wasn't. She had already chosen me, I could tell, watching me through the readings, coming up to me and chatting at the breaks. By the end of the day she'd learned where I lived, that I was single, unattached, and straight, and that I'd been bucking for eight years to get a part this good. She told me that she lived only a block away from my building (a lie, I later found out), and, after the rehearsal, suggested we take a cab together and split the expense. I agreed, and the cab left us out on West 72nd next to the park.

It was dark and cold, and I saw her shiver under her down-filled jacket. I shivered too, for we were alone at last, somewhat hidden by the trees, and there were no passersby to be seen, only the taxis and buses and cars hurtling past.

I turned to her, the smile gone from my face. "I know what you've done," I said. "I talked to Guy Taylor. He told me all about it. And warned me."

Her face didn't change. She just hung on to that soft half smile of hers, and watched me with those liquid eyes.

"He said . . . you'd be after me. He told me not to take the part. But I had to. I had to know if it's true, all he said."

Her smile faded, she looked down at the dirty, ice-covered sidewalk, and nodded, creases of sadness at the corners of her eyes. I reached out and did what I had planned, said what I had wanted to say to her ever since leaving Guy Taylor crying without tears at the table in Charlie's.

"Teach me," I said, taking her hand as gently as I knew how. "I'd be no threat to you, no competition for roles. In fact, you may need me, need a man who can equal you on stage. Because there aren't any now. You can take what you want from me as long as you can teach me how to get it back again.

"Please. Teach me."

When she looked up at me, her face was wet with tears. I kissed them away, neither knowing nor caring whose they were.

Chet Williamson's books include *Soulstorm, Ash Wednesday,* and *Lowland Riders.* His stories have appeared in *The New Yorker, Twilight Zone,* and *Alfred Hitchcock's Mystery Magazine,* among other periodicals.

Who says vampires don't know a thing about romance . . .

Softly While You're Sleeping

BY EVELYN E. SMITH

et's not take a cab," Ann proposed, as they came out of the coffee shop. "Let's walk; it's only ten blocks or so. Or don't you like walking?"

Tom squeezed her arm. "Doll, I'm a country boy. Walked ten miles every day through roaring blizzards and raging hurricanes and all that jazz just to get myself an education. But I never expected to find a city girl who liked to walk. Don't tell me you like to cook, too?" He grinned down at her. "Or am I asking too much?"

"Much too much!" Ann hated cooking, and the truth was she hated walking, too. On a blistering hot night like that, the prospect was—well—not sheer horror, because she knew what that could be like, but bad enough. She wasn't masochistic, but it was just after midnight, and, if they walked, they might run into Mr. Varri starting on his nightly rounds. She was desperately anxious to meet him face to face. If Tom was with her, she wouldn't be afraid . . . anyhow, she'd be less afraid.

"You must live right by the river," Tom observed, as they pushed further and further east. "One of those big new luxury apartment houses, eh?"

"I live a block away from the river. But not in a new house."

"They've done a nice job converting some of those old mansions," he said.

She smiled. When they reached the cobbled street with its two rows of white-trimmed black brick tenements, it was empty, and the incandescent moonlight bathing it only emphasized its desolation. Mr. Varri must have gone already.

"Cobblestones in New York—can you beat that?" Tom said wonderingly. And he shivered, though perspiration was streaking his ruddy face. "They ought to do something, though—plant some trees or *something!* It looks . . . dead. What kind of people would want to live in a place like this?"

"People like me, for instance," she said, stopping in front of one of the black brick houses.

"Gosh, Ann I—I'm sorry; I—" And suddenly something swooped down at them from overhead. Tom pushed her violently up the steps and into the tiny vestibule. "Those things can be dangerous!" His voice was shaking.

And her laugh was cracked. "Some country boy—afraid of a bird!"

He glanced over his shoulder, through the protecting glass of the outer door. "That wasn't a bird," he said. "It was a bat."

She had known, of course, but she had to keep on pretending to herself. "I thought bats were really harmless, afraid of people?"

"Normally, they are. A bat wouldn't come as close to people as that, not after dark, anyway, unless it was rabid . . ."

"I don't think it's rabid," Ann said.

A door down the hall creaked open; Mrs. Brumi's moon face glimmered from the shadows. "Sorry if we disturbed you, ma'am," Tom said, giving her the boyish-charm smile full-voltage. She stared at him expressionlessly.

"What on earth was that?" Tom demanded, as they started up the narrow stairs.

Ann waited until they'd climbed two flights before she answered, "My landlady. She worries about my morals, disapproves of my friends, and what can I do? She comes from the same tribe as my father."

"Tribe!" Tom squeaked.

"In Albania, *tribe* is just a word to—well—group people who come from the same part of the country. And everybody who lives in the same part is likely to be connected somehow." She wasn't being entirely truthful. A tribe was a tribe.

"Relatives can be hell," Tom agreed. "You ought to see my aunt Nonie—a real kook if ever there was one."

Ann lived on the third floor. Her apartment was in almost opulent contrast to the rest of the house, and she had come to expect a gasp of surprise from newcomers, as she switched on the light. "Well," Tom said. "We-ell, you really do have the place fixed up; you'd almost think . . ."

". . . you were in one of the new luxury apartment houses . . . ?" she finished for him.

He flushed. "Ann, I didn't mean—Honestly, I didn't realize—All the fellows said you must be making at least. . . ." His regular-featured face took on an exalted expression; he was posing for a statue—Champion of Women's Rights. "I didn't dream the firm paid women so much less than men. It's a darned shame."

"My salary isn't too bad. I just don't believe in spending money on rent." Then she smiled. "I'll go make us something cold to drink. First I'll turn on the fans, though; it's stifling in here." She had two fans, one at each end of the apartment, but though both sets of wings beat the air energetically, it remained always hot and stagnant.

"Keep on plugging; someday you'll have enough saved up to get an air-conditioner," he laughed, as she went into the kitchen. Then he was embarrassed again. "Hell, Ann," he called in after her, "I don't make so much money myself." She knew he didn't—less than half of what she herself made.

She started taking out ice, enjoying the cold touch of the cubes on her warm, sticky fingers. He came into the kitchen behind her. "What on earth is that?" he demanded staring.

"A bathtub," Ann said composedly. "Lots of the old houses have bathtubs in the kitchen. Someday I'll get a stall shower put in." She handed him a glass. "How are you on plumbing?"

He looked surprised. "I don't know; I never tried."

"No good," she decided.

They went back to the living room. Tom punctiliously waited

until she sat on the couch before he seated himself beside her. "I don't want to sound officious, Ann," he said, "but I don't think this is a good place for a girl living alone. Even if a relative of yours does own the house, the street isn't safe."

"Mrs. Brumi is not a relative of mine," she said emphatically. "And the street's safe enough. This is the East Side. It's over on the West Side that they have the street gangs and the muggings. Here, you hardly ever see anyone late at night."

"Oh, it's quiet, all right," he agreed, picking up his drink. His Adam's apple moved up and down contentedly as he swallowed. Then he transferred the drink to his other hand, and, moving closer on the couch, put the liberated hand—and the arm attached to it—around her waist. "Listen, doll, you probably think I have a hell of a nerve coming fresh from the hinterlands and starting to tell you how to run your life, but sometimes somebody from the outside can get a more objective look at things, If you know what I mean. I still say this isn't the kind of place a girl like you should be living in, and I don't mean the safety bit. Appearances are pretty important these days; no matter how nicely you've fixed up your apartment, the house is squalid—you can't get away from that. Why, I wouldn't be surprised if part of the reason you're not making the money a girl in your position ought to is because you're living like this, so the firm feels you don't have the top-executive outlook."

Now the boyish smile was for her alone. "Don't misunderstand me, doll. It doesn't matter at all about your folks' being Albanian. The only thing is, you've got to work twice as hard to prove you have the real American viewpoint."

He took another swallow of his drink. "You don't have to go out on a financial limb to live decently. If you teamed up with another nice girl, you could move into one of those efficiency apartments a lot of the better buildings are renting. Sure, you'd have less space, but you'd have modern plumbing, air-conditioning, *and* an address you'd be proud of. The whole deal probably wouldn't run you more than a few extra dollars each month, and you'll find it'll be worth every cent of it. . . ."

Something flopped against the window. "It's the bat!" she shrieked. "It's trying to get in! Do something, Tom!"

"For Pete's sake; it couldn't get through the screens, even if it wanted to." His arm tightened. "And this is a hell of a time to be talking about bats. How about dousing those lights, doll? They make the place even hotter."

"Look out of the window," she urged. "See if it is the bat."

He sighed, and then laughed. "Okay, little girl, anything to make you feel better. He strolled over to the window. "Must've been the wind," he reported. "Not a thing in sight."

"Not a thing?"

"There's a man out there. But I thought bats were what you were interested in."

"What kind of man?" she insisted.

"Tall, young, good-looking—if you like the Valentino type." He laughed comfortably, sure that she didn't. "He's wearing a T-shirt and slacks. They look white, but it could be the moonlight. Sensible fellow—wish I'd dressed that way myself." He grinned, because you didn't go to the theatre in T-shirt and slacks, not unless you sat in the balcony. "Very clean type," he finished kindly.

"It must be Mr. Varri."

"Is that so?" Tom flung his thick body heavily beside her. He took his drink in his right hand and her left breast in his left. "Now, where were we . . . ?"

It never gets too hot for them, she thought smolderingly.

It had been a burningly hot night when she first saw Mr. Varri. She couldn't sleep, and she was sitting by the window, hoping for a breeze from the river. He came walking down the street; in his T-shirt and slacks, he could have been anybody—from one of the tenements on the block or one of the "luxury" houses by the river. His face was pale and sad. He meant nothing to her, and soon after she fell asleep.

She was awakened by whistling outside. She got up and looked out of the window. It wasn't light yet; he was coming back along the cobblestones. He was less immaculate, but still very clean. There was a rosy joy in his face. Whatever he does, he can't have been working hard, she thought fretfully. But it was obvious that he hadn't been at work. He was either a lover or a criminal; she hoped a criminal and that he would be caught, not because of whatever else he might have done, but because he had robbed her of her sleep; she'd never be able to get back to it again that night. She sat at the window, watching a thick pink dawn spread stickily over the street trying to remember the name of the tune he had been whistling.

When she came downstairs later that morning, Mrs. Brumi was mopping the front steps. "I want to get finished with this before it gets too hot," she said, wiping sweat from her forehead. "You look tired, Anna; heat getting you?"

Only the middle-aged and the old let themselves be "gotten" by the heat. "It's because I haven't had enough sleep. Four o'clock in the morning, a man came walking down the street, whistling as if he were the only one in the world!"

"Some people got no consideration!" Mrs. Brumi agreed.

"He was dressed all in white," Ann said, wondering now why this should have seemed sinister to her the night before.

"Sounds like Mr. Varri; he works in one of the hospitals. Lives in Mrs. Lugat's place." Mrs. Brumi gave Ann a sly look. "A nice boy—clean and polite and quiet. And he comes from the old country, Anna, from the hills like your papa."

Ann wished Mrs. Brumi wouldn't call her *Anna*. But Mrs. Brumi had known her ever since she was born. Ann's family hadn't lived in Mrs. Brumi's house, but further down the street, in a house that had been torn down later to make room for the luxury apartments Tom admired. Ann had been still quite little when her family moved up to Washington Heights, to a steam-heated apartment with a private bathroom and a refrigerator that made its own ice. "But we can find all of these things in this neighborhood," Ann's father had complained. "Why must we move so far away?"

"I want my family to have a nice place to live in," her mother had said. "Even more, I don't want them to grow up in this neighborhood." Ann's mother had come from Tirana; she didn't like the hill people.

Time passed. Anna had gone to college and become Ann. Her parents had died, and she'd come back to the old neighborhood. The law had required Mrs. Brumi to put steam heat in her flats and install private toilets; having gone so far, she had put in electric refrigerators also. Rents were three times as high as they'd been when Anna was little, but they were still less than half that of most other apartments. They were in great demand, but Mrs. Brumi had given Ann preference.

The neighborhood had changed. The old-country people were still there, lurking implacably behind drawn blinds, but new-country people had moved in among them, interesting and Bohemian people—artists and actors and musicians and doctors from the nearby hospitals. Mrs. Brumi couldn't seem to get it through her head that Ann was now one of the interesting people and had no more old-country ties. She criticized everything Ann did. "Why do you want to fix up your apartment all arty-smarty? It's like paint on the face of an old lady; no matter how much she puts on, you can still see a hag underneath. When you get yourself a husband who makes a good salary, you'll move to a nice house in Long Island and fix it up. Silly to make this place like a department store, the way those arty-smarty pigs do." The arty-smarty pigs, of course, being the actors and artists and musicians.

She had commented freely and adversely upon the young men who came to help Ann paint walls and put up bookshelves. "They're not the kind of boys I'd like my daughters to go out with. . . . If they were still looking for husbands, of course," she added smugly. Her daughters had all been old-country-type girls and had made solid old-country-type marriages; one had even landed a dentist.

"I'm only saying this for your own good, Anna, but those boy friends of yours look like scum. They look like the kind that don't have any respect for a young girl. You can do better than them at least, Anna. You're not bad-looking, even if you are too skinny. All right, so maybe you don't have a dowry, but you've got a steady job."

Mrs. Brumi also disapproved of the long stretches when there were no young men at all, and Ann sat home evenings, reading and listening to her hi-fi. "That's no life for a young girl, specially when she isn't so very young any more and hasn't time to sit and wait. Now, I know a nice young man whose folks come from Scutari. He's a widower with a nice little butcher shop of his own. His mama lives with him and she'd be taking care of the two little boys, so he wouldn't stop you if you wanted to keep on working. . . ."

At this point, Ann had exploded, and told Mrs. Brumi firmly to mind her own business. Mrs. Brumi's broad face hadn't changed expression, but she stopped dropping in on Ann with fattening old-country dishes and nauseating old-country advice. Ann supposed she ought to be thankful that the old woman did no more now than call her by her first name. She had a feeling, though, that Mrs. Brumi was only quiescent, and that soon she'd erupt again with another small Albanian businessman.

However, Ann couldn't make herself move away. She'd already put too much into the apartment—not money but lots of time and taste. She'd never be able to get one as cheap anywhere else, and she needed her money for the costly annual winter vacations, the clothes from Bonwit's and Saks', and the warm, comfortable bank account.

Yet evenings, in the drenching heat of her apartment, self-doubts started to come at about the same time as darkness. Maybe the scheme of things she'd worked out for herself wasn't perfect; maybe an air-conditioner would be a better investment than a trip to Bermuda. She hadn't really enjoyed herself in Miami, the winter before, or in Mexico City, before that. She'd met young men, but she couldn't meet them on their own terms. Looks and clothes weren't enough—a girl had to be a slut also. Maybe there was something of the old country left in her, she thought.

It was foolish, she knew, not to give up one vacation for an air-conditioner. That didn't mean giving up the plan of things. She could go to Bermuda the year after. But she was afraid–break one link and the whole chain of dreams would fall apart.

The second night she saw Mr. Varri was even hotter than the first. She hadn't even tried to go to sleep but sat at her window, greedily sucking at an imaginary breeze. He came down the street, pale-faced and sad, his feet almost noiseless on the cobblestones. But the hospitals are all in the other direction, she thought. Not necessarily all, she reassured herself; there might be others.

When she fell asleep, her dreams were unlike any she'd ever had before. They would have been nightmares, but the necessary terror was lacking. Mr. Varri woke her up again just before dawn, singing the same tune he'd whistled the night before. The words brought recognition; her father sung it sometimes, and it always made her mother angry—why, Anna never knew. It seemed so silly and harmless; the words the same as in a thousand other folksongs. So, although Mr. Varri wasn't singing in English, she understood him. . . .

> Do not cry, my dearest one,
> There is no need for weeping.
> Happiness I'll bring to you,
> Softly while you're sleeping. . . .

As he passed beneath her window, he looked up, directly at where she was standing, and she felt awareness come alive between them, although she knew it was her imagination; he couldn't possibly see her in the darkness. Yet he smiled and moved his hand in a diffident wave. Mrs. Brumi must have told him about me, she assured herself. But she crossed her arms across her chest to cover the thin nightgown and the strap held up by a safety-pin, because his face looked as if he saw her quite clearly.

The next morning she deliberately sought out Mrs. Brumi. "That man—the one you said must be Mr. Varri—woke me up again. He was singing, and so loud it's a wonder the whole street didn't wake up. Can't you ask Mrs. Lugat to speak to him?"

"I didn't hear nothing," Mrs. Brumi said. "And I sleep to the front."

"But you must have heard," Ann insisted. "It was so loud."

Mrs. Brumi shook her stolid head. "Girls who aren't married think their dreams are real. . . ."

The nasty, lying old bitch, Ann thought. She's just getting even because I told her to mind her own business. On her way to work, she met several people whom she knew slightly. All of them lived on the street; none of them had heard any singing in the night.

After that, he sang every night as he came home, sang until the glass in all the windows on the street should have quivered and angry heads come popping out. But no one seemed to hear; it was as if his voice existed only in her head. She was eager to see him by daylight, to speak to him, not to stop his singing, but to have him assure her that he had sung. She never saw a sign of him.

One morning she went boldly into Mrs. Lugat's house and pressed the bell marked "Varri." When there was no answer, she tugged at the inner door—often the buzzers didn't work—but it was locked. Mrs. Lugat was there, behind the glass, tall, gaunt, with an incongruous red smile painted on her bony face. "Can I help you?"

"I—I wanted to speak to Mr. Varri," Ann said, clutching her handbag with claw fingers, wondering, in a panic, what she could possibly say to him.

"My tenants all work at night," Mrs. Lugat told her. "They don't like to be disturbed daytimes. Come back after dark, and I'll let you in."

When Ann came back to the house that evening, Mrs. Brumi gave her a gap-toothed grin. "I'm glad you went to see Mr. Varri," she said. "He's a shy boy—he needs encouragement."

"You said he came from the old country!" Ann stormed. "How could he? There hasn't been any travel between the United States and Albania for years. It's behind the Iron Curtain. How could he get here?"

Mrs. Brumi's smile broadened. "Maybe he flew," she suggested.

Mr. Varri seemed to be very much encouraged. All night he sang under her window, and she was afraid to try to go to sleep, afraid he might work his way into her dreams. . . .

You sit and long for one true love,
While true love you're denying,
The only kind of love that's true
Is the love that is undying. . . .

But maybe the translation wasn't quite right, she thought; maybe it should have been "the love of the undying." Maybe that was why her mother had hated the song.

What would they have done about this in the old country? Probably gone to an exorcist; and, in the new country . . . an analyst. But analysts were so expensive; besides, she wasn't sure they could cope with fantasies outside the mind.

She'd thought Tom would help, simply by being so solid and real. But he was a little too much of both. She looked at the hay-colored hair mown close to this blocky head and sprouting thickly on his soft-muscled arms, at the circles of sweat under the nylon shirt sleeves—for he'd taken off his coat. And she knew that he was as clean and sanitized and deodorized as a man could be, because odors were part of appearances. But it was a hot night, and he was a man.

"What's the matter with you, anyway?" he asked petulantly. "I thought New York girls were supposed to be—well—broad-minded, and, hell, you're worse than the chicks back home." He took hold of her again. "Don't you like me, doll?" he asked throatily. "Am I so hard to take?"

"I do like you, Tom," she said, trying to make her pulling away look more like a retreat than a reflex. "But it's so hot, and that thing flopping at the window . . ."

"It's been gone for ages." She didn't say anything. His voice rose. "The fellows at the office told me you were . . . funny, but I couldn't believe it; you didn't look like that kind of a girl to me. Now, I'm beginning to wonder."

She looked at him. He averted his eyes. "Ann, honestly, I didn't mean anything like that. I—oh, hell, why are you acting like this, then?"

She was no longer under any obligation to placate him. "Have you ever thought that perhaps you're not the most irresistible man in the world."

"But—but all the other fellows said you were the same with them."

"I'm glad to see you do such a thorough job of research before embarking on a new project," she said. "You should go far. Out that door, to begin with."

He got up, his face a fiery red. "For Pete's sake, Ann . . ." But it wasn't she he was upset about. He had fumbled the ball; he had goofed; he had failed to live up to his own picture of himself.

"Good-night, Tom." The door crashed shut. Then it opened a little way, and his head came apologetically through the aperture.

"Sorry, I didn't mean to slam it, but the wind—Ann, I truly am sor—"

"For God's sake go!" She almost pushed him down the stairs. "A storm's coming up; you wouldn't want to get caught in it and spoil that pretty new silk suit."

Watching from the window, she saw him come out into the empty street. Not quite empty . . . as he walked west, something swooped out of the shadows and fluttered after him. Yes, I'm . . . funny, she thought. And I have funny acquaintances.

Lightning streaked the sky; thunder crashed, and the rain did come, in wild sweet gusts. She slept peacefully and comfortably. When Mr. Varri's singing awakened her just before dawn, the rain had stopped, and it was cooler. She looked down from her window, and he grinned up at her, with a face that was darkly handsome, and, at the same time curiously innocent. His shining immaculacy was gone; great dark stains marred the whiteness of his clothes. "Mud," she said to herself, "just mud . . ." She began to giggle.

Tom didn't come to the office the next day. "He's in the hospital," Bill Cullen, the sales manager, Tom's boss, told her.

"Oh, poor Tom." She tried to sound convincingly surprised and regretful. "Awfully sudden, wasn't it? I hope it's nothing serious."

"He was attacked, or something, last night. Got his throat slashed." And Bill looked at her curiously. "He had a date with you, didn't he?"

"Do you think I'm that desperate?" Bill's face took on a "this is no joking matter" expression. She changed her tack. "And how do you happen to know I had a date with him?"

He turned pink. "Well, he just happened to mention to a few of the fellows that he was taking you to see *Gypsy.*"

She could almost hear Tom's confident voice: "So you guys couldn't make any headway with her, eh? Well, maybe we country boys can teach you city fellows a trick or two. . . ." She choked back unseemly laughter. "He was all right when he left my place," she said demurely. "I suppose it must have happened on his way back."

"Looks like it." Bill ran a hand through his thinning crew cut.

"But what's funny is he says he's not coming back here afterward. He's quitting. Just like that. And he seemed so happy here, so anxious to get ahead."

"Big city must've been too much for him," she said, and she wondered dreamily what the doctors at the hospital had made of the marks on Tom's throat.

◊◊◊

That night the bat hovered outside her window, plaintively begging, "Please let me in, Anna. Please. . . ."

She wasn't afraid any more. "That would be very foolish of me," she told him calmly, "after what you did to Tom." But she doubted that Tom had invited him either, so why did Mr. Varri ask her permission? Was it because he came from the same tribe as her father . . . or because she was a woman?

"It's because I love you, Anna. That Tom, he was just food; all I wanted from him was his blood, and that I did not need to ask for. I took what I wanted, and I hurt him because he hurt you. But with you, Anna, it is different. I want your love; so I can come to you only if you ask me. Ask me, Anna, please ask me; I will show you a happiness greater than you have ever dreamed could be possible."

For three nights she held out against him, but, on the fourth, she moved slowly through a fog that seemed to swirl around the room and took out the screen. The black wings swooped in, beating the air into coolness, fluttering against her cheeks in a caress. "I love you, Anna; don't fear me."

Her body relaxed into trembling quietness; her throat throbbed expectantly even before she felt the prickle of the two tiny sharp teeth gently piercing the thin skin, gently drawing out her blood and, with it, her fears and anxieties and self-doubts. This *is* love, she thought wonderingly as her throat swelled to meet the vampire's kiss—a true kiss, not the clumsy suction of damp lips and the thrust of slimy tongue, not the disgusting fumble of sweating, odorous human bodies. She wanted it to go on until every drop of blood was drained from her body, leaving her utterly clean, utterly pure.

"No, no, not yet," she moaned, as the pressure started to slacken. Reaching out, she tried to grasp the wings, but they eluded her.

"No more tonight, dearest," he whispered. "It would be too dangerous for you. But I will come to you again tomorrow night . . . and every night."

All day at the office she sat surrounded by filing cabinets and telephones and typewriters, dictating letters and memorandums and making decisions with her body, while her mind dreamed of the night that had passed and the night that was to come. Through her fog, she heard little secretaries talking ecstatically about their dates that evening. For the first time in her life, she had a date she was looking forward to; for the first time in her life she had tasted ecstasy. . . .

Night after night, the vampire returned to bring her all the happiness he had promised—and more. As the days and night passed, she changed, but she wasn't aware of it, or that the change was visible, not until the day Bill Cullen came into her office and asked if she were free that evening. . . . Bill, who had dated her several times when he'd first joined the firm; then became merely an office friend.

He had to ask twice before his words filtered through the golden fog that insulated her all the time now. "Sorry, Bill," she murmured. "I'm busy tonight. I'm busy every night. . . ."

"You're in love," he told her. "There's something about you, something different. You're softer, more—more human, more like a woman."

She wasn't angry or annoyed or . . . anything. "Yes, I am in love." She knew that the word had no real meaning for him, and she did feel a faint emotion—pity.

He looked at her. "Better watch yourself, kid. Don't overdo it. You look wonderful, but you don't look good, if you know what I mean."

The one thing the fog couldn't completely insulate her from was vanity. She went and looked at herself in the washroom mirror. She had always been pale and slender and pretty; now she was chalk-white, gaunt . . . and beautiful. But it was a distinctly necrotic loveliness. Shock began to grow in her, dissipating the fog. Almost with clarity, she started wondering what would happen when all the blood had been drained out of her.

That evening, when she got home, she was close to being awake for the first time in days. "I'm so glad everything's turning out so nice for you, Anna!" Mrs. Brumi was beaming from the doorstep.

Ann looked at her, unable to put the questions she wanted to ask into words. "It won't be long," Mrs. Brumi said reassuringly.

The words came, then, and, with them, the fears—new fears piled upon the old. "It won't be long until what? Until I'll be of no use to him any more? Until I'm—" and still that was the lesser horror—"dead."

Mrs. Brumi looked appalled. "What a thing to say, Anna! Of course you won't be dead. You just won't be alive—that's all."

That's all. Ann was becoming her old bitter self. "What will happen then? Will he buy that house in Long Island, so we'll have a nice place to keep our coffins?"

"You can't expect that, Anna. For a skinny girl who isn't so young and who hasn't any dowry, it's a good match. And there's always room in Mrs. Lugat's house."

"The bride was white," Ann said hysterically, "and a coffin was her dowry." And this is how folksongs start. How had she let herself slip into this? Calm Ann, cool Ann, collected Ann? She was lonely and romantic and she had the heritage . . . but that was no reason to have let herself go primitive. She should have known better than to accept a fantasy love. Of course it was more beautiful than a real love; otherwise fantasies would never have come into being. Weakness made them real, and she had let herself be weak, but, essentially, she knew, she was strong.

That night the vampire sobbed and pleaded outside her window. She wanted to let him in, but she rehardened her heart against him. "Why, Anna, why?" he moaned. "I love you so much. I thought you loved me."

"I do. But when all my blood is gone, then you won't love me any more."

"Of course I will!" he told her eagerly. "You'll become like me, then. We'll always be together. We'll go out every night, and, after we've drunk our fill, we'll dance together high above Central Park in the silvery moonlight."

"But you'll never be able to drink my blood again; you'll never be able to love me again."

"Of course I will love you, Anna—only in a different way. Love changes after marriage. Even for the others it does."

"Their kind of love isn't love. You taught me that."

"Anna," he wept, beating his head against the screen, "you can't leave me now; you can't leave me alone again. It's wrong; we are betrothed."

"This isn't the old country," she said, angry that he should take so much for granted. "In America, people make love casually, without being betrothed."

"But how could their kind of love be anything but casual? Our kind could never be. Anna, come with me. I'll give you your heart's desires, though you may not know them. . . ."

She thought of going out night after night and feeding on the coarse thick throats of strangers. Disgusting, she thought; what love could survive that? "Look," she said coldly, "my parents didn't come from the old country and work like slaves to give me a decent home and a good education so I should wind up spending my days in a coffin and my nights going out sucking people's blood."

He beat his wings frantically. "But, Anna, all the time you've been living in a coffin. By making you one of the undead, I am bringing you to life—"

Her tone was even chillier. "I despise cheap symbolism," she said, "even in a vampire."

He couldn't understand; his concern was only for himself. "Anna," he wept, "Anna, I'm so alone. I love you so much. Have pity on me—don't go away from me."

But she left him. The next day she rented another apartment—on the West Side, where luxury apartments were cheaper, because it was unfashionable. However, it was on West Seventy-second street, which is a broad, well-lit thoroughfare, full of patisseries and quite safe. And it wasn't only to save money that she moved across town; it was to be as far as she could get from the old neighborhood while still being conveniently situated with respect to her office.

She didn't give Mrs. Brumi notice, because she didn't want to give her time to hatch any new plots; she paid her a month's rent instead. And she hired professional packers; so the whole operation could be over in a day, and she wouldn't have to spend another night in the apartment. Not that she was afraid of Mr. Varri—she knew he wouldn't hurt her but of herself.

The new apartment was completely air-conditioned, so she would never need to open the windows. But sometimes, late at night, over the hum of the machinery, she thought she heard something flapping against the windows, and a tiny desperate voice singing . . .

> *Do not weep my dearest one,*
> *There is no need for weeping.*
> *Happiness I'll bring to you,*
> *Softly while you're sleeping.*

The words were appropriate now, because sometimes she found herself quite openly in tears. Just the same, she didn't open the windows. She was strong.

It took a long time for the marks on her neck to heal. But it was easy to hide them with tight wide necklaces, which were expensive, because everything she put on her body had to be of good quality. However, she got a new boyfriend who was a jeweler, and, while he lasted, she got substantial discounts.

———

Evelyn E. Smith is the author of *House of Four Windows, Flowers of Evil,* and *Phantom at Lost Lake,* among other novels. In the 1950s and '60s, her short stories appeared regularly in *Fantasy and Science Fiction, Fantastic Universe, Galaxy,* and other magazines.

Finding one's vocation can be a revelation.
And some callings have more bite to them than others.

Following the Way

BY ALAN RYAN

wenty years ago, in my senior year at Regis High School—a very fine and very private Jesuit preparatory school on the upper east side of Manhattan—vocations to the priesthood were the order of the day. As I recall, twenty-five or so of the one hundred and fifty members of my graduating class entered the seminary, most of them, not surprisingly, choosing the Society of Jesus. Not all of them are priests today. (For that matter, not all of the Jesuits who taught me at Regis are priests today.) But vocations were in the air in that school, then half a century old already, and I suspect that, even today, few boys pass through their four years of study without at least considering, however briefly, the possibility of the priesthood. I did. I think we all did. We had behind us, though immediate in our thoughts, a long and impressive tradition. And before us we had some very powerful male role models: priests whom we respected as teachers and scholars, men who had devoted their lives to God, to an ideal, and to us, men who were clearly happy in their work, and who were, at the same time, interesting. The exceptions—sadly and most notably, the headmaster of the school during my four years there—only emphasized the union of humanity and spirituality in the others. For a boy with the inclination, the lure was hard to resist.

Those boys who were so inclined naturally sought and found willing advisers among the priests and scholastics on the faculty. But the rest of us—a spiritually silent majority—were not over-looked by the ever-thorough Jesuits—oh, no—and, sometime during the first half of our senior year, each of us was invited into the office of the Jesuit student counselor for a private chat. (I should stress that there was no coercion here. At Regis we were seldom "ordered" to do things; rather, we were "invited.") I remember that, in my case, the priest—a kind, charming, very learned, and often sickly man named William Day—who will fig-ure prominently in this chronicle of my vocation—engaged me in polite conversation for some minutes without raising the question that I knew very well was at hand. The idea was that, if I had been reluctant to acknowledge interest in the priesthood before now, this would be my golden opportunity. I said nothing, and the poor man—as he had no doubt done a hundred times in the pre-vious two weeks—had to broach the subject himself. Had I, he wondered casually, ever considered becoming a priest? Yes, Father, I answered, I had. Ah ha, he said, nodding gently. You've thought about it? Oh, yes, I said. And what conclusion have you reached? It's not for me, I said. Oh, he said, I see, and stopped nodding. And why is that? He asked. Sex, I said. Apparently I said it with such conviction that he was thoroughly convinced of my thinking on the subject and ended the conversation there and then.

But times and people change.

I went from four years with the Jesuits at Regis High School to four years with the Jesuits at Fordham University. The Lincoln Center campus was then only in the planning stage, and I was always glad I missed it. (Leave it to the Jebbies, we joked in the cafeteria, to luck into expensive real estate and a good address.) Like my classmates who accompanied me from Regis, I was happy to exchange East 84th Street for the Rose Hill campus in the north Bronx. The Third Avenue El still rattled past the campus then and the traffic was heavy and noisy on Fordham Road and Webster Avenue, but the campus itself was an island, a green and peaceful island apart from the world outside, firmly anchored in bedrock by the pylons of handsome Keating Hall, its gray field-stone blocks and clock tower so quintessentially representative of American college architecture that fashion photographers and TV crews filming commercials were often to be found on its steps. It was a lovely place: the green expanse of Edwards Parade, the rose-covered trellis in the square beside Dealy Hall, the musty antique air of Collins Theatre, the richly detailed chapel that sang aloud to God, all of it peaceful and lovely.

The Jesuit priests there were much the same as those at Regis—a little more worldly, perhaps, a little wittier, a little more acerbic, a little more eccentric, but, in all that mattered, essentially the same. I admired them, admired the wit and the learning and the grace with which they moved through the world, the casual self-assurance, the *flair*. My father had died when I was a child and there were no other male relatives close by, so, lacking a model at home, and primed by four years at Regis, I naturally turned toward these men and sought to emulate them. It was not a bad choice.

I spent most of my time in college—intellectually, at least, and psychologically, I suppose—as a young gentleman in a nineteenth-century novel might have spent his time at Oxford. I wrote some poetry, submitted some stories to *The New Yorker* and the *Atlantic Monthly*, and spent a great deal of time pursuing women. I read—in Greek—Plato and Aristotle and Euripides and, to lighten the mood, Sappho and the poets. (Xenophon and Homer had been amply translated at Regis.) Horace, Catullus, and Livy held sway in Latin class. Ronsard, Racine, Flaubert, Camus, Ionesco, were read in French; Dante in Italian; Chaucer in Middle English. I majored in French for three of the four years, studied linguistics and the gothic novel and early American literature and European history and "gentlemen's biology" and did some Russian on the side, in addition to the equivalent of full majors in philosophy and theology that were required of all undergraduates at the time. Most of my teachers were Jesuit priests.

One afternoon in the spring of my junior year, I was coming down the steps of Keating Hall when I met that same Jesuit who had offered me my golden opportunity to confess a vocation at Regis. I had heard through the Jesuit grapevine that he'd been unwell and was now at Fordham, taking courses and regaining his strength. It was a warm day—not warm by summer standards, but warm for April after winter's chill–but the priest was buttoned up tight in a black raincoat that obviously still had its winter lining in place. I knew him to be in his early forties, but a casual observer might have guessed him ten years older than that. Looks can be deceiving.

"Hello, Father Day."

He slowed his already slow progress up the shallow steps of Keating and mumbled the half-smiled greeting teachers offer former students whom they no longer recall. But I had stopped where I was an apparently something compelled him to raise his eyes to my face, and when he did so, he halted too. Eyes momentarily alive, he scrutinized my face.

"Regis," he said.

I smiled and said yes.

"Three years ago?"

"Yes."

"Of course," he said. His eyes narrowed, and before I could remind him myself, he told me my name, as casually as if I'd last been with him yesterday.

These Jesuits, I thought.

I was about to ask him how he was, but he spoke before I could.

"Sex," he said, and we laughed together, remembering. "Most succinct answer I ever had," he said, "and a good one, a good one."

We stood on the steps, chatting easily and pleasantly. He seemed eager to know how I was doing at Fordham, what I was studying, who my teachers were, what plans I had for the future. In high school there had been much talk about "the Regis spirit," one manifestation of which was the invisible but substantial tie that links alumni whenever they encounter each other in the world in later years. It can make confidants of strangers, this common baggage of shared learning, assumptions, attitudes. Father Day, I knew, was a Regis man himself, and I was warmed by this tangible evidence of the Regis spirit in action. After a few minutes, he suggested that we go to the Campus Center for coffee—his treat—and since I had been heading there myself when we met, I readily agreed.

We sat for two hours, happily telling stories about mutual acquaintances at Regis, stories that often made us laugh as we compared quite different versions of the same events as seen from the sides of students and faculty. Then the conversation gradually drifted back to me and my life at Fordham and my future and I wasn't even surprised when Father Day inquired casually if I had ever thought again about the possibility of a priestly vocation. I had, of course. In a setting like that—spiritual, intellectual, psychological—one does. It was—and here I measure my words with extra caution—a not unattractive possibility. But, still, it was not attractive enough to win me over. My interest in that direction was based primarily on practical and pragmatic considerations, and definitely not on any "call from God to His service" that I had felt. He smiled understandingly when I told him I had thought about it but my conclusion remained the same.

"No harm in asking," he said, and maintained his slight smile.

I agreed.

"And no harm in thinking about it further," he said, the smile unchanged.

I agreed again.

"Will you?" he asked.

"Think about it further?"

"Yes."

"All right," I said, my smile matching his. "Couldn't hurt."

"Right," he said. "Couldn't hurt. Which is the punch line of an old vaudeville joke." He leaned back in his chair. "Ten minutes before he's going on stage, see, this famous comedian dies in his dressing room and the stage manager has to . . ."

We talked another twenty minutes or so before I had to leave for a late class. Even then, as I rose and gathered my books, it did not occur to me that Father Day, when we first met on the steps of Keating Hall, had been heading into the building and had changed his direction entirely to spend two and a half hours talking with me in the cafeteria.

When we parted at the front doors of the Campus Center, we assured each other how good it had been to talk and sincerely wished each other well. We both felt it, I was certain: the Regis spirit, made flesh.

It was three years later and I was twenty-four, a graduate student at UCLA, before I saw him again. Either because I had promised or because it was inevitable, I had indeed been thinking further about the priesthood.

Los Angeles, UCLA, Westwood Village, and Santa Monica (where I had a furnished apartment just off Wilshire Boulevard, about ten blocks from the beach), seem unlikely places to be thinking about withdrawing—to a degree at least—from the world and devoting one's life to the service of God. I did, however, and although I was aware of the contrast between my own thinking and that of those around me, I continued to consider, if only in a pragmatic way, the possibility of becoming a priest.

The idea had much to recommend it. I was alone in the world now, my mother having died in an automobile accident in Switzerland during the summer following my graduation from Fordham. I went to California an orphan, lacking even brothers, sisters, aunts, uncles, cousins, to form a family. There was, in that regard, no one to take into account but myself. On the other hand, a religious community could readily fill the need for a structure and a sense of purpose and continuity in my life.

Furthermore, my mother's death had left me financially independent as well, thanks to her firm belief in large amounts of travel insurance, and my independence and self-sufficiency made me, I think it fair to say, rather more mature in my judgments than others in their early twenties, and rather more than I might have been myself in different circumstances.

As for the "sex" I had mentioned to Father Day half a dozen years earlier as an overriding factor in my negative decision, it had proved, as I grew older, less of a problem. To speak the truth, I was no virgin, and I think my needs and appetites at the time, during those years, were as normal as anyone else's, which may prove a mystery to laymen who think that priests and future priests are sometimes spared their hunger. They are not; I can vouch for it. But I did find, through necessity of time and circumstance, that the urge can be controlled, not through any secret vice, which is most often only a form of self-torture, serving merely to remind us of what we lack, but through a careful discipline of the will.

In a practical sense, my life was right for the priesthood. In a psychological sense—and a practical one—I was comfortable with the idea; I would teach in any case. In a spiritual sense, it meant nothing at all; I felt no infusion of god's spirit, no call to His service, and began truly to wonder if that last were really needed.

And then, once again, I ran into Father Day.

It was early May, the end of the academic year, the oral exams for my master's degree successfully completed, and nothing before me but a summer of travel. I had driven back to the campus to return some books and was sitting near the entrance to Royce Hall, enjoying the California sun, reading a newspaper, and listening to the noon carillon concert from the undergraduate library. I had nothing to do for the afternoon, nothing to do, in fact, for a week until my plane left for Europe.

I heard a voice speak my name and say, "Well, hello."

I raised my head and there was Father Day.

He looked much the same as he had three years before, In fact, we might almost have been back on the steps of Keating Hall at Fordham, amid the elms and the dogwood, rather than here beside the Spanish architecture of Royce Hall, amid the bird of paradise plants and the palms. He still looked older than his years—the same observation I had made at Fordham, the last time I'd seen him. And he was still somewhat overdressed. The sun was warm, with only a gentle breeze blowing across the campus, but Father Day wore black woolen slacks and a black turtleneck shirt under a battered gray tweed sport jacket. Even discarding the standard clerical garb, as Jesuits feel so free to do, he had not indulged in any great license. He looked, as he had before, like a man recovering from a long illness, which indeed he was. Thin blood, I thought, meant to thicken in the sun. I said it was good to see him and that he was looking well.

We satisfied each other's curiosity and quickly provided basic information. He told me he had been on campus the whole spring term. Nominally, he was here to take courses in comparative religion. Actually, he was in California for a rest to build up his strength. He spent part of his time helping out with light duties—mass and confession—in a parish church in North Hollywood, where he was living now. He was thinking of accepting a teaching position he'd been offered at Loyola University. I told him that, unless a decent teaching position came along for me, I planned to start work on my doctorate in the fall term and, in that case, would no doubt turn into the archetypal perennial student. He smiled a little ruefully and said that it wasn't such a bad life, and then we were laughing together.

And before I realized it, we were once again talking about me and I was, once again, admitting that thoughts of the priesthood were still in my mind. And, again before I realized it, we had strolled from the campus out to Westwood village and had found a quiet booth in a bar near the Bruin Theatre.

"You keep turning up in my life," I said when we had beers in front of us.

"Twice," he said.

"Twice is almost a pattern."

"Almost," he agreed.

"Maybe you're haunting me."

"Maybe," he said and took a long drink from his glass. "Or maybe God is haunting you through me."

I thought of all the practical reasons I had for taking Holy Orders, and of all the spiritual reasons I lacked. "Not bloody likely," I said.

"Oh?" It's a Jesuit habit to say that; it offers nothing but elicits much.

So I told him, told him all the wide range of my thoughts on the subject, told him how, although I had not reached a definitive conclusion, the inevitable answer, born of inertia, seemed certainly negative. He listened patiently, his face without expression, until I finished.

"So, then, you feel no call to the priesthood, no compulsion. Is that right?"

I shook my head. "None."

"The call can come in any variety of ways," he said. "The path to God is not a straight one."

"And there are many doors in the castle, yes, I know, Father."

"Don't be impatient."

"Sorry."

"Maybe I'm your call."

I looked at him then and, for a long moment, and for the first time, seriously wondered if perhaps he was right, perhaps he was truly haunting me.

"The path to God is not a straight one," I said, and we both smiled and relaxed, the moment of tension gone.

"If we run into each other like this again," he said, "it will definitely be a pattern."

"Indeed," I said.

"Patterns like that must be considered."

"All right," I said, "if we run into each other like this again, I'll grant you it constitutes a pattern."

"And you'll consider it?"

"The pattern?"

"The priesthood."

"Ah," I said. And a moment later: "All right."

"Good," he said. "I think this calls for another beer."

It was not three years this time, but six weeks, before I saw him again.

I took a place in the queue for tickets to the Royal Ballet at Covent Garden and there he was just in front of me. Neither of us realized it until he'd bought his ticket and turned away from the counter. Suddenly there we were. I quickly purchased my own ticket and followed him outside into Floral Street. A minute later, we were established in the Nag's Head a few doors away, two pints of lager before us.

"You're following me," I said. "It's beginning to look slightly sinister."

"Is it?" Jesuits love to ask questions.

"A bit. What are you doing here? I thought you were in Los Angeles."

"I was. Actually, in a way, I still am. I took the faculty position at Loyola and then rather lucked into a university travel grant. It was none of my doing, actually."

"I'll bet," I said lightly.

"Actually," he replied.

He looked, it hardly seems necessary to mention, quite the same as before. The weather in London was cool and damp even in summer, but he was still overdressed. It seemed a permanent feature of his appearance. Apparently the California sun had not succeeded in thickening his blood. I didn't imagine the chilly air of London would accomplish much in that line, but the thought seemed not to have occurred to him.

"Did you follow me here?"

He shook his head, a gentle smile on his lips. "Impossible," he said.

That, of course, was the truth, and I knew it already. Apart from the obvious reasons, if he'd appeared just behind me in the queue, I might have doubted, but he had been there in front of me when I arrived, no question about it, and I did not.

"Then you're haunting me," I said.

"So it appears," he replied. He lifted his glass and in one long drink finished off the beer. "I have to be on my way," he said. "Let's meet for dinner."

We agreed on seven-thirty at Romano Santi in Soho, and a moment later he was gone. I stayed longer in the Nag's Head, ordered another pint and drank it as slowly as the first. After that, I walked over to Charing Cross Road and spent the rest of the afternoon in the National Portrait Gallery. I barely saw the faces in the paintings. I could see only the face of Father Day, haunting me wherever I went.

During the meal, we limited the conversation to general topics. Afterward, he invited me back to his house for drinks. As we rode in the taxi the length of Oxford Street from Soho to Notting Hill Gate, and then pulled up in front of a lovely home in Kensington Park Road which he was renting for the summer, I wondered what sort of travel grant provided that sort of living allowance.

These Jesuits, I thought. They're like some fine old family, ripe with old money.

"Shall we sit in the sitting room?" he said as he gestured me inside. "It seems only proper."

By that point, I was half expecting servants, but the house was empty. We'd had Chianti with the meal and he suggested a lighter burgundy now. He poured the wine himself. When we were settled in easy chairs, he wasted no time.

"I think you have a vocation," he said. "Perhaps you feel no call, nothing of the sort you've thought all along you ought to feel, but a vocation nonetheless."

"Why?" I asked. I tried to sip my drink calmly.

"Why do you have a vocation or why do I say that?"

"Both." These Jesuits, I thought again. They never stop. It comes with long practice.

"Both," he repeated, in a tone that reminded me of the classroom. "As for the first, why you have a vocation, I couldn't begin to tell you. I almost hate to say it because it sounds entirely too pat, but it's not for us to question the ways of God."

"Just lucky, I guess." I said it as much to provoke him as for anything else.

"I guess," he said, and studied me curiously, as if wondering at the oddness of God's dealings among men. While he studied me, I had the opportunity to do the same with him, and realized that, at least for the moment, he no longer looked as sickly as he had before. He looked, rather, like a man with a definite job to do, a man with a clear purpose.

"As for the second point," he said, "why I'm telling you this, remember that Christ taught us to be fishers of men."

"The wise fisherman doesn't cast his net at random," I said.

"Nicely put."

"Why me, Father?"

"You're the type."

"*What* type?"

"Why, the priestly type, of course."

"That's a tautology."

"You'll make a splendid Jesuit," he laughed. "Here, let me top up your glass."

We sat together in silence for a while, with only the wine and our thoughts.

"Have you not noticed," he said at last, "that I seem to keep recurring in your life? Oh, never mind, of course you have." He leaned forward in his chair. "Answer a question. The Church will last forever, will it not? Until, would it be safe to say, the end of time, at least? Agreed?"

I nodded.

"Why?" he snapped. "How can that be?"

I hesitated, answers that had once seemed so clear—or at least so thoroughly assumed—now failing me.

"I've forgotten a lot of my catechism," I said to cover my hesitation.

"You haven't forgotten *this* catechism," he said. "These are answers you never knew. What is the central fact in your belief?"

"That Christ was the Son of God."

"And?"

"That He died on the cross. The sacrifice of the cross."

"The sacrifice of the cross," he repeated. "And what is the central practice, the central event, of your worship?"

"The Eucharist," I said. "The sacrifice of the mass."

"The sacrifice of the mass. Can you live forever?"

"Yes."

"How?"

"My soul is eternal. Listen, I—"

"You can live forever," he said.

I looked at him.

He said it again, more slowly. "You can live forever."

It was my turn. "How?" I said.

He raised his wine glass toward me. It reflected the light from a lamp and glowed ruby red.

"This is the cup of my blood," he said. "Take and drink of it." He was smiling.

I looked from his face to the glass of wine, held aloft as it might be held above the altar, offered to God and displayed to the faithful, with the words of consecration transforming it to blood.

Of course. At last. Here was the epiphany I'd sought, the obvious thing, long regarded but never seen till now: the realization, revelation, moment, insight, the ancient sacred secret of the Church. I was surprised only in that I felt no surprise.

I thought of all the priests I'd known, thought of all the times I'd been at mass and heard a priest murmur those words, transforming wine into the blood of Jesus Christ. Thought of the cross. Thought of the ages of the Church, alone of all institutions, had lasted already. Thought of the ages ahead. And, again very practical, thought of myself standing before an altar, speaking those very same words, ordained with the power of transforming ordinary wine into sacred blood, an endless supply for an endless lifetime. I held my breath a moment, then looked back at Father Day.

"Do the others know?" I asked. "Or is it only the Jesuits?"

When he was done laughing, he caught his breath and said, "Oh, this is definitely not a perfect world. Yes, the others know." And he was off again into gales of laughter.

When he'd caught his breath a second time, he raised his glass in a silent toast. Then he set it down, rose from his chair, and came and stood beside me. He bent forward and gently—very gently—placed his lips against my neck.

This was all some years ago.

What follows is forever.

I am a priest and shall remain so. I rest eternal in the bosom of the Lord. I am following the way, I am satisfied.

Alan Ryan is the editor of *The Penguin Book of Vampire Stories* and the author of *Quadriphobia, Panther!, The Kill*, and many other novels and collections. His story "The Bones Wizard" won the World Fantasy Award.

He always thought he'd be happy to lose the hunger . . .
but he never thought it would happen this way.

Appetites

BY LAWRENCE SCHIMEL

stretched, cracking my back, and finally opened my eyes. The alarm clock's glow was the only light in my tiny studio. 8:47 P.M. Still early. I figured I'd head to the gym for a quick workout before starting my shift as a cabbie. In this city that never sleeps, there're folks who need a cab at all hours—although certainly fewer at night than during the day. But there's also less traffic, which is a relief, and I drive my cab as much for something to do as for the money. I don't need much, in terms of possessions and things, lifestyle—I have a rent-stabilized apartment in a neighborhood that has only recently become fashionable—but I do need something to keep me going. I'm such a creature of habit, to the point where I almost fetishize the normalcy of routine. The gym was definitely a part of that fetishized jumble of habits.

Lately the "in" crowd has moved over to American Fitness, that great, big, subterranean complex of exercise equipment and such (with too much emphasis on the such—stuff like aerobics classes and a "health" bar and too many men and women cruising one another). At least there're fewer crowds at my gym now.

I'm still at the Chelsea Gym, if for no other reason than it's open until midnight, which better fits my schedule. Until something comes along to disrupt my inertia, it's where I plan to stay. There's something unpretentious about this all-male gym, it's two small floors of freeweights. It's top-heavy in its focus because that's what most men want: big pecs and biceps. I think it's tied to the fact that you can't change the size of your dick, but you can change the rest of your body—insecurities being such a natural part of our psyches, we've become size queens about those muscles you do see in day-to-day life.

Of course, vanity and narcissism also play a heavy role, I reflected as I gathered my gym clothes into a knapsack. I flexed my bicep and thought how this—my looks, my body—helped get me laid more than "personality" or any other trait. I went to the gym to keep these charms as best I could, although I did also enjoy the endorphin rush of the workout.

And part of me was concerned about putting on or at least maintaining my weight, in case the HIV ever got the upper hand.

Not that I needed to justify my going to the gym to anyone, myself included. Lately, however, I was reconsidering all of my actions. Which was another reason I went to the gym: It was a good place for me to think. When the body was occupied with some simple, repetitive task like pumping iron, the mind was left free to roam, the subconscious liberated as the front brain kept the body in motion.

It was a quick trip from my miniscule, fifth-floor walk-up with an airshaft view on West Twenty-Fifth Street down to the gym, but I took my time, strolling lazily along Eighth Avenue and looking at the passersby. A crowd of scantily-clad guys on roller blades lingered outside the Big Cup, while those inside the cafe ogled at them through the glass as they sipped their cappuccinos and iced teas. A blonde walking a Dalmatian caught my eye as she turned the corner at Nineteenth, but I already had a destination I felt committed to, and her pooch tugged her on toward home, so we merely locked gazes for a moment and chalked each other up as "the one who got away."

I made small talk in the lobby with Carlos, who was just leaving the gym as I got there. For someone like me who didn't hold down a normal job—as a cabbie, people came into my life in five minute

STREETS OF BLOOD

intervals—the gym provided some social stability: that group of people I saw regularly, even though they weren't especially important in my life. They were one of my routines. I looked forward to the gossip and interchanges, but when they switched gyms or moved to San Francisco or Los Angeles or (God alone knows why) Salt Lake City, there was always someone new to take their place. Their familiarity was comforting, reassuring in a way. And these days I felt I needed all the comforting and reassurance I could get.

I felt at home here.

The Chelsea Gym was also the cheapest of any of the neighborhood gyms; even the Y on Twenty-Third was more expensive. In fact, the only problem I had with the Chelsea Gym were the mirrors. Practically the entire place was mirrored so the men could preen and pose while they pump.

I'm always afraid someone will notice I don't have a reflection.

I try hard to make it less obvious, keeping some piece of equipment between me and the mirrors whenever possible and ignoring their existence when I can't.

I gave my ID to Sam and went in. The locker room was crowded with naked men, as the abs workout class (the Chelsea Gym's token semi-aerobic item) had just let out and they were hitting the showers at the same time a chunk of the post-work lifters were coming upstairs from the steam room and sauna. I loved to be in that whirl and press of bodies, their blood racing from the workout or the heat, tantalizing, but I didn't linger long. I was studiously ignoring the scale over by the sunlamps and then pretending to myself that I wasn't ignoring it and would weigh myself after my workout. The sooner I was out of the locker room, the easier it was to put out of mind.

I was working shoulders and back today. Generally I like to start with some rowing, vigorous exercise to get everything going, but both machines were occupied. I began with some front pull downs instead, grateful that all the machines faced inward, away from the mirrors. I had barely begun my first set when a stunning young woman I'd never seen before wandered into view. A curious enough sight in this all-male environment, she would've caught my attention anywhere with those long legs. She was dressed in a short skirt, which showed them off to nice advantage. What was she doing here, I wondered, as she walked to the far end of the workout floor, her gaze flicking over the equipment and men as she passed. I stared at her, lusted at her, thought a flicker of interest was returned as she walked by. I was grateful I had only just begun my workout, that I wasn't sweaty and smelly, my face flushed with exertion—I still held my charms.

For a moment I grappled with the existential problem of loneliness: not just as a man, but as a vampire. What would it be like if we were to date, move in together, join our lives? I could share immortality with her.

It was a ludicrous fantasy, of course. I didn't even know this woman, had just seen her for the first time in my life, and already I was planning an eternity for us! I didn't even know her serostatus.

It was natural, though, to want desperately to fill my life with someone else at the drop of a hat. "This is no country for old men," Yeats wrote of Byzantium. That sort of loneliness is even more cosmically acute for someone like myself, destined always to be alone, to outlive anyone I might know or love, to be constantly dependent on humans for nourishment.

I continued my set, not wanting to be so obvious in my infatuation. It was an appealing fantasy: the romance we might have, as much as the pleasure our bodies might take in sex.

I was procrastinating, thinking about so much else, and I knew it. I wanted to pretend everything was as it had always been, didn't want to face what was happening to me.

I've been HIV positive for at least a decade, with no adverse affects. I'm not sure when exactly I was infected, or even whether it was from unsafe sex or from drinking infected blood. Probably both.

There's a taste to infected blood that's different from anything else. It's like drinking lowfat or skim milk in some ways, thin and watery because there're usually fewer t-cells. But it's got an extra flavor from all that virus, richer in taste the higher the viral load. So infected blood is like drinking skim chocolate milk. I'm partial to the taste of it, but I try not to indulge too much, for a bunch of reasons. I'm less concerned about multiple strains of HIV, although with the changes now happening to me perhaps I should've been more wary. Infected persons often have other diseases and afflictions, which I want to avoid. And perhaps most importantly, one of the ways that the HIV hasn't affected me is that, thanks to my vampirism, I am constantly replenishing my t-cell levels with the blood I feed on. So I stay healthy by drinking healthy blood. I do also feel guilty, taking the few remaining t-cells from people who're already losing them to the disease.

And thus I've been asymptomatic for at least a decade, maybe more, depending on when I was first infected. Until now.

I've begun losing my appetite, my first signs of the disease taking its toll on my body.

This terrifies me. I'm not replenishing my immune system with fresh, healthy blood and all that it contains.

And what frightens me even worse is that I'm afraid the virus is now attacking whatever it is that makes me biologically a vampire. The cellular changes that happened that night when I was drained completely of blood and then restored with his blood, making me like him, a creature of the night. It wasn't at all scientific, although that's how I'm thinking about it now since there's such a science surrounding the virus these days; it's how we're trained to think about it, in numbers and chemicals and not at all its devastatingly human effects.

I'd been able to ignore much of that techno stuff since my vampirism has been operating like an immune system, keeping me healthy from the HIV infection. Until now, when it seems a mutation of the HIV is attacking what makes me a vampire, my immune system equivalent.

And I've no idea what to feel.

The HIV might "cure" my vampirism. But the cure itself will kill me, since my vampirism is the only thing keeping me alive now.

I'm not exactly discontent being a vampire, but I don't know if that's just because I'm so used to it now. I'd be happy to give up the bloodletting and the deaths. It's been a long time since I've killed anyone, though at first I didn't know how to stop feeding, how not to gorge myself past satiation until I was bloated into a torpor—a dangerous state for me to be in since I so frequently had to flee the scenes of my hunger-crimes.

And as I, once immortal, confront my sudden mortality, certain questions from my past begin to recur: Did I have a soul? Was there an afterlife? Was I damned for all the lives I took to feed myself? Even though they were all in self defense, my body's natural instinct for survival and self-preservation.

Would I again become mortal when I lost my vampirism, or would I instead die? But I was not alive now; I was undead. A quibble, perhaps, but an important one: I was not alive now, and I had once been dead. If I lost the state I was in, would I not revert to being dead?

And what would be the difference if I did become mortal? I'd sicken and die soon enough. I've never relished the idea of wasting away to this disease and being unable to die, on account of being undead already. I railed against the cruelties of fate, ignoring for the moment the fact that so many others had died before me and would yet die from this disease, men and women who would've killed for the prolonged years my vampirism had given me.

I'd been sitting blankly at the machine, lost in these reflections. That young woman wandered through my view again, drawing my mind back into my body as my body began to respond to the sight of her, arousal stirring my cock within my shorts.

I stood, deciding to skip the rest of my workout, and followed her down the stairs, determined to meet her, talk to her, maybe more.

I had no answers to any of my questions. And I did not know if there was anything I could do to change what was happening. I was hoping the exercise would increase my appetite, which might prolong my un-life some while longer. I did not, could not, know what would come.

So I followed this woman, whose gaze met mine and in whose eyes I felt happy to be lost for all eternity, responding to those appetites that still lay within me.

Lawrence Schimel is the editor of The American Vampire Series, in addition to more than twenty other anthologies, including *Tarot Fantastic, The Fortune Teller,* and *Camelot Fantastic.* His stories and poems have appeared in over one hundred anthologies, ranging from *The Time of the Vampires* to *The Random House Treasury of Light Verse,* and in numerous periodicals.

Come sit by the fire and warm your bones as you listen to this tale. . . .

Ken's Mystery

BY JULIAN HAWTHORNE

ne cool October evening—it was the last day of the month, and unusually cool for the time of year—I made up my mind to go and spend an hour or two with my friend Keningale. Keningale was an artist (as well as a musical amateur and poet), and had a very delightful studio built onto his house, in which he was wont to sit of an evening. The studio had a cavernous fireplace, designed in imitation of the old-fashioned fireplaces of Elizabethan manor-houses, and in it, when the temperature out-doors warranted, he would build up a cheerful fire of dry logs. It would suit me particularly well, I thought, to go and have a quiet pipe and chat in front of that fire with my friend.

I had not had such a chat for a very long time—not, in fact, since Keningale (or Ken, as his friends called him) had returned from his visit to Europe the year before. He went abroad, as he affirmed at the time, "for purposes of study," whereat we all smiled, for Ken, as far as we knew him, was more likely to do anything else than to study. He was a young fellow of buoyant temperament, lively and social in his habits, of a brilliant and versatile mind, and possessing an income of twelve or fifteen thousand dollars a year; he could sing, play, scribble, and paint very cleverly, and some of his heads and figure-pieces were really well done, considering that he never had any regular training in art; but he was not a worker. Personally he was fine-looking, of good height and figure, active, healthy, and with a remarkably fine brow, and clear, full-gazing eye. Nobody was surprised at his going to Europe, nobody expected him to do anything there except amuse himself, and few anticipated that he would be soon again seen in New York. He was one of the sort that find Europe agree with them. Off he went, therefore; and in the course of a few months the rumor reached us that he was engaged to a handsome and wealthy New York girl whom he had met in London. This was nearly all we did hear of him until, not very long afterward, he turned up again on Fifth Avenue, to every one's astonishment; made no satisfactory answer to those who wanted to know how he happened to tire so soon of the Old World; while, as to the reported engagement, he cut short all allusion to that in so peremptory a manner as to show that it was not a permissible topic of conversation with him. It was surmised that the lady had jilted him; but, on the other hand, she herself returned home not a great while after, and, though she had plenty of opportunities she has never married to this day.

Be the rights of that matter what they may, it was soon remarked that Ken was no longer the careless and merry fellow he used to be; on the contrary, he appeared grave, moody, averse from general society, and habitually taciturn and undemonstrative even in the company of his most intimate friends. Evidently something had happened to him or he had done something. What? Had he committed a murder? or joined the Nihilists? or was his unsuccessful love affair at the bottom of it? Some declared that the cloud was only temporary, and would soon pass away. Nevertheless, up to the period of which I am writing, it had not passed away, but had rather gathered additional gloom, and threatened to become permanent.

Meanwhile I had met him twice or thrice at the club, at the opera, or in the street, but had as yet had no opportunity of regularly renewing my acquaintance with him. We had been on a footing of more than common intimacy in the old days, and I was not disposed to think that he would refuse to renew the former relations now. But what I had heard and myself seen of his

STREETS OF BLOOD

changed condition imparted a stimulating tinge of suspense or curiosity to the pleasure with which I looked forward to the prospects of this evening. His house stood at a distance of two or three miles beyond the general range of habitation sin New York at this time, and as I walked briskly along in the clear twilight air I had leisure to go over in my mind all that I had known of Ken and had divined of his character. After all, had there not always been something in his nature—deep down, and held in abeyance by the activity of his animal spirits—but something strange and separate, and capable of developing under suitable conditions into—into what? As I asked myself this question I arrived at his door; and it was with a feeling of relief that I felt the next moment the cordial grasp of his hand, and his voice bidding me welcome in a tone that indicated unaffected gratification at my presence. He drew me at once into the studio, relieved me of my hat and cane, and then put his hand on my shoulder.

"I am glad to see you," he repeated, with singular earnestness—"glad to see you and to feel you; and tonight of all nights in the year."

"Why tonight especially?"

"Oh, never mind. It's just as well, too, you didn't let me know beforehand you were coming; the unreadiness is all, to paraphrase the poet. Now, with you to help me, I can drink a glass of whisky and water and take a bit draw of the pipe. This would have been a grim night for me if I'd been left to myself."

"In such a lap of luxury as this, too!" said I, looking round at the glowing fireplace, the low, luxurious chairs, and all the rich and sumptuous fittings of the room. "I should have thought a condemned murderer might make himself comfortable here."

"Perhaps; but that's not exactly my category at present. But have you forgotten what night this is? This November-eve, when, as tradition asserts, the dead arise and walk about, and fairies, goblins, and spiritual beings of all kinds have more freedom and power than on any other day of the year. One can see you've never been in Ireland."

"I wasn't aware till now that you had been there, either."

"Yes, I have been in Ireland. Yes—" He paused, sighed, and fell into a reverie, from which, however, he soon roused himself by an effort and went to a cabinet in a corner of the room for the liquor and tobacco. While he was thus employed I sauntered about the studio, taking note of the various beautifies, grotesquenesses, and curiosities that it contained. Many things were there to repay study and arouse admiration; for Ken was a good collector, having excellent taste as well as means to back it. But, upon the whole, nothing interested me more than some studies of a female head, roughly done in oils, and, judging from the sequestered positions in which I found them, not intended by the artist for exhibition or criticism. There were three or four of these studies, all of the same face, but in different poses and costumes. In one the head was enveloped in a dark hood, overshadowing and partly concealing the features; in another she seemed to be peering duskily through a latticed casement, lit by a faint moonlight; a third showed her splendidly attired in evening costume, with jewels in her hair and ears, and sparkling on her snowy bosom. The expressions were as various as the poses; now it was demure penetration, now a subtle inviting glance, now burning passion, and again a look of elfish and elusive mockery. In whatever phase, the countenance possessed a singular and poignant fascination, not of beauty merely, though that was very striking, but of character and quality likewise.

"Did you find this model abroad?" I inquired at length. "She has evidently inspired you, and I don't wonder at it."

Ken, who had been mixing the punch, and had not noticed my movements, now looked up, and said: "I didn't mean those to be seen. They don't satisfy me, and I am going to destroy them; but I couldn't rest till I'd made some attempts to reproduce— What was it you asked? Abroad? Yes—or no. They were all painted here within the last six weeks."

"Whether they satisfy you or not, they are by far the best things of yours I have ever seen."

"Well, let them alone, and tell me what you think of this beverage. To my thinking, it goes to the right spot. It owes its existence to your coming here. I can't drink alone, and those portraits are not company, though, for aught I know, she might have come out of the canvas tonight and sat down in that chair." Then, seeing my inquiring look, he added, with a hasty laugh, "It's November-eve, you know, when anything may happen, provided it's strange enough. Well, here's to ourselves."

We each swallowed a deep draught of the smoking and aromatic liquor, and set down our glasses with approval. The punch was excellent. Ken now opened a box of cigars, and we seated ourselves before the fireplace.

"All we need now," I remarked, after a short silence, "is a little music. By-the-by, Ken, have you still got the banjo I gave you before you went abroad?"

He paused so long before replying that I supposed he had not heard my question. "I have got it," he said, at length, "but it will never make any more music."

"Got broken, eh? Can't it be mended? It was a fine instrument."

"It's not broken, but it's past mending. You shall see for yourself."

He arose as he spoke, and going to another part of the studio, opened a black oak coffer, and took out of it a long object wrapped up in a piece of faded yellow silk. He handed it to me, and when I had unwrapped it, there appeared a thing that might once have been a banjo, but had little resemblance to one now. It bore every sign of extreme age. The wood of the handle was honey-combed with the gnawing of worms, and dusty with dry-rot. The parchment head was green with mold, and hung in shriveled tatters. The hoop, which was of solid silver, was so blackened and tarnished that it looked like dilapidated iron. The strings were gone, and most of the tuning-screws had dropped out of their decayed sockets. Altogether it had the appearance of having been made before the Flood, and been forgotten in the forecastle of Noah's Ark ever since.

"It is a curious relic, certainly," I said. "Where did you come across it? I had no idea that the banjo was invented so long ago as this. It certainly can't be less than two hundred years old, and may be much older than that."

Ken smiled gloomily. "You are quite right," he said; "it is at least two hundred years old, and yet it is the very same banjo that you gave me a year ago."

"Hardly," I returned, smiling in my turn, "since that was made to my order with a view to presenting it to you."

"I know that; but the two hundred years have passed since then.

Yes; it is absurd and impossible, I know, but nothing is truer. That banjo, which was made last year, existed in the sixteenth century, and has been rotting ever since. Stay. Give it to me a moment, and I'll convince you. You recollect that your name and mine, with the date, were engraved on the silver hoop?"

"Yes; and there was a private mark of my own there, also."

"Very well," said Ken, who had been rubbing a place on the hoop with a corner of the yellow silk wrapper; "look at that."

I took the decrepit instrument from him, and examined the spot which he had rubbed. It was incredible, sure enough; but there were the names and the date precisely as I had caused them to be engraved; and there, moreover, was my own private mark, which I had idly made with an old etching point not more than eighteen months before. After convincing myself that there was no mistake, I laid the banjo across my knees, and stared at my friend in bewilderment. He sat smoking with a kind of grim composure, his eyes fixed upon the blazing logs.

"I'm mystified, I confess," said I. "Come; what is the joke? What method have you discovered of producing the decay of centuries on this unfortunate banjo in a few months? And why did you do it? I have heard of an elixir to counteract the effects of time, but your recipe seems to work the other way—to make time rush forward at two hundred times his usual rate, in one place, while he jogs on at his usual gait elsewhere. Unfold your mystery, magician. Seriously, Ken, how on earth did the thing happen?"

"I know no more about it than you do," was his reply. "Either you and I and all the rest of the living world are insane, or else there has been wrought a miracle strange as any in tradition. How can I explain it? It is a common saying—a common experience, if you will—that we may, on certain trying or tremendous occasions, live years in one moment. But that's a mental experience, not a physical one, and one that applies, at all events, only to human beings, not to senseless things of wood and metal. You imagine the thing is some trick or jugglery. If it be, I don't know the secret of it. There's no chemical appliance that I ever heard of that will get a piece of solid wood into that condition in a few months, or a few years. And it wasn't done in a few years, or a few months either. A year ago today at this very hour that banjo was as sound as when it left the maker's hands, and twenty-four hours afterward—I'm telling you the simple truth—it was as you see it now."

The gravity and earnestness with which Ken made this astounding statement were evidently not assumed. He believed every word that he uttered. I knew not what to think. Of course my friend might be insane, though he betrayed none of the ordinary symptoms of mania; but, however that might be, there was the banjo, a witness whose silent testimony there was no gainsaying. The more I meditated on the matter the more inconceivable did it appear. Two hundred years—twenty-four hours; these were the terms of the proposed equation. Ken and the banjo both affirmed that the equation had been made; all worldly knowledge and experience affirmed it to be impossible. What was the explanation? What is time? What is life? I felt myself beginning to doubt the reality of all things. And so this was the mystery which my friend had been brooding over since his return from abroad? No wonder it had changed him. More to be wondered at was that it had not changed him more.

"Can you tell me the whole story?" I demanded at length.

Ken quaffed another draught from his glass of whisky and water and rubbed his hand through his thick brown beard. "I have never spoken to any one of it heretofore," he said, "and I have never meant to speak of it. But I'll try and give you some idea of what it was. You know me better than any one else; you'll understand the thing as far as it can ever be understood, and perhaps I may be relieved of some of the oppression it has caused me. For it is rather a ghastly memory to grapple with alone, I can tell you."

Hereupon, without further preface, Ken related the following tale. He was, I may observe in passing, a naturally fine narrator. There were deep, lingering tones in his voice, and he could strikingly enhance the comic or pathetic effect of a sentence by dwelling here and there upon some syllable. His features were equally susceptible of humorous and of solemn expressions, and his eyes were in form and hue wonderfully adapted to showing great varities of emotion. Their mournful aspect was extremely earnest and affecting; and when Ken was giving utterance to some mysterious passage of the tale they had a doubtful, melancholy, exploring look which appealed irresistibly to the imagination. But the interest of his story was too pressing to allow of noticing these incidental embellishments at the time, though they doubtless had their influence upon me all the same.

"I left New York on an Inman Line steamer, you remember," began Ken, "and landed at Havre. I went the usual round of sightseeing on the Continent, and got round to London in July, at the height of the season. I had good introductions, and met any number of agreeable and famous people. Among others was a young lady, a countrywoman of my own—you know whom I mean—who interested me very much and before her family left London she and I were engaged. We parted there for the time, because she had the Continental trip still to make, while I wanted to take the opportunity to visit the north of England and Ireland. I landed at Dublin about the 1st of October, and, zigzagging about the country, I found myself in County Cork about two weeks later.

"There is in that region some of the most lovely scenery that human eyes ever rested on, and it seems to be less known to tourists than many places of infinitely less picturesque value. A lonely region too: during my rambles I met not a single stranger like myself, and few enough natives. It seems incredible that so beautiful a country should be so deserted. After walking a dozen Irish miles you come across a group of two or three one-roomed cottages, and, like as not, one or more of these will have the roof off and the walls in ruins. The few peasants whom one sees, however, are affable and hospitable, especially when they hear you are from that terrestrial heaven whither most of their friends and relatives have gone before them. They seem simple and primitive enough at first sight, and yet they are as strange and incomprehensible a race as any in the world. They are as superstitious, as credulous of marvels, fairies, magicians, and omens, as the men whom St. Patrick preached to, and at the same time they are shrewd, skeptical, sensible, and bottomless liars. Upon the whole, I met with no nation on my travels whose company I enjoyed so much, or who inspired me with so much kindliness, curiosity, and repugnance.

"At length I got to a place on the sea-coast, which I will not further specify than to say that it is not many miles from Ballymacheen, on the south shore. I have seen Venice and Naples, I have driven along the Cornice road, I have spent a month at our own Mount Desert, and I say that all of them together are not so beautiful as this glowing, deep-hued, soft-gleaming, silvery-lighted, ancient harbor and town, with the tall hills crowding round it and the black cliffs and headlands planting their iron feet in the blue, transparent sea. It is a very old place, and has had a history which it has outlived ages since. It may once have had two or three thousand inhabitants; it has scarce five or six hundred today. Half the houses are in ruins or have disappeared; many of the remainder are standing empty. All the people are poor, most of them abjectly so; they saunter about with bare feet and uncovered heads, the women in quaint black or dark-blue cloaks, the men in such anomalous attire as only an Irishman knows how to get together, the children half naked. The only comfortable-looking people are the monks and the priests, and the soldiers in the fort. For there is a fort there, constructed on the huge ruins of one which may have done duty in the rein of Edward the Black Prince, or earlier, in whose mossy embrasures are mounted a couple of cannon, which occasionally sent a practice-shot or two at the cliff on the other side of the harbor. The garrison consists of a dozen men and three or four officers and non-commissioned officers. I suppose they are relieved occasionally, but those I saw seemed to have become component parts of their surroundings.

"I put up at a wonderful little old inn, the only one in the place, and took my meals in a dining-saloon fifteen feet by nine, with a portrait of George I (a print varnished to preserve it) hanging over the mantel-piece. On the second evening after dinner a young gentleman came in—the dining-saloon being public property of course—and ordered some bread and cheese and a bottle of Dublin stout. We presently fell into talk; he turned out to be an officer from the fort, Lieutenant O'Connor, and a fine young specimen of the Irish soldier he was. After telling me all he knew about the town, the surrounding country, his friends, and himself, he intimated a readiness to sympathize with whatever tale I might choose to pour into his ear; and I had pleasure in trying to rival his own outspokenness. We became excellent friends; we had up a half-pint of Kinahan's whisky, and the lieutenant expressed himself in terms of high praise of my countrymen, my country, and my own particular cigars. When it became time for him to depart I accompanied him—for there was a splendid moon abroad—and bade him farewell at the fort entrance, having promised to come over the next day and make the acquaintance of the other fellows. 'And mind your eye, now, going back, my dear boy,' he called out, as I turned my face homeward, "Faith, 'tis a spooky place, that graveyard, and you'll as likely meet the black woman there as anywhere else!'

"The graveyard was a forlorn and barren spot on the hill-side, just the hither side of the fort; thirty or forty rough head-stones, few of which retained any semblance of the perpendicular, while many were so shattered and decayed as to seem nothing more than irregular natural projections from the ground. Who the black woman might be I knew not, and did not stay to inquire. I had never been subject to ghostly apprehensions, and as a matter of fact, though the path I had to follow was in places very bad going, not to mention a haphazard scramble over a ruined bridge that covered a deep-lying brook, I reached my inn without any adventure whatever.

"The next day I kept my appointment at the fort, and found no reason to regret it; and my friendly sentiments were abundantly reciprocated, thanks more especially, perhaps, to the success of my banjo, which I carried with me, and which was as novel as it was popular with those who listened to it. The chief personages in the social circle besides my friend the lieutenant were Major Molloy, who was in command, a racy and juicy old campaigner, with a face like a sunset, and the surgeon, Dr. Dudeen, a long, dry, humorous genius, with a wealth of anecdotical and traditional lore at his command that I have never seen surpassed. We had a jolly time of it, and it was the precursor of many more like it. The remains of October slipped away rapidly, and I was obliged to remember that I was a traveler in Europe, and not a resident in Ireland. The major, the surgeon, and the lieutenant all protested cordially against my proposed departure, but, as there was no help for it, they arranged a farewell dinner to take place in the fort on All-halloween.

"I wish you could have been at that dinner with me! It was the essence of Irish good-fellowship. Dr. Dudeen was in great force; the major was better than the best of Lever's novels; the lieutenant was overflowing with hearty good-humor, merry chaff, and sentimental rhapsodies anent this or the other pretty girl of the neighborhood. For my part I made the banjo ring as it had never rung before, and the others joined in the chorus with a mellow strength of lungs such as you don't often hear outside of Ireland. Among the stories that Dr. Dudeen regaled us with was one about the Kern of Querin and his wife, Ethelind Fionguala—which being interpreted signifies 'the white-shouldered.' The lady, it appears, was originally betrothed to one O'Connor (here the lieutenant smacked his lips), but was stolen away on the wedding night by a party of vampires, who, it would seem, were at that period a prominent feature among the troubles of Ireland. But as they were bearing her along—she being unconscious—to that supper where she was not to eat but to be eaten, the young Kern of Querin, who happened to be out duck-shooting, met the party, and emptied his gun at it. The vampires fled, the Kern carried the fair lady, still in a state of insensibility, to his house. 'And by the same token, Mr. Keningale,' observed the doctor, knocking the ashes out of his pipe, 'ye're after passing that very house on your way here. The one with the dark archway underneath it, and the big mullioned window at the corner, ye recollect, hanging over the street as I might say—'

"'Go 'long wid the house, Dr. Dudeen, dear,' interrupted the lieutenant; 'sure can't you see we're all dying to know what happened to sweet Miss Fionguala, God be good to her, when I was after getting her safe upstairs—'

"'Faith, then, I can tell ye that myself, Mr. O'Connor,' exclaimed the major, imparting a rotary motion to the remnants of whisky in his tumbler. ''Tis a question to be solved on general principles, as Colonel O'Halloran said that time he was asked what he'd do if he'd been the Dook o'Wellington, and the Prussians hadn't come up in the nick o'time at Waterloo. "Faith,' says the colonel, 'I'll tell ye—'

"'Arrah, then, major, why would ye be interruptin' the doctor, and Mr. Keningale there lettin' his glass stay empty till he hears—The Lord save us! The bottle's empty!'

"In the excitement consequent upon this discovery, the thread of the doctor' story was lost; and before it could be recovered the evening had advanced so far that I felt obliged to withdraw. It took some time to make my proposition heard and comprehended; and a still longer time to put it in execution; so that it was fully midnight before I found myself standing in the cool pure air outside the fort, with the farewells of my boon companions ringing in my ears.

"Considering that it had been rather a wet evening indoors, I was in a remarkably good state of preservation, and I therefore ascribed it rather to the roughness of the road than to the smoothness of the liquor, when, after advancing a few rods, I stumbled and fell. As I picked myself up I fancied I had heard a laugh, and supposed that the lieutenant, who had accompanied me to the gate, was making merry over my mishap; but on looking round I saw that the gate was closed and no one was visible. The laugh, moreover, had seemed to be close at hand, and to be even pitched in a key that was rather feminine than masculine. Of course I must have been deceived; nobody was near me: my imagination ha play me a trick or else there was more truth than poetry in the tradition that Halloween is the carnival-time of disembodied spirits. It did not occur to me at the time that a stumble is held by the superstitious Irish to be an evil omen, and had I remembered it it would only have been to laugh at it. At all events, I was physically none the worse for my fall, and I resumed my way immediately.

"But the path was singularly difficult to find, or rather the path I was following did not seem to be the right one. I did not recognize it; I could have sworn (except I knew the contrary) that I had never seen it before. The moon had risen, though her light was yet obscured by clouds, but neither my immediate surroundings nor the general aspect of the region appeared familiar. Dark, silent hillsides mounted up on either hand, and the road, for the most part, plunged downward, as if to conduct me into the bowels of the earth. The place was alive with strange echoes, so that at times I seemed to be walking through the midst of muttering voices and mysterious whispers, and a wild, faint sound of laughter seemed ever and anon to reverberate among the passes of the hills. Currents of colder air sighing up through narrow defiles and dark crevices touched my face as with airy fingers. A certain feeling of anxiety and insecurity began to take possession of me, though there was no definable cause for it, unless that I might be belated in getting home. With the perverse instinct of those who are lost I hastened my steps, but was impelled now and then to glance back over my shoulder, with a sensation of being pursued. But no living creature was in sight. The moon, however, had now risen higher, and the clouds that were drifting slowly across the sky flung into the naked valley dusky shadows, which occasionally assumed shapes that looked like the vague semblance of gigantic human forms.

"How long I had been hurrying onward I know not, when, with a kind of suddenness, I found myself approaching a graveyard. It was situated on the spur of a hill, and there was no fence around it, nor anything to protect it from the incursions of passers-by. There was something in the general appearance of this spot that made me half fancy I had seen it before; and I should have taken it to be the same that I had often noticed on my way to the fort, but that the latter was only a few hundred yards distant therefrom, whereas I must have traversed several miles at least. As I drew near, moreover, I observed that the head-stones did not appear so ancient and decayed as those of the other. But what chiefly attracted my attention was the figure that was leaning or half sitting upon one of the largest of the upright slabs near the road. It was a female figure draped in black, and a closer inspection—for I was soon within a few yards of her—showed that she wore the calla, or long hooded cloak, the most common as well as the most ancient garment of Irish women, and doubtless of Spanish origin.

"I was a trifle startled by this apparition, so unexpected as it was, and so strange did it seem that any human creature should be at that hour of the night in so desolate and sinister a place. Involuntarily I paused as I came opposite her, and gazed at her intently. But the moonlight fell behind her, and the deep hood of her cloak so completely shadowed her face that I was unable to discern anything but the sparkle of a pair of eyes, which appeared to be returning my gaze with much vivacity.

"'You seem to be at home here,' I said, at length. 'Can you tell me where I am?'

"Hereupon the mysterious personage broke into a light laugh, which, though in itself musical and agreeable, was of a timber and intonation that caused my heart to beat faster than my late pedestrian exertions warranted; for it was the identical laugh (or so my imagination persuaded me) that had echoed in my ears as I arose from my tumble an hour or two ago. For the rest, it was the laugh of a young woman, and presumably of a pretty one; and yet it had a wild, airy, mocking quality, that seemed hardly human at all, or not, at any rate, characteristic of a being of affections and limitations like unto ours. But this impression of mine was fostered, no doubt, by the unusual and uncanny circumstances of the occasion.

"'Sure, sir,' said she, 'you're at the grave of Ethelind Fionguala.'

"As she spoke she rose to her feet, and pointed to the inscription on the stone. I bent forward, and was able, without much difficulty, to decipher the name, and a date which disembodied state between two and three centuries ago.

"'And who are you?' was my next question.

"'I'm called Elsie,' she replied. 'But where would your honor be going November-eve?'

"I mentioned my destination, and asked her whether she could direct me thither.

"'Indeed, then, 'tis there I'm going myself,' Elsie replied, 'and if your honor'll follow me, and play me a tune on the pretty instrument, 'tisn't long we'll be on the road.'

"She pointed to the banjo which I carried wrapped up under my arm. How she knew that it was a musical instrument I could not imagine; possibly, I thought, she may have seen me playing on it as I strolled about the environs of the town. Be that as it may, I offered no opposition to the bargain, and further intimated that I would reward her more substantially on our arrival. At that she laughed again, and made a peculiar gesture with her hand above her head. I uncovered my banjo, swept my fingers across the strings, and struck into a fantastic dance-measure, to the music of which we proceeded along the path. Elsie slightly in advance, her feet keeping time to the airy measure. In fact, she trod so lightly, with an elastic, undulating movement, that with a little more it seemed as if she might float onward like a spirit. The extreme whiteness of her feet attracted my eye, and I was surprised to find that instead of being bare, as I had supposed, these were encased in white satin slippers quaintly embroidered with gold thread.

"'Elsie," said I, lengthening my steps so as to come up with her, 'where do you live, and what do you do for a living?'

"'Sure, I live by myself,' she answered; 'and if you'd be after knowing how, you must come and see for yourself.'

"'Are you in the habit of walking over the hills at night in shoes like that?'

"'And why would I not?' she asked, in her turn. 'And where did your honor get the pretty gold ring on your finger?'

"The ring, which was of no great intrinsic value, had struck my eye in an old curiosity-ship in Cork. It was an antique of very old-fashioned design, and might have belonged (as the vender assured me was the case) to one of the early kings or queens of Ireland.

"'Do you like it?' said I.

"'Will your honor be after making a present of it to Elsie?' she returned, with an insinuating tone and turn of the head.

"'Maybe I will, Elsie, on one condition. I am an artist; I make pictures of people. If you will promise to come to my studio and let me paint your portrait, I'll give you the ring, and some money besides.'

"'And will you give me the ring now?' said Elsie.

"'Yes, if you'll promise.'

"'And will you play the music to me?' she continued.

"'As much as you like.'

"'But maybe I'll not be handsome enough for ye,' said she, with a glance of her eyes beneath the dark hood.

"'I'll take the risk of that,' I answered laughing, though, all the same, I don't mind taking a peep beforehand to remember you by.' So saying, I put forth a hand to draw back the concealing hood. But Elsie eluded me, I scarce know how, and laughed a third time, with the same airy, mocking cadence.

"'Give me the ring first, and then you shall see me,' she said, coaxingly.

"'Stretch out your hand, then,' returned I, removing the ring from my finger. 'When we are better acquainted, Elsie, you won't be so suspicious.'

"She held out a slender, delicate hand, on the forefinger of which I slipped the ring. As I did so, the folds of her cloak fell a little apart, affording me a glimpse of a white shoulder and of a dress that seemed in that deceptive semi-darkness to be wrought of rich and costly material; and I caught, too, or so I fancied, the frosty sparkle of precious stones.

"'Arrah, mind where ye tread!' said Elsie, in a sudden, sharp tone.

"I looked round, and became aware for the first time that we were standing near the middle of a ruined bridge which spanned a rapid stream that flowed at a considerable depth below. The parapet of the bridge on one side was broken down, and I must have been, in fact, in imminent danger of stepping over into empty air. I made my way cautiously across the decaying structure; but, when I turned to assist Elsie, she was nowhere to be seen.

"What had become of the girl? I called, but no answer came, I gazed about on every side, but no trace of her was visible. Unless, she had plunged into the narrow abyss at my feet, there was no place where she could have concealed herself—none at least that I could discover. She had vanished, nevertheless; and since her disappearance must have been premeditated, I finally came to the conclusion that it was useless to attempt to find her. She would present herself again in her own good time, or not at all. She had given me the slip very cleverly, and I must make the best of it. The adventure was perhaps worth the ring.

"On resuming my way, I was not a little relieved to find that I once more knew where I was. The bridge that I had just crossed was none other than the one I mentioned some time back; I was within a mile of the town, and my way lay clear before me. The moon, moreover, had now quite dispersed the clouds, and shone down with exquisite brilliance. Whatever her other failings, Elsie had been a trustworthy guide; she had brought me out of the depth of elf-land into the material world again. It had been a singular adventure, certainly, and I mused over it with a sense of mysterious pleasure as I sauntered along, humming snatches of airs, and accompanying myself on the strings. Hark! What light step was that behind me? It sounded like Elsie's; but no, Elsie was not there. The same impression of hallucination, however, recurred several times before I reached the outskirts of the town—the tread of an airy foot behind or beside my own. The fancy did not make me nervous; on the contrary, I was pleased with the notion of being thus haunted, and gave myself up to a romantic and genial vein of reverie.

"After passing one or two roofless and moss-grown cottages, I entered the narrow and rambling street which leads through the town. This street a short distance down widens a little, as if to afford the wayfarer space to observe a remarkable old house that stands on the northern side. The house was built of stone, and in a noble style of architecture; it reminded me somewhat of certain palaces of the old Italian nobility that I had seen on the Continent, and it may very probably have been built by one of the Italian or Spanish immigrants of the sixteenth or seventeenth century. The molding of the projecting windows and arched doorway was richly carved, and upon the front of the building was an escutcheon wrought in high relief, though I could not make out the purport of the device. The moonlight falling upon this picturesque pile enhanced all its beauties, and at the same time made it seem like a vision that might dissolve away when the light ceased to shine. I must often have seen the house before, and yet I retained no definite recollection of it; I had never until now examined it with my eyes open, so to speak. Leaning against the wall on the opposite side of the street, I contemplated it for a long while at my leisure. The window at the corner was really a very fine and massive affair. It projected over the pavement below, throwing a heavy shadow aslant; the frames of the diamond-paned lattices were heavily mullioned. How often in past ages had that lattice been pushed open by some fair hand, revealing the charming countenances of his high-born mistress! Those were brave days. They had passed away long since. The great house had stood empty for who could tell how many years; only bats and vermin were its inhabitants. Where now were those who had built it? And who were they? Probably the very name of them was forgotten.

"As I continued to stare upward, however, a conjecture presented itself to my mind which rapidly ripened into a conviction. Was not this the house that Dr. Dudeen had described that very evening as having been formerly the abode of the Kern of Querin and his mysterious bride? There was the projecting window, the arched doorway. Yes, beyond a doubt this was the very house. I emitted a low exclamation of renewed interest and pleasure and my speculations took a still more imaginative, but also a more definite turn.

"What had been the fate of that lovely lady after the Kern had brought her home insensible in his arms? Did she recover, and were they married and made happy ever after; or had the sequel been a tragic one? I remember to have read that the victims of vampires generally became vampires themselves. Then my thoughts went back to that grave on the hill-side. Surely that was unconsecrated ground. Why had they buried her there? Ethelind of the white shoulder! Ah! Why not not I lived in those days; or why might not some magic cause them to live again for me? Then would I seek this street at midnight, and standing here beneath her window, I would lightly touch the strings of my bandore until the casement opened cautiously and she looked down. A sweet vision indeed! And who prevented my realizing it? Only a matter of a couple of centuries or so. And was time, then, at which poets and philosophers sneer, so rigid and real a matter that a little faith and imagination might not overcome it? At all events, I had my banjo, the bandore's legitimate and lineal descendant, and the memory of Fionguala should have the love-ditty.

"Hereupon, having retuned the instrument, I launched forth into an old Spanish love-song, which I had met with in some moldy library during my travels, and had set to music of my own. I sang low, for the deserted street re-echoed the lightest sound, and what I sang must reach only my lady's ears. The words were warm with the fire of the ancient Spanish chivalry, and I threw into their expression all the passion of the lovers of romance. Surely Fionguala, the white-shouldered, would hear, and awaken from her sleep of centuries, and come to the latticed casement and look down! Hist! See yonder! What light—what shadow is that that seems to flit from room to room within the abandoned house, and now approaches the mullioned window? Are my eyes dazzled by the play of the moonlight, or does the casement move—does it open? Nay, this is no delusion; there is no error of the senses here. There is simply a woman, young, beautiful, and richly attired, bending forward from the window, and silently beckoning me to approach.

"Too much amazed to be conscious of amazement, I advanced until I stood directly beneath the casement, and the lady's face, as she stooped toward me, was not more than twice a man's height from my own. She smiled and kissed her finger-tips; something white fluttered in her hand, then fell through the air to the ground at my feet. The next moment she had withdrawn, and I heard the lattice close.

"I picked up what she had let fall; it was a delicate lace handkerchief, tied to the handle of an elaborately wrought bronze key. It was evidently the key of the house, and invited me to enter, I loosened it from the handkerchief, which bore a faint, delicious perfume, like the aroma of flowers in an ancient garden, and turned to the arched doorway. I felt no misgiving, and scarcely any sense of strangeness. All was as I had wished it to be, and as it should be; the medieval age was alive once more, and as for myself, I almost felt the velvet cloak hanging from my shoulder and the long rapier dangling at my belt. Standing in front of the door I thrust the key into the lock, turned it, and felt the bolt yield. The next instant the door was opened, apparently from within; I stepped across the threshold, the door closed again, and I was alone in the house, and in darkness.

"Not alone, however! As I extended my hand to grope my way it was met by another hand, soft, slender, and cold, which insinuated itself gently into mine and drew me forward. Forward I went, nothing loath; the darkness was impenetrable, but I could hear the light rustle of a dress close to me, and the same delicious perfume that had emanated from the handkerchief enriched the air that I breathed, while the little hand that clasped and was clasped by my own alternately tightened and half relaxed the hold of its soft cold fingers. In this manner, and treading lightly, we traversed that I presumed to be a long, irregular passageway, and ascended a staircase. Then another corridor, until finally we paused, a door opened, emitting a flood of soft light, into which we entered, still hand in hand. The darkness and the doubt were at an end.

"The room was of imposing dimensions, and was furnished and decorated in a style of antique splendor. The walls were draped with mellow hues of tapestry; clusters of candles burned in polished silver sconces, and were reflected and multiplied in tall mirrors placed in the four corners of the room. The heavy beams of the dark oaken ceiling crossed each other in squares, and were laboriously carved; the curtains and the drapery of the chairs were of heavy-figured damask. At one end of the room was a broad ottoman, and in front of it a table, on which was set forth, in massive silver dishes, a sumptuous repast, with wines in crystal beakers. At the side was a vast and deep fireplace, with space enough on the broad hearth to burn whole trunks of trees. No fire, however, was there, but only a great heap of dead embers; and the room, for all its magnificence, was cold—cold as a tomb, or as my lady's hand—and it sent a subtle chill creeping to my heart.

"But my lady! how fair she was! I gave but a passing glance at the room; my eyes and my thoughts were all for her. She was dressed in white, like a bride; diamonds sparkled in her dark hair and on her snowy bosom; her lovely face and slender lips were pale, and all the paler for the dusky glow of her eyes. She gazed at me with a strange, elusive smile; and yet there was, in her aspect and bearing, something familiar in the midst of strangeness, like the burden of a song heard long ago and recalled among other conditions and surroundings. It seemed to me that something in me recognized her and knew her, had known her always. She was the woman of whom I had dreamed, whom I had beheld in visions, whose voice and face had haunted me from boyhood up. Whether we had ever met before, as human beings meet, I knew not; perhaps I had been blindly seeking her all over the world, and she had been awaiting me in this splendid room, sitting by those dead embers until all the warmth had gone out of her blood, only to be restored by the heat with which my love might supply her.

"'I thought you had forgotten me,' she said, nodding as if in answer to my thought. 'The night was so late—our one night of the year! How my heart rejoiced when I heard your dear voice singing the song I know so well! Kiss me—my lips are cold!'

"Cold indeed they were–cold as the lips of death. But the warmth of my own seemed to revive them. They were now tinged with a faint color, and in her cheeks also appeared a delicate shade of pink. She drew fuller breath, as one who recovers from a long lethargy. Was it my life that was feeding her? I was ready to give her all. She drew me to the table and pointed to the viands and the wine.

"'Eat and drink,' she said. 'You have traveled far, and you need food.'

"'Will you eat and drink with me?' said I, pouring out the wine.

"'You are the only nourishment I want,' was her answer. 'This wine is thin and cold. Give me wine as red as your blood and as warm, and I will drain a goblet to the dregs.'

"At these words, I know not why, a slight shiver passed through me. She seemed to gain vitality and strength at every instant, but the chill of the great room stuck into me more and more.

"She broke into a fantastic flow of spirits, clapping her hands, and dancing about me like a child. Who was she? And was I myself, or was she mocking me when she implied that we had belonged to each other of old? At length she stood still before me, crossing her hands over her breast. I saw upon the forefinger of her right hand the gleam of an antique ring.

"'Where did you get that ring?' I demanded.

"She shook her head and laughed. 'Have you been faithful?' she asked. "It is my ring; it is the ring that unites us; it is the ring you gave when you loved me first. It is the ring of the Kern—the fairy ring, and I am your Ethelind—Ethelind Fionguala.'

"'So be it,' I said, casting aside all doubt and fear, and yielding myself wholly to the spell of her inscrutable eyes and wooing lips. 'You are mine, and I am yours, and let us be happy while the hours last.'

"'You are mine, and I am yours,' she repeated, nodding her head with an elfish smile. 'Come and sit beside me, and sing that sweet song again that you sang to me so long ago. Ah, now I shall live a hundred years.'

"We seated ourselves on the ottoman, and while she nestled luxuriously among the cushions, I took my banjo and sang to her. The song and the music resounded through the lofty room, and came back in throbbing echoes. And before me as I sang I saw the face and form of Ethelind Fionguala, in her jeweled bridal dress, gazing at me with burning eyes. She was pale no longer, but ruddy and warm, and life was like a flame within her. It was I who had become cold and bloodless, yet with the last life that was in me I would have sung to her of love that can never die. But at length my eyes grew dim, the room seemed to darken, the form of Ethelind alternately brightened and waxed indistinct, like the last flickerings of a fire; I swayed toward her, and felt myself lapsing into unconsciousness, with my head resting on her white shoulder."

Here Keningale paused a few moments in his story, flung a

fresh log upon the fire, and then continued:

"I awoke, I know not how long afterward. I was in a vast empty room in a ruined building. Rotten shreds of drapery depended from the walls, and heavy festoons of spiders' webs gray with dust covered the windows, which were destitute of glass or sash; they had been boarded up with rough planks which had themselves become rotten with age, and admitted through their holes and crevices pallid rays of light and chilly draughts of air. A bat, disturbed by these rays or by my own movement, detached himself from his hold on a remnant of moldy tapestry near me, and after circling dizzily around my head, wheeled the flickering noiselessness of his flight into a darker corner. As I arose unsteadily from the heap of miscellaneous rubbish on which I had been lying, something which had been resting across my knees fell to the floor with a rattle. I picked it up, and found it to be my banjo—as you see it now.

"Well, that is all I have to tell. My health was seriously impaired; all the blood seemed to have been drawn out of my veins; I was pale and haggard and the chill— Ah, that chill," murmured Keningale, drawing nearer to the fire, and spreading out his hands to catch the warmth— "I shall never get over it; I shall carry it to my grave."

Julian Hawthorne inherited from his father—Nathaniel Hawthorne—a talent for writing and a penchant for the supernatural and the macabre. He was acquainted with Bram Stoker, and in fact "Ken's Mystery" was published in 1888, nine years before *Dracula*.

Children growing up in New York City need to be tough to survive.

Good Kids

BY EDWARD BRYANT

hat blood?" said Donnie, appalled. "That's grossss."

Angelique was peeking over her shoulder at the lurid paperback vampire novel. "Don't draw out your consonants. You sound like a geek."

"I'm not a geek," said Donnie. "I'm only eleven years old, you jerk. I get to draw out my esses if I want to."

"We're all too goddamned bright," said Camelia gloomily. "The last place I went to school, everybody just played with dolls or talked all day about crack."

"Public schools," Angelique snorted.

Donnie flipped the page and squinted. "Yep, he's lapping up her menstrual blood, all right. This vampire's a real gink."

"Wonderful. So her arching, lily-white swan throat wasn't enough," said Cammie. "Oh boy. I can hardly wait til I start having my period."

The lights flashed and the four of us involuntarily glanced up. Ms. Yukoshi, one of the Center's three night supervisors, stood framed in the doorway. "Okay, girls, lights out in there. Put away the book. Hit those bunks. Good night, now." She started to exit, but then apparently changed her mind. "I suppose I ought to mention that this is my last night taking care of you."

Were we supposed to clap? I wondered. Maybe give her a four-part harmony chorus of "Thank you, Ms. Yukoshi"? What was appropriate behavior?

"No thanks are necessary," said Ms. Yukoshi. "I just know I need a long, long vacation. Lots of R and R." We could all see her sharp, white teeth gleaming in the light from the overhead. "You'll have a new person to bedevil tomorrow night. His name is Mr. Vladisov."

"So why don't we ever get a good WASP?" Cammie whispered.

The other two giggled. I guess I did too. It's easy to forget that Camelia is black.

Ms. Yukoshi looked at us sharply. Donnie giggled again and dog-eared a page before setting the vampire book down. "Good night, girls." Ms. Yukoshi retreated into the hall. We listened to the click and echo of her stylish heels moving on to the next room, the next island of kids. Boys in that one.

"I wonder what Mr. Vladisov will be like," Donnie said.

Angelique smiled. "At least he's a guy."

"Good night, girls." Donnie mimicked Ms. Yukoshi.

I snapped off the lamp. And that was it for another fun evening at the renovated brownstone that was the Work-at-Night Child Care Center and Parenting Service. Wick Pus, we called it, all of us who had night-shift parents with no other place to put their kids.

"Good night," I said to everybody in general. I lay back in the bunk and pulled the covers up to my chin. The wool blanket scratched my neck.

"I'm hungry," said Angelique plaintively. "Cookies and milk aren't enough."

"Perhaps you want some blooood?" said Donnie, snickering.

"Good night," I said again. But I was hungry too.

The next day was Wednesday. Hump day. Didn't matter. No big plans for the week—or for the weekend. It wasn't one of the court-set times for my dad to visit, so I figured probably I'd be spending the time reading. That was okay too. I like to read. Maybe I'd finish the last thousand pages of Stephen King's new novel and get on to some of the stuff I needed to read for school.

We were studying urban legends and old wives' tales—a side issue was the class figuring out a nonsexist term for the latter.

We'd gone through a lot of the stuff that most of us had heard—and even believed at one time—like the hook killer and the Kentucky Fried Rat and the expensive car that was on sale unbelievably cheap because nobody could get the smell out of the upholstery after the former owner killed himself and the body wasn't discovered for three hot days. Then there was the rattlesnake in the K-Mart jeans and the killer spiders in the bouffant. Most of that didn't interest me. What I liked were the older myths, things like keeping cats out of the nursery and forbidding adults to sleep in the presence of children.

Now I've always liked cats, so I know where my sympathy lies with that one. Kitties love to snuggle up to warm little faces on chilly nights. No surprise, right? But the bit about sucking the breath from babies' lungs is a load of crap. Well, most of the time. As for the idea that adults syphon energy from children, that's probably just a cleaner way of talking about the incest taboo.

It's a way of speaking metaphorically. That's what the teacher said.

I can see why adults would want to steal kids' energy. Then they could rule the world, live forever, win all the Olympics. See what I mean? So maybe some adults do. You ever feel just how much energy is generated by a roomful of hyper kids? I know. But then, I'm a kid. I expect I'll lose it all when I grow up. I'm not looking forward to that. It'll be like death. Or maybe undeath.

It all sounds sort of dull gray and drab, just like living in the book *1984*.

The thing about energy is that what goes out has to come in first. Another lesson. First Law of Thermodynamics. Or maybe the Second. I didn't pay much attention that day. I guess I was too busy daydreaming about horses, or maybe sneaking a few pages of the paperback hidden in my vinyl binder.

Don't even ask what I'm going to do when I grow up. I've got lots of time to figure it out.

Mr. Vladisov had done his homework. He addressed us all by name. Evidently he'd sucked Ms. Yukoshi dry of all the necessary information.

"And you would be Shauna-Laurel Andersen," he said to me, smiling faintly.

I felt like I ought to curtsy at least. Mr. Vladisov was tall and courtly, just like characters in any number of books I'd read. His hair was jet-black and fixed in one of those widow's peaks. Just like a novel. His eyes were sharp and black too, though the whites were all bloodshot. They didn't look comfortable. He spoke with some kind of Slavic accent. Good English, but the kind of accent I've heard actors working in restaurants goofing around with.

Shauna-Laurel, I thought. "My friends call me SL," I said.

"Then I hope we shall be friends," said Mr. Vladisov.

"Do we have to call you 'sir'?" said Angelique. I knew she was just being funny. I wondered if Mr. Vladisov knew that.

"No." His gaze flickered from one of us to the next. "I know we shall *all* be very close. Ms. Yukoshi told me you were all . . ." He seemed to be searching for the correct phrase. ". . . good kids."

"Sure," said Donnie giggling just a little.

"I believe," said Mr. Vladisov, "that it is customary to devour milk and cookies before your bedtime."

"Oh, that's not for a while yet," said Angelique.

"Hours," chimed in Donnie.

Our new guardian consulted his watch. "Perhaps twenty-three minutes?"

We slowly nodded.

"SL," he said to me, "will you help me distribute the snacks?"

I followed Mr. Vladisov out the door.

"Be careful," said Angelique so softly that only I could hear. I wondered if I really knew what she meant.

Mr. Vladisov preceded me down the corridor leading to the playroom and then to the adjacent kitchenette. Other inmates looked at us through the doorways as we passed. I didn't know most of their names. There were about three dozen of them. Our crowd—the four of us—was pretty tight.

He slowed so I could catch up to his side. "Your friends seem very nice," he said. "Well behaved."

"Uh, yes," I answered. "They're great. Smart too."

"And healthy."

"As horses."

"My carriage," mused Mr. Vladisov, "used to be pulled by a fine black team."

"Beg pardon?"

"Nothing," he said sharply. His tone moderated. "I sometimes slip into the past, SL. It's nothing."

"Me," I said. "I love horses. My dad says he'll get me a colt for my graduation from middle school. We'll have to stable it out in Long Island."

Mr. Vladisov didn't comment. We had reached the closetlike kitchenette. He didn't bother to turn on the light. When he opened the refrigerator and took out a carton of milk, I could see well enough to open the cabinet where I knew the cookies were stored.

"Chocolate chip?" I said. "Double Stuf Oreos?"

Mr. Vladisov said, "I never eat . . . cookies. Choose what you like."

I took both packages. Mr. Vladisov hovered over the milk, assembling quartets of napkins and glasses. "Don't bother with a straw for Donnie," I said. "She's not supposed to drink through a straw. Doctor's orders."

Mr. Vladisov nodded. "Do these things help you sleep more soundly?"

I shrugged. "I 'spose so. The nurse told me once that a high-carb snack before bed would drug us out. It's okay. Cookies taste better than Ritalin anyway."

"Ritalin?"

"An upper that works like a downer for the hypers."

"I beg your pardon?"

I decided to drop it. "The cookies help us all sleep."

"Good," said Mr. Vladisov. "I want everyone to have a good night's rest. I take my responsibility here quite seriously. It would be unfortunate were anyone to be so disturbed she woke up in the early morning with nightmares."

"We all sleep very soundly," I said.

Mr. Vladisov smiled down at me. In the dim light from the hall, it seemed to me that his eyes gleamed a dusky red.

〈〈〈

I passed around the Double Stuf Oreos and the chocolate-chip cookies. Mr. Vladisov poured and distributed the glasses of milk as solemnly as if he were setting out communion wine.

Cammie held up her milk in a toast. "We enjoyed Ms. Yukoshi, but we know we'll like you much better."

Mr. Vladisov smiled without parting his teeth and raised an empty hand as though holding a wine glass. "A toast to you as well. To life everlasting, and to the dreams which make it bearable."

Angelique and I exchanged glances. I looked at Donnie. Her face was saying nothing at all. We all raised our glasses and then drank. The milk was cold and good, but it wasn't the taste I wished. I wanted chocolate.

Mr. Vladisov wished us a more conventional good night, then smoothly excused himself from the room to see to his other charges. We listened hard but couldn't hear his heels click on the hallway tile.

"Slick," said Angelique, nibbling delicately around the edge of her chocolate-chip cookie.

"Who's he remind me of?" mused Cammie. "That old guy—I saw him in a play once. Frank Langella."

"I don't know about this," said Donnie.

"What don't you know?" I said.

"I don't know whether maybe one of us ought to stay up all night on watch." Her words came out slowly. Then more eagerly, "Maybe we could take turns."

"We all need our rest," I said, "It's a school night."

"I sure need all the energy I can get," said Cammie. "I've got a geography test tomorrow. We're supposed to know all the capitals of those weird little states west of New Jersey."

I said, "I don't think we have anything to worry about for a while. Mr. Vladisov's new. It'll take him a little while to settle in and get used to us."

Cammie cocked her head. "So you think we got ourselves a live one?"

"So to speak." I nodded. "Metaphorically speaking . . ."

So I was wrong. Not about what Mr. Vladisov was. Rather that he would wait to get accustomed to how things ran at Wick Pus. He must have been very hungry.

In the morning, it took Donnie forever to get up. She groaned when Cammie shook her, but didn't seem to want to move. "I feel shitty," she said, when her eyes finally opened and started to focus. "I think I've got the flu."

"Only if bats got viruses in their spit," said Cammie grimly. She gestured at Donnie's neck, gingerly zeroing in with her index finger.

Angelique and I leaned forward, inspecting the throat.

Donnie's brown eyes widened in alarm. "What's wrong?" she said weakly.

"What's wrong ain't pimples," said Cammie. "And there's two of them."

"Damn," said Angelique.

"Shit," said Donnie.

I disagreed with nobody.

The four of us agreed to try not to get too upset about all of this until we'd had time to confer tonight after our parents dropped us off at the Center. Donnie was the hardest to convince. But then, it was her throat that showed the pair of matched red marks.

Mrs. Maloney was the morning-shift lady who saw us off to our various bus and subways to school. Mr. Vladisov had gone off duty sometime before dawn. Naturally. He would return after dark. Double naturally.

"I'm gonna tell my mom I don't want to come back to the Center tonight," Donnie had said.

"Don't be such a little kid," said Cammie. "We'll take care of things."

"It'll be all right," Angelique chimed in.

Donnie looked at me as though begging silently for permission to chicken out. "SL?"

"It'll be okay," I said as reassuringly as I could. I wasn't so sure it would be that okay. Why was everyone staring at me as though I were the leader?

"I trust you," Donnie said softly.

I knew I was blushing. "It'll be all right." I wished I knew whether I was telling the truth.

◇◇◇

At school, I couldn't concentrate. I didn't even sneak reads from my Stephen King paperback. I guess I sort of just sat there like a wooden dummy while lessons were talked about and assignments handed out.

I started waking up in the afternoon during my folklore class.

"The thing you should all remember," said Mrs. Dancey, my teacher, "is that myths never really change. Sometimes they're garbled and they certainly appear in different guises to different generations who recount them. But the basic lessons don't alter. We're talking about truths."

The truth was, I thought, I didn't know what we were all going to do about Mr. Vladisov. That was the long and short of it, and no urban myth Mrs. Dancey tempted me with was going to take my mind off that.

Time. Things like Mr. Vladisov, they figured they had all the time in the world, so they usually seemed to take things easy. Given time, we'd figure something out. Cammie, Donnie, Angelique, and me. We could handle anything. Always had.

"Shauna-Laurel?" It was Mrs. Dancey. Talking to me.

I didn't know what she had asked. "Ma'am?" I said. "Sorry."

But it was too late. I'd lost my chance. Too much daydreaming. I hoped it wouldn't be too late tonight.

◇◇◇

Donnie's twin red marks had started to fade when the four of us huddled in our room at the Center to talk.

"So maybe they *are* zits," said Cammie hopefully.

Donnie irritably scratched at them. "They itch."

I sat on the edge of the bunk and swung my legs back and forth. "Don't scratch. They'll get infected."

"You sound like my mother."

"Good evening, my good kids." Mr. Vladisov filled the doorway. He was all dark clothing and angular shadows. "I hope you are all feeling well tonight?"

"Aren't you a little early?" said Angelique.

Mr. Vladisov made a show of consulting his watch. It was the old-fashioned kind, round and gold, on a chain. It had hands. I glanced out the window toward the street. The light had gone while we were talking. I wondered where Mr. Vladisov spent his days.

"Early? No. Perhaps just a bit," he corrected himself. "I find my position here at the Center so pleasant, I don't wish to be late." He smiled at us. We stared back at him. "What? You're not all glad to see me?"

"I have the flu," said Donnie dully.

"The rest of us will probably get it too," Angelique said.

Cammie and I nodded in agreement.

"Oh, I'm sorry," said Mr. Vladisov. "I see why this should trouble you. Perhaps I can obtain for you an elixir?"

"Huh?" That was Cammie.

"For your blood," he said. "Something to strengthen your resistance. Tomato juice, perhaps? Or V-8? Some other healthful beverage?"

"No," said Donnie. "No thank you. I don't think so. No." She hiccuped.

"Oh, you poor child." Mr. Vladisov started forward. Donnie drew back. "Is there something I can do?" he said, checking himself in midstride. "Perhaps I should call for a doctor?" His voice sounded so solicitous. "Your parent?"

"No!" Donnie came close to shouting.

"She'll be okay," said Cammie.

Mr. Vladisov looked indecisive. "I don't know . . ."

"We do," I said. "Everything will be fine. Donnie just needs a good night's sleep."

"I'm sure she will get that," said Mr. Vladisov. "The night is quiet." Then he excused himself to fetch our milk and cookies. This time he didn't ask for volunteer help.

Cammie was stroking Donnie's hair. "We'll see nothin' happens. You'll be just fine."

"That's right," said Angelique. "We'll all stay up."

"No need," I said. "We can take turns. No use everybody killing themselves."

"Bad phrasing," said Cammie. "Taking turns sounds good to me."

I volunteered, "I'll take the first watch."

"Yeah." Cammie grinned. "That way the rest of us got to stay up in the scariest part of the night."

"Okay, so you go first and wake me up later."

"Naw. Just kidding."

I liked being friends with Cammie and the others. But then we were so much alike. More than you might think.

The daughter of a widowed Harlem mortician.

The daughter of the divorced assistant French consul.

The daughter of an ambitious off-Broadway director.

The daughter of a divorced famous novelist.

All of us denied latch-keys and dumped at Wick Pus. Handier than boarding school if a parent wanted us. But still out of their hair.

One of us used to love drugs. One of us was thinking about loving God. Another was afraid of being the baby of the group. And another just wanted peace and a horse. I smiled.

Donnie actually did look reassured.

After a while, Mr. Vladisov came back with our nightly snacks. He seemed less exuberant. Maybe he was catching on to the fact that we were on to him. Maybe not. It's hard to tell with adults.

At any rate, he bid us all a good evening and that was the last we saw of him until he came around to deliver a soft, "Lights out, girls. Sleep well. Sleep well, indeed."

We listened for his footsteps, didn't hear any, heard him repeating his message to the boys down the hall. Finally we started to relax just a little.

Through the darkness, Cammie whispered, "Three hours, SL. That's it. Don't knock yourself out, okay? Wake me up in three hours."

"Okay."

I heard Donnie's younger, softer whisper. "Thanks, guys. I'm glad you're all here. I'm even going to try to sleep."

"Want a ghost story first?" That was Angelique.

"No!" Donnie giggled.

We were all silent.

I listened for steady, regular breathing. I waited for anything strange. I eventually heard the sounds of the others sleeping.

I guess I really hadn't expected them to drift off like that.

And then I went to sleep.

I hadn't expected that either.

I woke up sweaty, dreaming someone was slapping me with big slabs of lunch meat. Someone *was* slapping me. Cammie.

"Wake up, you gink! She's gone!"

"Who's gone?" The lamp was on and I tried to focus on Cammie's angry face.

"Donnie! The honky blood-sucker stole her."

I struggled free of the tangled sheet. I didn't remember lying down in my bed. The last thing I recalled was sitting bolt upright, listening for anything that sounded like Mr. Vladisov skulking around. "I think he—he put me to sleep." I felt terrible.

"He put us all to sleep," said Angelique. "No time to worry about that. We've got to find Donnie before he drains her down to those cute little slippers." Donnie had been wearing a pair of plush Felix the Cat foot warmers.

"Where we gonna look?" Cammie looked about ready to pull Mr. Vladisov apart with her bare fingers with their crimson paint-ed nails.

"Follow running blood downhill," I said.

"Jeez," Cammie said disgustedly.

"I mean it. Try the basement. I bet he's got his coffin down there."

"Traditionalist, huh?"

"Maybe. I hope so." I pulled on one Adidas, wound the laces around my ankle, reached for the other. "What time is it, any-way?"

"Not quite midnight. Sucker didn't even wait for the witching hour."

I stood up. "Come on."

"What about the others?" Angelique paused by the door to the hall.

I quickly thought about that. We'd always been pretty self-sufficient. But this wasn't your ordinary situation. "Wake 'em up," I said, "We can use the help." Cammie started for the door, "But be quiet. Don't wake up the supervisors."

On the way to the door, I grabbed two Oreos I'd saved from my bedtime snack. I figured I'd need the energy.

I realized there were thirty or thirty-five kids trailing just behind as my roommates and I found one of Donnie's Felix slippers on the landing in the fire stairs. It was just before the final flight down to the dark rooms where the furnace and all the pipes were. The white eyes stared up at me. The whiskers didn't twitch.

"Okay," I said unnecessarily, "come on. Hurry!"

Both of them were in a storage room, just up the corridor from the place where the furnace roared like some giant dinosaur. Mr. Vladisov sat on a case of toilet paper. It was like he was waiting for us. He expected us. He sat there with Donnie cradled in his arms and was already looking up at the doorway when we burst through.

"SL . . ." Donnie's voice was weak. She tried to reach out toward me, but Mr. Vladisov held her tightly. "I don't want to be here."

"Me neither," muttered Cammie from beside me.

"Ah, my good kids," said Mr. Vladisov. "My lambs, my fat little calves. I am sorry that you found me."

It didn't sound like he was sorry. I had the feeling he'd expected it, maybe even wanted it to happen. I began to wonder if this one was totally crazy. A psychotic. "Let Donnie go," I said, trying for a firmness I don't think was really showing in my voice.

"No." That was simple enough.

"Let her go," I repeated.

"I'm not . . . don't," he said, baring his fangs in a jolly grin.

I said, "Please?"

"You really don't understand." Mr. Vladisov sighed theatrically. "There are two dozen or more of you and only one of me; but I am a man of some power. When I finish snacking on this one, I will kill most of the rest of you. Perhaps all. I'll kill you and I will drink you."

"Horseshit," said Cammie.

"You will be first," said Mr. Vladisov, "after your friend." He stared directly at me, his eyes shining like rubies.

"Get fucked." I surprised myself by saying that. I don't usually talk that way.

Mr. Vladisov looked shocked. "Shauna-Laurel, my dear, you are not a child of *my* generation."

I definitely wasn't. "Let. Her. Loose," I said distinctly.

"Don't be tiresome, my child. Now be patient. I'll be with you in just a moment." He lowered his mouth toward Donnie's throat.

"You're dead," I told him.

He paused, smiling horribly. "No news to me."

"I mean *really* dead. For keeps."

"I doubt that. Others have tried. Rather more mature specimens than all of you." He returned his attention to Donnie's neck.

Though I didn't turn away from Mr. Vladisov, I sensed the presence of the other kids behind me. We had all crowded into the storage room, and now the thirty-odd of us spread in a sort of semicircle. If Mr. Vladisov wondered why none of us was trying to run away, he didn't show it. I guess maybe like most adults, he figured he controlled us all.

I took Cammie's hand with my right, Angelique's with my left. All our fingers felt very warm. I could sense us starting to relax into that fuzzy-feeling receptive state that we usually only feel when we're asleep. I knew we were teaming up with the other kids in the room.

It's funny sometimes about old folktales (we'd finally come up in class with a nonsexist term). Like the one forbidding adults to sleep in the same room with a child. They had it right. They just had it backwards. It's us who suck up the energy like batteries charging . . .

Mr. Vladisov must have felt it start. He hesitated, teeth just a little ways from Donnie's skin. He looked at us from the corners of his eyes without raising his head. "I feel . . ." he started to say, and then trailed off. "You're taking something. You're feeding—"

"Let her go." I shouldn't even have said that. It was too late for making bargains.

"My . . . blood?" Mr. Vladisov whispered.

"Don't be gross," said Cammie.

I thought I could see Donnie smile wanly.

"I'm sorry," said Angelique. "I thought you were going to work out okay. We wouldn't have taken much. Just enough. You wouldn't have suspected a thing. Finally you would have moved on and someone else would have taken your place."

Mr. Vladisov didn't look well. "Perhaps—" he started to say. He looked like he was struggling against quicksand. Weakly.

"No," I said. "Not on your life."

And then we fed.

Edward Bryant is the author of many novels and short story collections, including *Cinnabar, The Man of the Future, Fetish,* and *The Thermals of August*. His stories "giANTSs" and "Stone" have both won the Nebula Award. He lives in Denver, Colorado.

Sometimes celebrities attract a different kind of admirer.

Sweet Dreams, Norma Jeane

BY BARBARA COLLINS

e hid in the recess of a doorway, a tall, thin young man with a thatch of wild sandy hair that sprang from his head like leaves on a palm tree. His face was pale, pockmarked, his brown eyes intent, as he stared across the boulevard at the elegant whitestone apartment building on East 57th Street. It was a hot July day in 1961, and even though the sun was concealed behind the high Manhattan buildings, there was little relief from the heat. A bead of sweat ran from the young man's forehead down the side of his cheek, but he wasn't uncomfortable. He was used to waiting for her.

Every afternoon was the same. At about 4:30 a cab would pull up in front of number 444 (where she now lived alone in apartment 13E, having recently divorced her playwright husband) and the driver would honk. And wait. And curse, and honk again. And just when it seemed the cabbie was about to leave, she would come out—a vision of loveliness—wearing a beige skirt and blouse, or orange slacks and top, or a blue polka-dot dress . . . but always the same white scarf covering that silky platinum hair, and black sunglasses shading those luminous blue eyes.

Quickly she would climb into the back seat of the cab, removing her sunglasses, and when the driver turned to snarl at his inconsiderate passenger, his eyes would bug out in disbelief, and his mouth would drop open as his lips formed her name: *Marilyn Monroe!* And they would drive off—she apologizing profusely for keeping him waiting and he gushing boyishly about seeing all her movies.

But this afternoon would be different. This afternoon the young man was not standing in his usual spot, which was on the sidewalk in front of her building, where day after day she ignored him. Yes, today would be different, he thought, he hoped, as he watched from across the street.

A cab pulled up. The driver, a big man, almost obese, with a face like a catcher's mitt, honked his horn. And waited. And cursed. And just as he looked ready to give up, the door to the apartment building opened and Marilyn came out.

The young man across the street in the doorway leaned forward excitedly because she had on an outfit he had never seen her in before: a tight yellow dress with a plunging neckline, and matching high heels.

Like butter sizzling on the hot cement, she wiggled toward the waiting cab. She opened the back door, and her head disappeared from view as she ducked down to enter the car. Then, suddenly, her head reappeared as she backed out of the cab and turned slowly to look at the spot where the young man had stood, week after week, but not today.

She took a few halting high-heeled steps toward that spot, and removing her sunglasses, looked up the sidewalk toward Lexington, and down the sidewalk to the East River, her face a combination of puzzlement and worry.

The young man could almost read her mind.

I wonder where that kid is? I hope nothing's wrong.

And the young man smiled.

She returned to the cab and got in back. And the taxi drove off, its driver now having recognized her, yakking away, a big grin on his face. . . .

But Marilyn wasn't paying any attention to him. No, she was looking over her shoulder, out the back window of the cab, at the place on the sidewalk where the young man should have been.

The following afternoon the young man stood in a downpour on the sidewalk in front of Marilyn's apartment, his sandy hair matted to his head, his white knit shirt and tan chino pants, soaked and clinging to his body.

It wasn't that he didn't have an umbrella . . . it was just that he knew he'd seem more pathetic without one.

But he was a little surprised—and pleasantly so—when the door to the building opened and Marilyn came out. The taxi wasn't due for another ten minutes.

She was wearing a beige raincoat, cinched at her waist (he'd seen it before), but missing were the white scarf and sunglasses. Her right hand held an umbrella.

The young man's heart thumped wildly as she came toward him, and then her face—that lovely, lovely face—was just inches away.

He held his breath.

"For God's sake!" she snapped. "Don't you have an umbrella?"

He couldn't tell whether she was mad-*mad*, or mad-*concerned*. But it didn't matter; she was talking to him!

She thrust the umbrella—a black one with a wooden curved handle—at him, and he took it, thrilled to be holding something she owned, yet wondering which husband the umbrella had originally belonged to.

"I want you to stop coming here," she said sternly, then added, as if it would deter him, "I'm not worth it."

The rain, hitting her face, made it seem like she was crying.

He opened the umbrella and gallantly covered her.

There was an awkward silence.

Then Marilyn's eyes softened, and her voice became a mere whisper as she asked, "Where were you yesterday?"

He faked a cough. "Sick."

"And you're out here in the rain today?"

The taxi pulled up.

"You should be at home in bed!" she scolded. "Where do you live?"

"Ninety-third and Lexington."

Her eyes lit up. "That's where I'm headed," she said brightly. "You can ride along."

"Thank you."

"What's your name?"

"Johnny."

"Johnny . . ." She repeated the name slowly, her eyes now getting a faraway look.

He knew she was thinking of a long-ago lover. He even knew which one.

"Well, Johnny," she sighed, gesturing to the cab, "get in."

And they climbed in the back seat of the car.

She told the cabbie Lexington and 93rd, but would he mind very much if they stopped for a moment at the little park just ahead?

The cabbie, a handsome, dark Italian man, answered he'd be glad to drive Marilyn Monroe to hell and back if that's what she wanted.

And she laughed, a musical giggle, almost a squeal, as the cab pulled away from the curb.

At the end of 57th, just a half a block away, was a pocket park facing the East River. Not big enough for playground toys, but a nice place to sit and watch the boats sail by, which Marilyn did a lot.

The cab stopped.

Marilyn, sitting on the left side of the young man, leaned across him, putting the fingertips of her hand (and she had such spectacular hands—long fingers with platinum colored nails) on the foggy window, moving those fingers back and forth in the wetness so that she could see out. . . .

She was close to him, so very, very close, that he could feel the electricity coming off her voluptuous body, and see the fine hairs on her flawless face—like fuzz on a ripened peach—and smell the intoxicating scent of her perfume, Chanel No. 5.

He stared at her throat. It was so white, so soft and supple, speckled here and there with cute little moles. . . .

"They're not there," Marilyn said disappointedly. She pulled away from the window and sat back with a sigh.

"You can go on," she told the driver.

They rode in silence, rain pattering on the top of the car, fingers on a drumhead. Then the young man said, "How do you know these boys aren't taking your money *and* selling the pigeons to the meat market?"

Her eyes went wide with surprise, then narrowed with annoyance.

Quickly he tried to recover. "I mean, I'm just asking," he said apologetically. "I'd hate to think you were being fooled. . . ."

"They promised me," she said flatly, "and I believe them."

"Okay," he sighed. "But I think you're too trusting."

They rode in strained silence.

As they approached Lexington and 93rd, the young man, seeing his time with Marilyn was running out, said, "About you going down to the Bowery . . . you may have been able to do that five years ago, but it's too dangerous now . . . and besides, what good does it do?"

Marilyn turned to him, her eyes flashing, clearly irritated. "I don't see that's any of your business!" she said, enunciating each word, lips moving like no other lips could.

The cab came to a stop.

"This is where *you* get out," she said icily.

Boy, he thought, *she* sure was in a rotten mood!

She paid the driver, overtipping him, and climbed out of the cab. The young man followed her onto the street.

He grabbed her arm.

"I know where you're going," he said. "I know who you're seeing."

Shocked, she wrenched out of his grasp and backed up a few steps.

"He's *bad*, Marilyn!" the young man said desperately. "Please, I beg you, don't go to him!"

"Stay *away* from me!" she shouted. And she turned and ran down the street, toward the big brown building where she went every afternoon at four-thirty.

Crestfallen, the young man stared after her. He had worked so hard to meet her, to warn her . . . and in a matter of minutes it had deteriorated to this! What could he do to make her believe him? How could he reach her?

"Norma Jeane!" he called out.

She stopped in her tracks, one hand on the door handle of the apartment building she was about to enter.

"Norma Jeane," he repeated, softer, "please . . . be careful."

She stood frozen for a moment, then, without looking back, opened the door and disappeared inside.

Marilyn was upset, shaking, as she entered the lobby of the building.

As usual, she avoided the elevator and took the stairs; she liked to arrive out of breath, flushed and radiant—it was one of her tricks.

But she was *already* out of breath and flushed—though certainly not radiant—thanks to that Johnny! There was something very weird and very sad about that kid.

Her legs trembled as she climbed the stairs.

Just who did he think he was, anyway? What gave him the right to say just anything to her, of any nature, like it wouldn't hurt her feelings, as if he were talking to her clothing?

And how dare he give her advice on who she should or shouldn't be seeing? Acting like he was a friend. Not that some fans didn't eventually become friends, but she had neither the desire nor the energy to make any new ones. Especially when the fans were becoming more and more aggressive—taking one bite out of her after another. . . .

And Johnny was *wrong* about those two teenage boys in the park, because she could see them from her apartment window, letting the birds go. . . .

It all started one day last month when she sat on a bench in the little park, watching them catching pigeons in a net and putting the poor creatures in cages. When she asked the boys why they were doing that, they said a meat market paid them fifty cents for each one. So she offered to match the meat market's price, if they promised to let the birds go. Now she met the boys every couple of days or so, and paid for the pigeons they caught.

But Johnny was *right* about the Bowery. She shuddered, as she climbed the stairs, thinking about what *could* have happened to her last week, when she went down there in her usual black-wigged disguise, if that policeman hadn't come to her rescue. The policeman said someone called the precinct and told them what she was doing—handing out money to "bums"—otherwise, the cop wouldn't have been there to save her from that knife-wielding nut.

Could the anonymous caller have been her new "friend," Johnny?

Manhattan was changing. She could feel it moving restlessly under her feet, shifting in a frightening way. She had the ability to sense this—the way she could walk into a room full of people and tell right away who was an orphan.

The city was beginning to scare her, because in it she saw so much of herself. It was as if she and Manhattan were becoming one: on the verge of a nervous breakdown and unable to sleep at night. . . .

Marilyn rang the buzzer of apartment 6A.

Almost immediately the door opened and a large man, in a black suit with vest and tie, filled its frame. He was somewhere between fifty and sixty years old, bespectacled, with dark hair and neatly trimmed beard.

To her, he looked like a more handsome Abraham Lincoln. And a little like her ex-husband.

He ushered her in, and she took off her raincoat, revealing a sleeveless blue polka-dot dress. He hung the coat up in a closet, and together they walked down a short, narrow hallway to a living room dominated by Victorian furniture.

The thick, dark drapes were closed, and the only light came from candles flickering on the fireplace mantel. A stereo provided a soothing whisper of classical music.

She turned to face the man.

"Can we please just skip the psychoanalysis today, Doctor Hilgenfeldt," she pleaded, "and get right to the injection?"

He looked down at her, over the top of his glasses. "Bad night, my dear?" he asked, concerned.

"I didn't sleep a wink," she answered wearily. "Sometimes I wonder what the nighttime is for. It almost doesn't exist for me—

it all seems like one long, long horrible day."

She turned away from him, now, hugging herself as if she were cold. "And I'm building up such a tolerance to the Nembutal. I have to keep taking more and more . . . I'm just afraid one of these days. . . ." She didn't finish the sentence.

"Yes, yes," he nodded. "This is not good."

They entered his office, a dimly lit room with a leather psychiatrist's couch, a large mahogany desk littered with papers, and a bookcase crammed with medical journals. In one corner was a glass cabinet where the doctor kept his drugs. On the wall next to the cabinet hung a picture of Sigmund Freud; the stern Freud frowned toward the drugs, as if giving his opinion of them.

Marilyn lay down on the couch.

The doctor crossed the room to the cabinet.

"I'm moving back to Hollywood next week," she told him.

Busy getting the injection ready, the doctor stopped and turned to look at her.

"Are you sure this is wise?" he asked, his voice as sharp as the needle. "We have made such progress together. . . ."

"Yes, well," she said apologetically, "I'm sorry, but I have no choice. I owe those bastards at Fox one last picture."

The doctor approached Marilyn, syringe in one hand, needle up, and loomed over her.

"I was wondering," she said, looking up at him, searching his face, "if you could recommend another psychiatrist for me?"

He thought for a moment. "Yes," he answered slowly, "I know someone I think you'd like in Beverly Hills."

Marilyn partially rose from the couch, supporting herself with both elbows. "It's not a *woman*, is it?" she asked bitterly.

Her previous psychiatrist—a female—had locked her up just six months ago in a New York loony bin. If it hadn't been for Joe—thank God for Joe!—flying up from Florida, threatening to tear the place apart brick by brick, she never would have gotten out.

"No, my dear," the doctor said calmingly, "this is a man." Then he added, gesturing toward the picture of Freud, "As a matter of fact, he told me that he was once psychoanalyzed by Sigmund Freud."

Marilyn, a real Freud fan, liked that, and smiled and lay back on the couch.

"I'm giving you a higher dosage," the doctor explained, rubbing an alcohol-soaked cotton ball on her arm. "I think you could use a little more rest."

She nodded, closing her eyes, sighing in anticipation of the drug.

The needle entered her creamy white flesh.

What Marilyn liked about the Brevital was the quickness of it; one second she was awake and miserable, the next she was plunged into a cool pool of nothingness—void of exhausting and debilitating dreams. It was a deep, peaceful sleep that only a patient on an operating table—or a stiff on a morgue slab—was lucky enough to enjoy.

But as Marilyn slowly came out of the darkness, she thought she was having a dream—or rather, a *nightmare,* for she felt as if she were suffocating; there was a terrible weight on her body. And a hand on her dress caressing one breast. Then a mouth began kissing her neck.

Willing herself to swim up, up, to break the surface of that cool pool of nothingness, she realized, to her horror, that the person on top of her was Doctor Hilgenfeldt!

She squirmed and tried to throw him off, but he was heavy, and she was so weak from the drug.

How sad, Marilyn thought, *if only he'd asked nicely, I would have gladly . . .*

But now the doctor was no different than all the other men who used and betrayed her.

She screamed.

And Johnny was there pulling him off of her, and throwing the doctor across the room with such force that the man crashed into the medicine cabinet, smashing it, glass shards flying, drugs spilling out on to the floor, as he crumpled, bleeding, one hand reaching out to the wall for support, taking the picture of Freud down with him.

Marilyn, on the edge of the couch, shrieked, both hands to her cheeks, terrified of what she sensed the young man might do next, as he approached the doctor, who was sprawled on the floor.

Because Johnny looked different: larger, not thin and frail, skin even whiter, eyes somehow slanted, nearly yellow in color, lips curled back showing sharp white teeth.

The young man moved closer, a wild animal coming in for the kill. . . .

Marilyn jumped off of the couch, thrusting one hand toward him, fingers spread wide. "No, Johnny, no!"

She grabbed the young man's arm. It was ice cold.

"He didn't hurt me," she sobbed, tugging at that arm. "Please, let's just go."

She repeated her plea, instinctively, until the strange look went out of Johnny's eyes, and color returned to his face. Maybe she'd imagined the seeming transformation; maybe the drug had distorted her perceptions. . . .

"Only for you," was all the young man said. "Only for you."

And with a parting look of hatred at the slumped semiconscious doctor, Johnny put an arm around Marilyn and walked her out of the room.

They sat in the dark on one of the benches in the pocket park. The rain had turned to drizzle. Out on the East River, a boat sailed forlornly by in the mist.

"I'm not going to press any charges," Marilyn said in a small voice. "I don't want the publicity."

The young man looked at her. She was no longer the glamorous Marilyn Monroe he had ridden with earlier in the cab. The rain, and her tears, had washed all the makeup away—and along with it, that artificial woman—revealing just a frightened, vulnerable girl, who, to him, was even more intoxicatingly beautiful than the movie star image.

"He'll never bother you again," the young man told her.

Or any other woman. The young man would see to that. He'd return some night soon to the doctor's apartment—gaining entrance in another form—and finish him off. The doctor would not, however, walk the night with the others. He was not worthy. He would be, instead, simply another physician who sadly abused and overindulged and consequently overdosed on his own drugs.

Marilyn, however, *was* worthy—tonight—soon—very soon—he would bestow on her this gift of death, that was life. . . .

STREETS OF BLOOD

Marilyn turned to the young man. "How did you know about Doctor Hilgenfeldt?" she asked.

"You mean, how did I know you were seeing him? Or how did I know he was a fiend?"

"Both."

"I followed you, when you first went to see him . . . then checked him out." The young man gestured with one hand. "There'd been a few complaints by female patients, which nothing ever came of. . . . He either paid them off or had connections."

Marilyn looked startled, which he assumed was in response to the revelation about the doctor's unethical behavior, but then she said indignantly, "You've been spying on me!"

"Well . . . yes," he said.

She stared at him.

"Look," he sighed, gesturing with both hands. "I'll level with you. I wasn't really sick yesterday, I don't live on Lexington and 93rd, and my name isn't Johnny."

He wasn't sure how she'd take that, but he wasn't prepared for what happened next.

She slapped his face.

It stung, and he closed his eyes for a minute to let the rain take the hurt out.

Then he said softly, "Okay, I deserved that. But if someone you'd never met approached you on the street and said your shrink was a rapist, would you have believed it?"

She looked away from him.

"Well? Would you have?"

"No."

"See? I was just trying to protect you."

She looked back at him. "Why?" she asked defiantly.

He was silent for a moment, then said, "Because of something you did."

"And what was that?" she asked, but not so defiantly.

He looked out at the river, its surface choppy and murky. "It was almost a year ago," he said. "You'd been playing here in the park one evening with a girl who had polio . . . remember?"

"Suzie. Mrs. Jensen's granddaughter. She was visiting from Ohio."

"The old woman came to take her home because a storm was coming. . . ."

Marilyn nodded. "A really bad one."

"Yet still you sat, while the wind howled and the rain poured. . . ."

"I was thinking, 'My marriage is over.'"

"Suddenly, lightning struck that tree." The young man pointed to the large oak, nearby; an ugly gash in the bark—a gaping wound—ran down the trunk to its roots.

Marilyn turned to him excitedly. "That was the most incredible thing!" she said in a breathless little girl voice. "I was sitting with one foot on the ground, like this . . ." She crossed one leg over the other, to show him. ". . . and when the lightning came shooting out of the bottom of that tree, and skittered across the grass in front of my foot, it actually blew out a hole in my shoe!"

She smiled, wiggling one foot; then she frowned.

"But then I saw the bat, there on the ground," she continued. "It must have been hanging from a branch, when the lightning struck. At first, I thought it was dead, but when I got closer, I could see its little breast moving in and out. . . ."

"And you picked it up and took it home."

She nodded. "Did you know," she said, turning her body even more toward his, putting one arm on the back of the bench, "that bats can't see very well, but the reason they don't go bumping into everything is because they make this little squeaking noise—humans almost can't hear it—and the noise echoes off even the smallest thing, and bounces back and tells them something's there." She smiled. "You know, sonar, *before* sonar." Her eyes lit up. "Hey! Do you suppose that's where they got the idea from?"

He smiled. How he loved her. How he would love being with her forever. . . .

"And did you know," she went on, "that most bats are really very sweet creatures and can even be kept as pets?" She put one beautifully manicured finger to her lips, bit on it, then gestured outward with the finger. "The only problem is, though, they eat a lot of insects. You have to feed them an awful lot of bugs."

Which she got for him, rooting around in the park after dark, with those same beautifully manicured nails.

Marilyn sat back on the bench. "After I let the bat go, I found out it wasn't the kind of bat usually found in the United States. It was a *vampire bat*—from South America! They suck blood, you know. I read it in a book."

"Really?"

She looked at him. "Now *how* do you suppose it got way up here?"

He shrugged. "It happens."

"I guess it could have bitten me."

He leaned toward her. "Would that have been so bad?" he whispered, lips almost brushing her throat. "If it was a vampire bat, you could live forever."

She was silent for a moment, then said softly, "To live forever . . . what an awful thought."

He looked at her curiously. "Living forever doesn't appeal to you?"

She shook her head. "Maybe on celluloid. But for me, the *real* me, not the r-e-e-l me, the only thing that makes life worth living is knowing that someday it will end."

"But I don't understand. . . ."

"The fact that I'm famous gives me a feeling of happiness," she explained, "but it's only temporary. It's like caviar: Caviar is nice, but to have it every day at every meal, forever. . . ."

She stood up and looked down at him.

"I live for my work and for the few people I can count on, but one day my fame will be over and I will say 'good-bye, fame; I have had you, and I always knew you were fickle.' And it will be a relief to be done." She smiled sadly. "Don't you see?"

Still seated on the bench, he looked up at her. "I guess bats *are* blind . . . in more ways than one."

She held out one hand. "Walk me home?"

They walked slowly down 57th street, arm in arm. The rain let up, and the clouds parted, revealing a brilliant moon, which reflected in the puddles on the sidewalk. But the mirror images in the puddles were only of Marilyn.

She would have made a lousy vampire. Compassion was a bad trait for a child of the night—as he knew all too well.

They stopped in front of her building. She turned to him.

"Good night, Johnny. Sweet dreams. Wish me the same?"

"Good night, Marilyn," he said. "Sweet dreams." Then he added, "But my name really isn't Johnny."

"That's okay," she said with a half-smile, half-smirk. "My name really isn't Marilyn."

He watched her walk to the door of her building where she stopped and looked back.

"Hey!" she said gaily. "Did you hear the one about the vampire who bit Marilyn Monroe?"

"No." He smiled.

"The poor fella died of a drug overdose!" And she laughed, that musical laugh. But it caught in her throat.

She blew him a mocking movie star kiss.

And then she was gone.

Barbara Collins' work has appeared in dozens of mystery and suspense anthologies such as *Cat Crimes, Murder for Father, Vengeance is Hers,* and *Murder Most Delicious.* She lives in Muscatine, Iowa, with her family.

Night is the time to let your hair down and lose yourself in the pulse of the moment. . . .

Night Laughter

BY ELLEN KUSHNER

he thing is, it's just that you start to hate the daytime. All the bad things happen during the day: rush hour, lines at the bank, unwanted phone calls, junk mail, overworked people being rotten to each other. Night is the time for lovers, for reading alone by lamplight, for dancing, for cool breezes. It doesn't matter if your blood is hot or cold; it's the time for you.

"Come on," I say, tugging at his wrist, "come on, let's have fun!" He holds back, reluctant. "Come on, let's dance!"

All over the city the lights are blinking off and on all the time. Night laughter. "Come on into the night!"

"Crazy," he says, "that's what you are."

Rich nighttime laughter bubbles in me. I let a little of it show in the corners of my mouth to scare him. He's scared. He says, "You wanna dance?"

I turned away, shrug nonchalantly. "Nah, not really."

"You wanna . . . go for a ride?"

"Nah." I lick my lips, trite, unmistakable. "Let's go for a walk. In the park."

"No one's in the park at this hour."

"We'll be. Just the two of us, alone. With the long paths all to ourselves."

He rises, follows. The night is like that.

He's wearing a good suit, the best he's got. The night's the time for dressing up, dressing high, dressing fine. Your real night clothes, those are the pressed black and starched white that a gentleman wore, with maybe a touch of gold or a bright ribbon sash setting it off. And a woman was always sleek and bright, lean and clean as a new machine, streamlined as a movie queen. My dress is like that; it clings and swirls so smooth, so long. I stride along beside him in my spiky heels, like a thoroughbred horse with tiny goat's hoofs. Long ago, in Achaea, God wore goat's hoofs and played the pipes all night long. Pipes of reed, like the mouth of a saxophone, blowing long and lonely down the wind between the standing trees.

The trees of Central Park are sparse, hanging over us in ordered rows, dark and tall as the street lamps between them, but under the trees is shadow. The circles of light, when you come to them, are bright enough to read by. Little insects buzz and flutter against their haloes.

Bums are asleep on the benches; poor guys, don't even know if it's night or day. I always avoid them. The only thing they want is money; they never knew how to have a good time, or they've forgotten how. I knew someone once who couldn't bear the light of day, quite right. He'd get out of his white jacket and into a velvet dressing gown, put on dark glasses and retire from the sunrise like poison, while we watched the lights going out in strings across the park, and he'd be making his jokes about what to do with the waking birds and their noise. Owl, I called him, and he called me Mouse. But finally we couldn't take it anymore, he took to sucking red life out of a wine bottle with thick glass, green as sunshades, and he lost the taste for real life altogether; now for all I know he's one of the bums on the benches. They know they're safe: we won't touch them if we don't have to.

This man I'm with, he keeps darting his eyes left and right, as if he's looking for a cop or a junkie or a mugger. I take his arm, press up against him. "You're cold," he says.

I flip my silver scarf twice around my throat. "No, I'm not."

Lights from the passing cars streak our path. I tilt my head back, eyes veiled against the glare of sky, the light bouncing off the clouds.

He says, "I think I see my office. There, over the trees."

I lead him deeper into the darkness, toward the boat pond.

He says, "Y'know it's really dangerous in here," coming all the time along with me.

I kick off my shoes, they go shooting up like silver rockets out over the old lake. My feet press the damp earth, soft and cool, perfect night feeling. Not just earth under them; there's old cigarette stubs moldering into clay and hard edges of glass and a little bird's bone.

Considerately I lean my back against a tree, unwrap my scarf and smile one of my dream smiles.

"Cigarette?" I ask huskily. He fumbles in his pocket, holds the white stick out to me; I just lean there, holding the pose, and finally he places the end between my polished lips. I look up sultry through my eyelashes, and he produces a light.

Oh, the gorgeousness of that tiny flame, orange and strong in the darkness! You don't get orange like that by daylight. I suck it to a perfect scarlet circle on the end of my cigarette, and then I give it back to him, trailing its ghostly wisp of smoke. Automatically he smokes it.

Automatic, still too nervous. He doesn't know how to have a good time! He was a mistake, a good-looking mistake. But then, not every night is perfect. I sigh so quietly only the wind hears me. Frogs are croaking in the pond, competing with crickets for airspace over the distant traffic roar. Another good night, opening itself to me. All you have to do is want it.

"C'mere," I say in my husky dusky cigarette voice. His tie so neatly tied, his shoes so clean they catch the little light on their rounded surface . . . He walks toward me. The expression on his face is steadier, more hopeful: here at last is something he thinks he'll understand. He buries his face in my neck. My white arms glow around his shoulders.

He's all pressed into me now, I'm like sandwich filling between him and the tree. There's a bubble of laughter in my throat; I'm thinking, What would happen if I swiftly stepped aside and all his hard softness were pressing against bark? But I just shift my weight, enjoying the way he picks up on it, shifting his body to conform to me. Now he likes the night. Now his hands have some life in them, running the maze between my dress and my skin. With my fingertips I touch his ears, his jaw, the rim of his collar, while he presses, presses, his breath playing like a brassy syncopated band, his life pulsing hard, trying to burst through his clothes. Owl always said, Let them do that.

He's working my dress up around my waist. His hands are hot. Ah, he's happy. He's fumbling with his buckle. I breathe on him and make him laugh.

"Fun?" I ask.

"Mm-hmmm."

"You're having a good time now."

I tickle the base of his throat and he throws back his head, face joyous in the mercury-colored cloudlight. Night laughter rises in me, too strong anymore to be contained. It wells through my mouth and fixes on his throat, laughter hard and sharp as the edge of a champagne glass, wet and bright as a puddle in neon.

It's fun, it's wild, it's night-blooming orchid and splashing fountains and the fastest car you've ever been in, speeding along the coast . . . It's *life*.

He hardly weighs anything now. I leave him under the tree; the bums can have what he's got left. I take a pair of slippers out of my bag; it's after midnight, but I won't be running home bare-foot, not like some unfortunate fairy-tale girl. Midnight's just the beginning for me.

In the distance a siren goes wailing by. Unsprung trucks speed across town, their trailers pounding as though they're beating the pavement to death. Moonlight and street light blend on the surface of the water.

I pass under the big statue of the hero on the horse, and walk jaunty and silent footed among his many lamplit shadows. Around the bend I see a white gleam, too white and sharp to be anything but a pressed evening jacket. For a moment I think that it is Owl again. But his face, when he turns to look at me, is different.

His jacket is a little rumpled but not dirty, and his black bow tie is perfectly in place. He is smiling. I catch up to him.

"Cigarette?" he says.

"No thanks, I just had one."

He takes one from a gold-plated case, lights it and inhales slowly and contentedly. Where his lips touched it I see a dark stain.

"Hungry?"

"Not a bit."

"Wonderful night," I say.

He nods, still smiling. "Let's go dancing," he says.

We'll have a good time.

Ellen Kushner is the author of the novels *Swordspoint* and *Thomas the Rhymer*, which won the World Fantasy Award, as well as various books for children. She is also a nationally syndicated radio talk show host.

Sometimes desperation makes unlikely allies. . . .

The Land of Lost Content

BY SUZY MCKEE CHARNAS

hese guys found this big old Mercedes-Benz sedan jammed into a clump of bushes in the county park, with the driver collapsed all bloody at the wheel," Wesley said. "They said they'd get the cops or take him to the hospital, but the guy said no. Well, they know Weinberg, and they called him. Figured the Mercedes man had his reasons and Weinberg might be able to make something out of it and tip them for it.

"Weinberg came and got this guy and tucked him up quiet at his U-Store-It near Hartford. He had the car hauled out and cleaned up, and he sold it for a nice price. Whoever this guy is, he took good care of his car."

Wesley paused to unwrap and break in a fresh stick of gum.

"But who is the guy?" he continued. "Nobody knows. I brought down everything they found on him, over in that paper bag. There's no wallet, no I.D., and he wouldn't give any name. Weinberg called this doctor he knows. The doctor took two slugs out of the Mercedes man, one here and one here." He touched his own chest and belly. "And he brought some whole blood to transfuse so the guy wouldn't drop dead while Weinberg was still trying to find out who might have a worthwhile interest in him.

"Now here's the weird part. They hung up the blood bottle and put the needle in, and the next thing you know the Mercedes man pulls the needle out again and busts it off, and he starts sucking the fuckin' tube. Sucking up the blood, you see what I mean? Drinking it. That's when Weinberg decided this one was for you, Roger. He said he didn't know anybody else who'd know what to do with a goddamn vampire."

Roger laughed delightedly, hugging his knees, and looked at Mark to see how he was taking all this.

The whole thing sounded to Mark like a loony hangover from the days when his Uncle Roger had been, in many of his successive crazes, a good market for outlandish items from Weinberg's unadvertised stock. Weinberg the fence was the only crook Mark knew and his first evidence that there were Jewish gangsters as well as all the other kinds.

Trust Roger to know people like that. Whenever things heated up too much between Mark's parents—this time it was over plans for his summer—he came to stay with Roger. He reveled in more freedom here than a fourteen-year-old school kid would be allowed anywhere else.

But what the heck was this? You walk into Roger's place, unannounced as usual, and everything looks like always: sliding door open to let in spring air from the yard, all the living-room plants looking wilted with neglect, Wesley sprawled on the couch chewing gum, and roger perched in the big leather chair bright as a jungle bird in his scarlet silk shirt and tie-dyed jeans. Roger owned a string of fashion outlets and liked to dress off the men's racks.

Then before you even have a chance to put away your pack and your school briefcase they tell you, straightfaced, that Roger has bought a vampire, and Wesley has just delivered him here, to Roger's garden apartment on the West Side of Manhattan. A vampire.

Mark kept his expression carefully noncommittal.

Roger said to Wesley, "Do you believe the guy really drank blood?"

Wesley shrugged. He was an ex-Marine, working these days as

a hospital attendant. In his spare time he did odd jobs for Roger. He said, "I seen guys do real weird things when they're shot."

Roger said, "Did this vampire say anything to them while they kept him at the U-Store-It?"

"Said he couldn't sleep. Who could, with two holes in him and no dope to put him out? Weinberg wanted some for him in case he started yelling, but the doctor said he wouldn't use anything without doing a bunch of tests first because the guy seemed to be built kind of odd, and he didn't know what the drugs would do. Real interested, this doctor was; I bet Weinberg told you that, Roger, to hurry you up—making out like he was worried the doctor would get hold of this vampire first to study him. Uh-huh, thought so. How much did you pay for this character, anyway?"

"Are you still game to help find out if he's worth the money?" Roger countered. Wesley shrugged again. They both got up. "Come on. Mark, you don't want to miss this."

It wasn't a joke. They were serious. All of a sudden the dim hallway to the guest rooms looked scary.

The living room was the center of the apartment. The kitchen and Roger's bedroom and bath were to the right, up front. On the short hallway leading left were closets, a guest bathroom, and two small spare rooms. One of the spare rooms was Mark's when he was staying here. Across the hall from it was a much smaller room, white and bare, with a tiny half-bath adjoining.

Mark opened the door to his own room and glanced in. Bed, dresser, drawing table, bookcase, old map prints hanging on the cool blue walls, window curtains with wild birds on them, Scandinavian striped fur rug on the floor—all reassured him. If use was made of the room in Mark's absence, Roger cleaned up any signs of it afterward. Mark never asked about that. He liked to think of the room as his own.

On the other side of the hallway the wooden door to the smaller bedroom stood open. No wonder the apartment smelled of plaster dust. Wesley had been at work here, installing square pipes flush against the sides of the doorway. Between the pipes hung a tall gate of metal bars. In the back wall there was one barred window glazed with frosted, wire-mesh glass, the kind used to keep out burglars. The bleak little chamber, transformed by the gate into a cage, contained a prisoner.

A man lay on his back on a cot against the wall. He was too tall for the cot; his feet hung over the end, and the blue blanket that covered them came up only to his chest. His face was turned away. He had gray hair. One arm hung down, the hand resting knuckles up on the linoleum.

Mark, inwardly braced to see a dangerous monster, felt relieved and disappointed. But maybe the man's face was awful with fangs and a million wrinkles, like the face on the Dracula book that Mark had browsed through on a Marboro bargain tale last week.

Roger, unlocking the gate, must have sensed Mark's reaction. "Doesn't look like much, does he?" he said uneasily. "I wonder if Weinberg's trying to put one over on me."

They went inside and walked over to the cot. The man turned his head. He had a long, lined face with hollow cheeks and sunken eyes that he seemed hardly able to hold open. His mouth looked dark and crusted, and Mark thought, *blood* and felt a twinge of nausea. Then he realized that it must be like when you have a bad fever, and your mouth gets so dry your lips blacken and crack.

Wesley rolled up the sleeve of his blue work shirt. Sitting down carefully at the head end of the cot, he slipped an arm under the man, raising his head and shoulders against his own side. The man's lips curled back in pain, showing plain teeth, no fangs. Wesley said in a soothing coaxing voice, "Okay now, you want to try a little, ah, drink?"

The man stared at nothing, ignoring the bared arm that Wesley held extended in front of him.

Mark said in a small voice, "Aren't you scared, Wesley?"

"Nope. I got lots of blood. Bled a fuckin' flood when I got hit in Nam, and I'm still here."

"I mean, if he bites you won't you turn into a vampire too?"

Roger said, "Don't be silly, Markie. If that were true, even if there was only one real vampire to start with, pretty soon we'd be all vampires and no people. It can't work like that, it doesn't make any sense. Wesley's safe."

Wesley grunted. "Only no biting on the neck, that's too personal. He can take it from my arm, like at the doctor's."

168   STREETS OF BLOOD

But the supposed vampire seemed disinclined to take it at all. Roger said furiously, "He's a fake! He must be some pal of Weinberg's who got shot up, so he's looking for a place to hide. I am not running a rest home for incompetent stick-up men or whatever this is—I'd rather sling him out in the street for the cops to find."

The man on the cot made no protest, no plea, but he gathered himself for an effort. His long, thin fingers closed on Wesley's forearm. The sound of his labored breathing filled the little room. He bent his face over the pale inner surface of Wesley's elbow.

Wesley jumped slightly and said, "Son-of-a-bitch?"

Roger stood rapt, lips parted, watching. Wesley sat there holding the man propped against him, watching too, cool again. God, Mark thought, Wesley was something: he never let anything really get to him.

At length the vampire drew back, licked his lips once, and subsided loosely onto the cot with a whispered sigh. Wesley got up, flexing his fingers. "Will you look at that," he said. There was a puncture in the vein in his arm, surrounded by a bruiselike discoloration.

Roger, gaping, said dazedly, "Uh, you want a Band-Aid?"

"No, it's only bleeding a little bit. Damnedest thing I ever saw. I better lie down a couple of minutes, though. I feel kind of dopey." Wesley ambled away toward the living room, still looking down at his arm.

They followed him out. "The gate locks automatically when you shut it," Roger said. He looked back at the man on the cot. "Jesus," he breathed, "it's true."

Wesley was lying on the couch. Roger crouched down next to him. "How did it feel?"

"Like giving fuckin' blood, what else?"

"You sure you're okay, Wesley?"

"Sure."

"I want you to get me supplies for him."

Wesley frowned. "I could lose my job, monkeying around with the hospital blood bank."

"I know you'll do what you can, Wesley," Roger said airily; which meant he had something on Wesley and wasn't interested in hearing about his problems. "I can store the stuff in the fridge, right? And if sometimes you can't get blood from the hospital, bring it on the hoof."

"Shit," Wesley said, clenching his fist and crooking his arm up. "I can't do this fountain-of-youth trick too often, you know."

"Then find somebody to fill in for you."

Wesley departed to return the rented van in which he had brought the vampire. Roger hung the key to the barred gate on a nail in a kitchen cabinet. "I'll leave this one here, Mark, but you won't need to use it unless there's an emergency."

Roger, an elfin thirty, had a heart-shaped face, fine-featured and lively. He wore his blue-black hair cut full, and he tossed it off his forehead with a dramatic gesture whenever possible. If angels had dark hair they would look like Roger, Mark thought, though an angel probably wouldn't get himself thrown out of four different schools as Roger had.

Mark knew himself to be plain and gangly and sallow, his appearance not helped at all by owlishly magnifying eyeglasses. He had realized fairly recently that Roger liked to have him around as a foil for Roger's own good looks, but Mark didn't mind much. He knew that he was going to make his own way with his brains. He knew, too, that Roger was a dabbler, never getting the benefit of his own intelligence, too easily bored, too greedy for the taste of the experiences he gobbled up.

Roger left Mark to unpack and in a little while came back down the hall carrying one of the kitchen chairs. This he set down outside the gate, and, sitting astraddle with his arms on the top of the chair back, he faced his new acquisition.

He had a portable tape recorder with him, and he switched it on and began asking questions: What's your name? How did you get to be a vampire? Are you in communication with other vampires? How much blood do you drink at a time? Who shot you?

Every time Mark looked up from arranging his bookshelves, he saw that the vampire was ignoring Roger and following with a sickly gaze what Mark was doing in the bedroom across the hall.

Once Roger had gone off to bed and there would be no interruptions, Mark got the plans for Skytown out of his briefcase and laid them out on the drawing table. This personal project ran currently to forty drawings depicting the systems of his one-man space station. Scientific accuracy was not his main concern, although he kept a tight rein on any impulse to outright fantasy. Mysterious vistas of space and carefully scaled perspectives and details of a space-going home were what fascinated him. Working with his Rapidograph under the fluorescent lamp, he forgot Roger, his parents, and even the vampire.

When he got up to brush his teeth in the bathroom down the hall, he was startled to find the vampire staring at him again. Returning, he shut his door and opened it only when he had turned out his light. Better to leave it open than lie in the dark wondering what was going on out there. Wesley had installed a night light in the cell, enclosed in a little wire cage and connected to a switch in the hallway. The vampire was illuminated, stretched motionless on the cot.

Mark turned on his side and lay listening to the muted sounds of traffic. In his head he tried to picture the details of the energy-gathering vanes of Skytown, sweeping shapes against a background of stars. Maybe there would be a special robot team to tend the vanes; or maybe he would reserve to himself the adventure of working outside in his space suit with stars for company.

Gradually, reluctantly, he became aware of a faint shuffling sound across the hall: movement, effort. Shivering slightly in his underwear, he got up and ghosted barefoot to the doorway.

The vampire stood leaning against the wall, facing in the direction of the little bathroom that adjoined his cell.

Mark sneezed.

The vampire looked at him.

Mark whispered, "I'll go get Roger."

But he didn't. Something in the vampire's posture, a faint shrinking in the already cramped shoulders, made it clear that he sensed what Mark knew—that Roger would make a humiliating joke out of this: a vampire who had to go to the bathroom just like everybody else and couldn't manage it on his own, poor thing. In acute discomfort Mark remembered how that last summer at camp had been. For no reason he'd found himself wetting the bed every night. Every morning he'd had to go rinse out his sheets and hang them outside to dry behind the cabin where everybody could see them. Very funny, ha ha.

He crossed the hallway and whispered through the bars, "I'll help, but if you try anything I'll yell my head off and Roger will come and—and beat you up. He keeps a hunk of lead pipe by his bed for burglars."

He padded toward the kitchen, already regretting the impulse. Cautiously he groped in the dark for the key. Not to wake Roger, not to invite Roger's mean side to come out, was important. He really hated Roger's mean side.

He unlocked the gate and entered the cell warily. He didn't want the vampire to get the idea that he could obtain favors just by looking weak and pathetic. He said, "Roger'd kill me if he knew I came in here. He'd send me home. What do I get for taking that chance?"

The vampire peered at him. Then came his rasping whisper, "You may, if you wish, put yourself on the level of attendant in a public lavatory. I was carrying change in my pockets."

The change would not be in the paper bag that Weinberg had given Wesley. That would do, though the vampire had tried to make it seem grungy to take payment. The main thing was not to let anybody reach you.

Mark moved nearer. The vampire draped a sinewy arm over his shoulders, and for a moment Mark thought in terror that he was being attacked. Then he realized that the man was so weak that he had to lean almost all of his weight on his helper. Maybe walking even these few steps would make him keel over. Maybe he'd die. It would have been better to have wakened Roger. Then if anything went wrong it wouldn't be Mark's fault.

"All right," gasped the vampire, transferring his grip to the corner of the sink.

Mark backed out of the tiny bathroom and stood against the wall. He heard the watery noises, the faint groan of relief, the fumbling for the flush handle. He thought, This is crazy: he pees like me or Roger, but he drinks people's blood.

Helping him back to his cot, Mark noticed that the vampire needed a bath and a change from his stained white shirt and rumpled pants. They had taken away his belt and his shoes.

"Wait," the vampire breathed.

Mark backed toward the gate. "Why?"

"Stay and talk. I must not sleep. If I do, I could easily drop into the sleep of years that takes me from one era to another. Then my life would sink to so low an ebb that my body would be unable to heal itself. I would die. Your Uncle Roger would be annoyed. So talk to me. Tell me things."

God, this was weird. "What things?"

"What do you do all day?"

"I'm in school, ninth grade."

A small silence, and then the vampire murmured, "That seems appropriate. I too am something of a student. Tell me about school."

Mark sat down on the floor across the room from the cot and talked about school. After a while he got a blanket from his closet and folded it under himself, and he brought a glass of water from the kitchen to moisten his throat.

The vampire lay still and listened. If Mark let a little time go by in silence, the vampire said, "Talk to me."

〈〉〈〉

When Mark got back from school the next day Wesley was there. "Your dad called, said he'd like to hear from you."

"Oh, yeah, thanks, Wesley." Both Mark's parents accepted Roger's apartment as Mark's neutral refuge from their endless hassling. Nevertheless they tried to keep tabs on him by phone.

"Okay," Wesley continued, "our friend is bathed and shaved, got clean pajamas on and fresh bandages. He's all set for a couple of days, except for the feeding. Now, you have to go inside his room for that. Even if you shove a glass of blood across the floor at him, he can't lean down and pick it up. He can sit up on his own, though—enough, anyhow, so you won't have to touch him. Carry the glass in and hand it to him, but keep clear of him."

Mark looked into the icebox for something to eat. There were plastic pouches of blood heaped up on the top shelf in back. He blinked fast and looked away. He said, "I thought you weren't scared of him."

"I wasn't scared to give him some of my blood yesterday, but he's healing awful fast. He's scary, all right. He's in a lot better shape than he should be, an old guy with two fuckin' bullet holes in him. Be careful." Wesley, washing his hands at the kitchen sink, laughed suddenly and turned off the water. "Look at me, washing up like after handling a patient at the hospital! I guess I'm just a natural for nursemaiding Roger's vampire, right? Roger sure thinks so."

He shook his head and tucked away the dish towel on which he had dried his hands. "Myself, I liked it better when I was just fixing this place up for Roger." With Wesley's help and at great expense, Roger had reconverted the entire ground floor of the brownstone from two tiny apartments to one comfortable one.

Shutting the icebox door on the sight of the blood, Mark said, "You give it to him cold, right out of the fridge? Isn't that sort of a shock?"

"Well, it's probably not a bad idea to heat the stuff up a little first—but not too hot."

"I know how. I used to heat up the bottle for Aunt Pat's baby that time I stayed with her." At the sink counter Mark spread peanut butter on a slice of bologna.

Wesley unwrapped fresh gum. "You'd make a good hospital attendant, thinking of a thing like that. If you could keep your distance, that is."

Mark felt ashamed that Wesley thought he wasn't cool enough. He considered telling Wesley about helping the vampire at night, how he kept his distance then all right, but decided not to say anything. Wesley might tell Roger.

He politely asked Wesley what was owing for the fresh blood supply, and Wesley went into the living room to wait while Mark got the money box out of the oven. Roger kept it there on the theory that no burglar would look inside a kitchen fixture. He avoided banks because they made reports of interest income for taxes, and he said he preferred to forgo the interest and the taxes both. The money was safe: the apartment was fortified New York City style with barred windows, grilles on the back doors, even strands of wire strung along the top of the wooden fence that enclosed the sour scrap of yard. It was like something out of a prison-camp story. Stalag Manhattan.

With only one prisoner.

As Wesley counted his bills in the hallway by the front door Mark said, "You know, I almost wish Mr. Weinberg's friend the doctor had taken this vampire away for the scientists to study. It feels funny, having somebody locked up here like this."

Wesley, chewing, looked at him. "You figure even a guy who drinks blood has a right not to be grabbed and shut up in Roger's apartment like he was a stray dog, is that it? That's Roger's lookout. You're a minor, you got no say, so don't go feeling all responsible. Stay laid back, all right? Right."

When Mark had the apartment to himself he got the paper bag and spread the vampire's belongings on the coffee table in the golden light of afternoon: a ball-point pen, blue; a felt-tipped pen, red; two pencils with broken points; four small index cards covered with unreadable handwriting; a rubber band, three paper clips, a horn-handled pocketknife; two keys; one case containing a pair of glasses with dark, heavy rims, the left lens cracked; and two quarters.

Mark passed up the knife after a moment's hesitation and pocketed one of the quarters as payment for last night's favor.

Then his mother phoned. She promised she wouldn't bring up the touchy subject of plans for his summer vacation, and he relaxed a bit. She sounded tired and anxious. How was he, she wanted to know, how was Roger? Did Mark need anything from home? Had his father called? Did Mark have enough pocket money? He was not to become any kind of a drain on Roger. How was school? Was he seeing that nice Maddox boy he'd brought home last week? Was he eating right? When was he planning to come home?

Never, he thought. He said, "I don't know, Mom. I just need to be able to settle down without a bunch of fighting going on all the time. I've got a lot of school work to do before the term ends."

"I wish your father wouldn't phone me when he knows you're probably home. He only does it so—"

"I have to go, Mom. I've got some things to do for Roger."

"Just remember, when your father calls you, you remind him that this little interlude that his foul temper provoked isn't coming off my time with you. When you leave Roger's you come back here to finish our six months together, darling. I love you, Markie."

Love you too, Mom; but you could never say that kind of thing out loud to either of them, because they'd put an edge on it and turn it around and cut you with it. She'd say later, He loves me, not you, he said so; and if Dad believed that even a little he'd think you were on her side. Then he'd take it out on you somehow, and you'd spend your time crying like Mom; crying and complaining.

He said, "Bye, Mom," and hung up. Then he sat there chewing his nails and wondering when he'd get used to his parents hating each other. Other kids got used to it with their folks. Maybe being an only child made it worse. On the other hand, Dad and Roger didn't seem to derive any special benefits from being brothers.

One time, one time only, he'd gone weeping to his father, begging him to patch it up, put the family back the way it was supposed to be. His father had said, "Is that what you do when you can't get what you want, cry like a girl? Who taught you that, your mother?"

The worst of it was that Mark had spoken as much out of feeling for his father as out of his own misery, knowing that his dad was wretched, too.

Thinking about them didn't help. He got up energetically and went into his room, where he pulled out the drawings for the botanical gardens of Skytown. He was working on plants picked up from different planets, right now one adapted from a book called *A Voyage To Arcturus* which was mostly boring but had this terrific tree that grabbed up small mammals in its branches and ate them. But what kind of an animal would it eat? A rat? A weasel? Weasels were vicious, you wouldn't mind if it ate a weasel. Inside the cage of branches he drew a weasel, working from the picture in his encyclopedia.

At last, reluctantly, he put the Skytown plans aside; there was work more pressing. He had to do a paper for Carol Kelly for her English class on a poem by A. E. Housman. If he didn't get to it soon, there wouldn't be enough time to work on it. Completing the job was important. Carol Kelly was getting awfully chummy lately. There was nothing like a cash transaction to push a relationship back into shape.

He settled down to the poem, trying to make sense of it.

◊◊◊

The evening after that, instead of packaged blood Wesley brought Bobbie, one of Roger's former girl friends. Going down the hall between Wesley and Roger, she kept laughing and saying, "It's just one of your theater friends fooling around, right, Roger? Come on, I know you—it's a joke, right?"

Then she was sitting there on the cot in the little white room and not laughing at all. She looked down with wide eyes at the vampire's head bent over her arm. Mark could only bear to watch out of the corner of his eye.

"Oh," she said softly. And then, still staring, "Oh, wow. Oh, Wesley, he's drinking my blood."

Wesley said, "I told you. No joke."

"Don't worry, Bobbie," Roger said, patting her shoulder. "You won't grow fangs afterward—Wesley hasn't, anyway."

She put her hand as if to push the vampire's head way, but instead she began to stroke his hair. She murmured, "I read my tarot this morning and I could see there would be fantastic new things, and I should get right behind them and be real positive, you know? But I never thought—oh, this is so far out, this is a real supernova, you know?" Until he finished she sat enthralled, whispering. "Oh, wow," at dreamy intervals.

When the vampire lifted his drowned, peaceful face, she said earnestly to him, "I'm a Scorpio; what's your sign?"

◊◊◊

Roger came home, having at last fired a store manager he disliked. He took Mark out for Chinese dinner and talked angrily about the mess the manager was leaving behind—unrecorded orders, evidence of pilfering and jacking around with receipts . . .

Mark handed him a note from school. "They want a signature on this." Roger was good at signing his brother's name.

The Land of Lost Content   177

"Sent home early for sleeping in class? What gives?"

Mark braced himself and explained.

Roger looked at him in openmouthed astonishment and the beginnings of outrage. "You mean you've been having midnight chats with our friend for the three nights he's been with us? What's he told you?"

"Nothing. He just listens. Last night I told him *Childhood's End, The Mysterious Island,* and some Ray Bradbury stories."

"And he doesn't say anything?"

"Nothing much."

Roger's mouth got thin and pressed together. "Tonight you take the tape recorder in with you, and you ask some questions and get some answers before you tell him a goddamn limerick."

Roger had been trying his questions on the vampire for shorter and shorter periods, perhaps because his efforts were always failures. Mark did no better. When he asked his memorized questions that night, they were ignored.

The vampire merely remarked, "Scheherezade has joined the Inquisition, I see. Fortunately, I can manage now without these diversions."

Roger was going away for the weekend, leaving Mark to look after the vampire. You had to keep Roger from taking advantage. He did it without thinking, really, he just sort of forgot about your interests in the pursuit of his own.

"Look, Roger," Mark said, "I'll take care of the place for you— water the plants and do some cleaning up and all that, like before, to pay you back for letting me stay here. But you're away a lot partying or checking out the shops, and that means I'm stuck with . . . him, in there. That's a big responsibility."

Roger was packing a rainbow sweater in nubbleknit acrylic he had borrowed from the uptown store for the weekend. "You can always go home," he said. Mark waited. Roger sighed. "Okay, okay. Five dollars a week."

"Ten."

"Bloodsucker!" Roger said. "All right, ten." So simple, no tear-ing your guts up over everything like at home. "Listen, there's a special reason why I'm going up to Boston. I want to consult with a few friends about this vampire. There must be ways to get incredibly rich on this thing."

With Roger gone, Mark settled down to the paper for Carol Kelly. Looking for a book of poetry criticism in the living room, he was distracted by a remnant from Roger's fling with superexotica, *The Two-Duck Pleasure Book: Balkan Folk Wisdom,* by R. Unpronounceable. Beguiled into browsing for enlightening dirty bits (" . . . method of contraception is for the woman to get up after intercourse, squat on the floor, and inserting her index finger . . ." Yuucchh), he spent a fascinating half hour.

Then he pulled out a book on Lapland and found the vampire's face looking at him from the back cover of the volume next to it.

No mistake; it was the same man, only in a three-piece suit with a beat-up raincoat slung around his shoulders. He was looking straight into the camera with an assertive stare, as if daring the photographer to soften his imperious features. Mark studied the strong planes of forehead and cheek, the jutting nose, the long, shapely mouth with lips muscular-looking as if slightly compressed on some inner tension. He could look at the photo as long and hard as he liked, while looking at the living man for any length of time made Mark nervous.

The book was called *Notes on a Vanished People,* the diaries of some hitherto unknown German traveler in South America. The translator and editor pictured on the book jacket was Dr. Edward Lewis Weyland, Ph.D., professor of anthropology and director of the Cayslin Center for the Study of Man at Cayslin College upstate. "New light on Pre-Columbian history," proclaimed the blurbs. "A stupendous find for anthropology, with erudite, provocative commentary by Dr. Weyland."

Mark recalled now having seen that forbidding face somewhere else recently—in the news, it had to be. He dug through the piled-up papers and magazines on the end tables until he found what he was looking for in a copy of *Time.* Then slowly, thoughtfully, heart pounding, he went down the hall, the book in his hand.

The vampire dozed, lying on his side with his knees sticking forward off the cot. Wearing pajamas and showing bandages at the opening of the collar, he looked a lot less impressive than in the photograph.

Mark said, "Dr. Weyland?"

The vampire opened his eyes. Mark let him see that he was holding *Notes on a Vanished People*. There was no observable reaction.

"I just thought you might be hungry," Mark said lamely.

"I am."

Mark had bought a stoneware mug so that he wouldn't have to see the blood being drained out of the glass. He stood carefully out of reach while Dr. Weyland drank.

"How'd you get shot?" he asked.

"You know my name. Do a minimum of research: look in the newspapers."

"I did. All anybody says is that you disappeared." Mark added aggressively, "I bet you did something dumb and somebody guessed about you and tried to kill you."

The vampire studied him a moment. "You would win your bet," he said, and he set the mug on the floor and lay back down.

Mark browsed through *Notes on a Vanished People* over a TV dinner that night. A lot of the book was boring, but there were some intriguing sections in the long introduction. Here Dr. Weyland described his suspicions that the German's notebooks existed, the search for them, and the struggle—against doubters whom Dr. Weyland demolished with a keen wit—to establish the authenticity of the documents once they were found. There were also some chilly passages about missionaries of the traveler's day and modern anthropologists. Pretty interesting background reading if you might be the first person to contact the inhabitants of the distant planets on scouting expeditions from Skytown . . .

Late on Sunday a stranger came to the door. "Bobbie tells me there's a vampire here," he said. "Show him to me." He stood not exactly with his foot in the door, but turned so that his thick shoulder seemed about to snap the chain.

"I'm sorry," Mark said quickly, "but my uncle isn't back yet from Boston, and I'm not allowed to let in anybody I don't know."

"My name is Alan Reese, Roger knows me. I'm sure he must have mentioned me to you."

"I have to keep the house rules," Mark said, putting a whine into his tone. He was thinking back to when Roger had been into sorcery. This must be the Reese he'd gotten mixed up with about that. Reese looked ready to bulldoze the door down, and capable of it, too, with a powerful torso and a wrestler's neck as broad as the head it supported.

But he only smiled, shrugged, and retired to sit on the steps into the areaway, reading a paperback book from his pocket. Plainly, he was going to wait for Roger.

Mark did the dishes and watched him from the window over the sink. Reese wore whipcord pants and an embroidered Mexican shirt, and he had brought a large black briefcase. His face was puffy and pale, the skin freckled and smooth like a boy's. There was more to be read in his thick hands than in his face. He tore out the pages of the book as he finished them, and before flipping them into the garbage can by the steps he absently crumpled them in his fist.

Leaving him unwatched didn't seem safe somehow. Mark stayed by the sink and sharpened the knives. Then he rearranged all the silver in the drawer.

Finally Roger came, arguing briefly with the cabby over the tip. Mark saw him turn to face Alan Reese with surprise. One of those big paws fell heavily on Roger's shoulder. The two men stood talking. Roger nodded a lot, hesitantly at first, then with vigor.

When he came in, Reese entered behind him, smiling.

"Mark, I want you to meet Alan Reese, an occultist I've known for a long time," Roger said. "He has some suggestions for managing our guest."

"I am, strictly speaking, a Satanist," Alan Reese introduced himself in a measured, theatrical voice. A light of triumph sparkled in his blue eyes, as if Mark had held a castle against him which he had blown down with a breath. "Does that make you nervous, Mark? It shouldn't. Having a vampire in an unprotected house with you is what should make you nervous. I'm going to help you keep control of him, using my knowledge of his Master."

Oh boy, Mark thought. He got the key from the cupboard door and went into the hall ahead of them to unlock the gate, determined to stick close. He wanted to see the man who had written the introduction to *Notes on a Vanished People* take this guy Reese apart with a sharp remark.

Dr. Weyland turned his head to watch them come in.

Ignoring him, Reese slipped on a black gown over his street clothes and took some objects from his briefcase. He murmured over them, kissed them, held them up to the four directions. One, a metal charm on a chain, he put around Roger's neck, it's twin around Mark's. The rest—a knife, a ring, a silver bowl, a withered brown thing that Mark couldn't identify—he placed carefully in the corners of the stark white cell.

Then he brought out a nest of trays and lit incense in them, and these Roger set down where Reese directed. Reese talked or chanted the whole time, projecting so that he seemed to fill the room. From a little pouch hung round his neck on a thong he rubbed something onto the window frame, the door frame, the drains of the bathroom appliances, and even the electric outlets. He made markings on the floor with a lump of red chalk.

Mark was given a censer and a candle to hold. He felt a fool and wished now he'd let them do all this weird stuff without him.

To his surprise and disappointment, Dr. Weyland made no comment. Mark had his first chance to observe the vampire without those chilly eyes staring back at him, and he felt an unpleasant shock. He thought he saw fear.

"All right, he's well bound. That's a start," Reese said finally, standing in the middle of the little room with his feet braced apart as if against a typhoon. He looked about him with a pleased expression.

"The funny thing is," Roger said, "he doesn't seem to have fangs, but he does—well, bite."

"So Bobbie said." Reese pulled back the sleeves of his gown from muscular forearms. "Hold him quiet—he can't hurt you, don't worry—and let me see."

Roger made a nervous grab for the vampire's wrists. Dr.

Weyland did not resist, not even when Reese hooked him under the armpits and dragged at him so that his head hung off the end of the cot. There was nothing silly in the scene anymore. Dr. Weyland's fear touched Mark like a cold breath.

Reese bent and clamped the vampire's head hard against his thick thigh with one arm. Seizing him by the jaw, he wrenched his mouth open.

A sound of protest escaped Mark.

Reese looked up. "This being is inhabited by a devil's strength. He only pretends weakness and pain to fool us. I may seem rough with him, but I know what I'm doing. I put all the force I have into encounters like this because that's the only way to keep control. He's all right; it would take a tank to hurt one of these."

Roger said, "You've come across vampires before?"

"I come across all kinds of abstruse things," Reese replied. "It's true there are no fangs, but here—see that? A sort of sting on the underside of the tongue. It probably erects itself at the prospect of dinner, makes the puncture through which he sucks blood, and then folds back out of sight again."

"Sexy." Roger said with new interest. "Maybe that's why he doesn't talk?"

"It shouldn't interfere," Reese said. "Let's have a look at his eyes." He shut the mouth and moved his hand to thumb back one of the vampire's eyelids.

Mark told himself they weren't really hurting Dr. Weyland. They were like zoologists or veterinarians immobilizing a dangerous animal so they could examine it. But Reese gripped and twisted the passive body of the vampire brutally, like a guy wrestling an alligator in a movie about the Everglades. Mark tried not to breathe the sharp odor from the censer and waited miserably for the examination to be over.

At last they finished, leaving the disheveled vampire—who had still spoken no word—stretched out on the cot, one arm over his eyes. Roger looked high, as if exhilarated by the defeat of someone who had scared him. Reese, smiling, packed up his gear and shed his gown. He came and sat in the verdant living room like any casual guest.

"Have you any plans for him?" he asked intently.

Roger scowled. "He's not very cooperative. I've been trying to get him to tell me things. Can you imagine what a best-seller it would be, a real vampire's story from his own lips? But he won't answer questions."

Reese stood up. "I was thinking of something more ambitious—some effort to cut through appearances to his essential self, the black and powerful heart of an existence beyond the laws of the life we know. Some way of taking over and harnessing this arcane and formidable nature to our own uses."

The atmosphere of the room seemed changed—darkened. Reese's bombast should have reduced him to an absurdity, but it didn't. He came across as not silly but scary. His melodramatic style was backed up by his beefy, aggressive muscularity and by the watchful stare of his small, cold eyes as he stood over the two of them.

"You have a marvelous find here," Reese said, "rich in possibilities. My High Priestess is skilled in hypnotism. With that and whatever rites and pressures seem appropriate, we'll have this creature begging to give up his secrets. Believe me, Roger, we'll wring him like a wet rag, he'll be our bridge to realms you can't even guess at yet. On May Eve, the night of April thirtieth, I and my group customarily hold a Great Sabbat, as you may remember. I want to hold it here and include your guest in the proceedings. Good, that's settled, then.

"Meanwhile, try to emphasize fresh supplies, like Bobble. I know some who'll volunteer for the experience, if I give the word. I agree there's no danger of the occasional donor becoming a vampire, especially now that I've mobilized my protective forces. Some trustworthy students of my arts would even pay to watch a vampire feed. The proceeds . . ."

The whole thing was building a crazy momentum. When Reese paused for breath, Mark cleared his throat and said, "I found out something about him today. His name is Edward Lewis Weyland and he's a famous anthropologist." Well, he certainly had their attention. He explained about the vampire's identity. "It's a kind of kidnapping already, don't you see? We could all get into a lot of trouble. He's not just some crazy tramp, he's an important professor."

Roger began to say something resentful, but Reese cut him off. "Be patient, Roger. Mark's young, he needs careful instruction." Reese's moon face looked placid, but he cracked the knuckles of his hands with muffled crunching noise. "He thinks what we have here is merely an ordinary man, albeit one of prominence, with a freakish taste for human blood—but basically a human being like ourselves to whom the laws of human societies apply.

"However; I am here to tell both of you—and qualified to tell both of you—that what you have behind bars in there is not simply a perverted human being. I felt the aura around it, and I arced my spells to subdue its real, its supernatural nature and render it docile."

"He didn't fight you because he's hurt," Mark blurted.

"Oh, I don't deny that the vampire has a fleshly carapace and that that shell has been damaged. But if you could see beyond the disguise, Mark, as I can, you'd know right away that this isn't a person at all. It's a bloodsucking devil, and it's subject to no laws but those of the Great One whose rites I study."

Argument was hopeless. Mark retreated to his own room, busying himself at his desk until the two men, still talking, left. Then he stepped into the hall, intending to go fix himself some dinner. He hadn't meant to look across into the cell, but he couldn't help himself.

The vampire sat elbows on knees, hands clasped at his mouth as if he'd been gnawing at his knuckles. His wide gaze seemed to leap to meet Mark.

In a low, tense voice Dr. Weyland said, "Let me out."

Face doggedly turned away, Mark shook his head, no.

"Why not?"

"Look," Mark said, "You don't understand. I'm just a kind of a guest here. Roger never messes around with my stuff and I don't mess around with his."

"Alan Reese will kill me."

"Roger wouldn't let anyone get hurt!" Mark was shocked. Did Dr. Weyland really misunderstand Roger so badly?

"Reese will bring a dozen or so of his followers here on May Eve. I think Roger, facing them, will be something less than brave."

"But this is his home. He wouldn't let them."

"He'll have no choice. Don't you recognize the kind of man Reese is?"

"He's just a weird friend of Roger's," Mark said uncomfortably. "Nothing terrible will happen."

"Nothing terrible?" Dr. Weyland seemed to look into space and to speak more to himself than to Mark. "I felt his hands on me, I saw his eyes. He's not the first man to lust after powers he imagines me to have."

Mark's scalp prickled. He said rapidly, "Look, you're forgetting—this is all Roger's idea, he's running things. He's taken care of you so far, hasn't he? I mean, Roger can be sort of inconsiderate and wild and Reese is definitely creepy, but they're not—they're not in a class with the person who shot you, for instance."

Dr. Weyland frowned. "Of course not. That was a matter of poor judgment on my part and self-defense on hers—an incident of the hunt, no more."

"It was a woman?" Mark was fascinated despite himself.

"Yes, a woman of more discernment and competence than I had thought. She acted as any intelligent prey acts. She wanted to escape me, and she succeeded.

"But this man Reese wants . . . to use me, to tear out my life and devour it, as men once ate the hearts of slain enemies in order to acquire their strength and skill in battle."

Overriding the vampire's final words, Mark said loudly, "That doesn't make sense. I'm not going to stand here and listen to a lot of crap that doesn't make sense." His face felt hot. He hurried up the hall to the kitchen.

His appetite was gone. He took off Reese's amulet and threw it into the garbage.

Later when he looked for *Notes on a Vanished People,* which he had used to prove Dr. Weyland's identity, he couldn't find it. Reese must have taken the book.

All the next morning Mark dreaded a resumption of that upsetting conversation with Dr. Weyland. He came home by a roundabout route from school and watched TV a while in the living room, but he couldn't put off the vampire's feeding indefinitely.

He delivered the mug full of blood with a tool that Wesley had contrived for the purpose the last time he was here by twisting a coat hanger around the end of a detachable mop handle. Reaching between the bars with this, Mark carefully pushed the mug across the floor toward the cot.

"Lunch," he announced in a tone he hoped would discourage conversation.

Moving very slowly, Dr. Weyland leaned down and took up the mug, emptied it, and carefully set it down on the floor again. He said, "Might you bring me something to read?"

Caught off balance, Mark blinked foolishly at him. "To read?"

"Yes. To read. Books, magazines, newspapers. Printed matter. Though of course I can't pay you for the service, since you've already 'earned' everything that I owned."

Those three nights of storytelling had transferred the second quarter and the pocketknife into Mark's possession. How else could he have made it unmistakably clear to Dr. Weyland that he operated on a strictly business basis?

"Now Roger pays me to look after you," he mumbled. He went to the living room and collected whatever was on the coffee table. The horn-rimmed glasses he placed on top of the pile before pushing it all into the cell.

Dr. Weyland picked up the glasses and put them on.

God, Mark thought suddenly, he's just an old guy with glasses, like Mr. Merman at school. "The lens was cracked when they came," he said.

He watched while the vampire, sitting with the blue blanket pulled around his shoulders, sorted through the untidy heap. "*Harpers. The Village Voice. Women's Wear Daily. The New Yorker. Prevention.* Does your uncle subscribe to everything published, regardless of the contents?"

"He doesn't have time to read most of it anyway," Mark said. "I have to do some homework now." It was long past time to do it, in fact.

He couldn't find his dictionary. Hesitantly he called, "How do you spell 'kinesthetic'?"

"Look it up," replied the vampire.

"Can't find my dictionary."

Dr. Weyland spelled out the word. Then he said, "'Kinesthetic'? What are you writing?"

"An assigned paper on some mushy poem," Mark said.

"May I see?" Dr. Weyland put aside the magazines.

With the mop handle Mark pushed in the book of poems. Dr. Weyland opened to the place marked with the flattened drinking straw. "'The Land of Lost Content,'" he murmured. "'Into my heart an air that kills from yon far country blows . . .'" Mark's outline for the paper was tucked inside the front cover. Dr. Weyland read this swiftly and looked up with a keen glance that made Mark uncomfortable.

"Interesting," the vampire said. "The second paragraph under the heading 'Kinesthetic Sense,' where you note, 'Poet writes about highways he went on, remembers moving muscles while going on highways . . .' That must be in response to a question from the teacher?"

"Yes, about what senses the poet uses in the poem."

"But when Housman writes of 'an air that kills,' I doubt he means he's smelling the air," Dr. Weyland said. "The deadly breeze seems to me to blow directly into Housman's heart, bypassing his senses altogether."

Mark fidgeted unhappily at the bars. He should have known better; there was nothing worse for school work than a grownup helping you with it. He said, "Well, without smell there's just sight and the kinesthetic sense. That's only two senses. I need more than that. The teacher wants at least two whole pages, double-spaced."

"I see," said Dr. Weyland dryly. "Nevertheless, while the point about muscular memory does have some minor value, you would do better without a paragraph on the senses altogether. Then the outline would flow much more easily from the first paragraph about the fairy-tale atmosphere of the poem, through the second on its childlike simplicity, to your conclusion concerning its meaning."

Mark remained mutinously silent.

Dr. Weyland flicked the edge of the page with his forefinger. "I see that you mean to conclude, 'I like the poem a lot.' But you called it a 'mushy poem' when you first mentioned it to me."

"I hate this assignment!" Mark burst out. "The poem doesn't even make sense. What's 'an air that kills,' anyway, poison gas? It's just dumb, a lot of babyish moaning around for no reason."

"Good, you do realize that you've avoided the main question," said Dr. Weyland; "what, precisely, 'an air that kills' might be and what it destroys in the poet. As for 'moaning around,' have you never had to leave behind an existence that suited you better than the one you moved on to?"

For no reason Mark felt a pressure of tears in his eyes. He turned away, angry and embarrassed.

"I have," Dr. Weyland added meditatively. "Often."

"That doesn't mean a person should go around whining all the time," Mark muttered. "Can I have that stuff back now? I have to go and type the paper up."

"You're not ready to," Dr. Weyland said. "Not until you at least consider the central question."

"I'm only in the ninth grade, you know. I'm not supposed to know everything."

"What is the air that kills?" asked Dr. Weyland inexorably. "Why does he let it into his heart?"

"I guess it's memory," Mark said sullenly, "and he lets it into his heart because he's a jerk. He's doing it to himself—making himself miserable by thinking about his happy childhood. Only a stupid jerk walks around thinking about his childhood. Most people's childhood's are actually pretty lousy anyhow."

"It isn't necessarily childhood that he means," Dr. Weyland said, "although you make a good case for that in your outline. I think the reference is more general—to the perils of looking backward on the times and the seductiveness of memory. Well." He fell for a moment into an abstracted silence. Then he added briskly, "I think, by the way, that if you really dislike the poem you should say so—and why—in your paper."

"I can't," Mark said. "This is for Carol Kelly, and she likes the crummy poem. She would."

"Who is Carol Kelly?"

Suddenly recalling that Dr. Weyland was a teacher himself,

Mark tried to brazen it out. "This is her assignment. I'm doing it for her."

"How kind of you," murmured Dr. Weyland, returning the book.

"She's paying me ten dollars. It's a business."

"My God," Dr. Weyland said, "a thesis mill! How old are you—fifteen?"

"Fifteen in June."

"Fifteen and rich, no doubt. Certainly enterprising."

"I'm not greedy," Mark said stoutly. "It's important to have an income of your own, that's all. Then you don't have to depend on other people. You should know—I bet you're rich yourself. I bet you've salted away all kinds of treasure from other times."

"Unfortunately, great wealth, like renown or exalted rank, attracts too much attention, most of it hostile," Dr. Weyland said. "I learned a long time ago to travel unencumbered and to depend on my wits. Now I'm not so sure. What a pity I have no diamonds about me, no purses of pirate gold. If I had, you and I could make a transaction of the kind you like, all business: my freedom for your enrichment."

"Money wouldn't change anything," Mark said. "I told you, I can't let you go."

Dr. Weyland drew back. He said harshly, "Of course. It was a mistake to ask you for help in the first place. I won't ask again."

For some time Mark sat at his drawing table, biting his pencil and working over the paper again and again. He couldn't read the poem now without thinking wretchedly of his parents.

God, Dr. Weyland would drive you crazy if you had him for a class. He was one of those never-satisfied types who beat out your brains under the mistaken impression that they're teaching you to think.

A kid from math class wanted to go to a movie after school. Mark begged off, saying he had chores to do. Actually, Wesley was coming today and would handle the feeding of Dr. Weyland. Mark used the time to go to a film and lecture about coyotes at the Museum of Natural History. He preferred seeing animals stuffed in the museum exhibits or on film to seeing them in a zoo. The zoo depressed him horribly.

The documentary film drove him out before the program was over. It first lovingly detailed the cleverness of the coyote, his beauty and his place as part of nature, and then settled into a barrage of hideous images: poisoned coyotes, trapped coyotes, burned coyotes, and coyotes mangled by ranchers' dogs. Mark didn't think he would ever be cool enough to stand that kind of stuff.

Wesley was still at Roger's when Mark got in. "I cleaned up our friend special for tonight," he said. "Roger called and said don't feed him. There's company coming."

Ugh, maybe that meant Alan Reese. Walking Wesley out, Mark told him about Reese's visit.

Wesley kicked at the base of the brownstone steps. "Shit," he said. "I thought Bobbie had quit running around with all those devil nuts. Didn't Roger and her do a trip with them once before?"

"He's getting into it again," Mark said.

Wesley shook his head. "Tell you one thing: Alan Reese is weird. He likes stagy stuff with all kinds of blood and crazy stunts. Him and his friends did something one time that left a whole apartment in Queens splashed with rooster blood. The chick who played altar for him and his friends that night said if he ever talked to her again she'd sue."

"Wesley, I'm sort of worried."

"Yeah, well, it'll be okay. Roger won't go as far as Reese will want to. It'll be okay." Wesley stuck a wad of gum under the curve of the stoop and went away whistling.

Dr. Weyland sat reading, dressed in dark trousers, socks and slippers. The cuffs of his white shirt were folded back the way Mark did his own cuffs when his arms got too long for the sleeves.

"Roger said not to give you anything to eat."

"Temporarily, I trust," Dr. Weyland said. "I need food badly when I'm healing. My hunger hurts."

Mark met his stare for as long as he could. "I can bring some water," he said. "But Roger said no food."

Just as he was about to settle into his work. Bobbie turned up at the front door with a short, stocky woman in a caftan who carried an embroidered knapsack by one broad strap. Bobbie smiled.

"Hi, Mark. This is my friend Julie. We called Roger and he said we could come see the vampire."

Mark hesitated. Julie had dark, haughty eyebrows and a determined-looking mouth. Bobbie wouldn't dare bring someone over without really getting Roger's permission, and anyway Roger was due back early. Mark let them in but asked them to wait to go back and see the vampire until Roger came.

Julie sat down in the big armchair by the avocado plant and surveyed the living room. "Roger must have good vibrations to be able to keep so many growing beings happy in his home."

Bobbie, curled on a hassock, smiled at Mark. "Mark takes care of it, mostly. When he's not around, it all goes to hell."

Turning to Mark, Julie said, "You wouldn't happen to have anything of the vampire's handy for me to look at while we're waiting—a hairbrush, used clothing? I can tell a lot about a person from those kind of things."

Another nut. Mark went to the cell. "Could you pass me your hairbrush, please?"

Dr. Weyland put down his book and brought the hairbrush from the tiny bathroom. The bare cell seemed more cramped than ever when his tall, stoop-shouldered form moved about in it.

Julie took the brush and drew a gray hair from among the bristles. "A man," she said firmly, "not a demon." She held the brush against her chest. "Tell me about the man, Bobbie."

Mark watered plants, listening as they talked. When he could no longer stand Bobbie's shapeless torrent of "wows" and "terrifics" and other general terms of awe that kept her from ever concluding a thought or a sentence, he relented and took them both down the hall for a quick glimpse of Dr. Weyland. The vampire looked up briefly from his reading but said nothing. The two women exchanged what Mark supposed was a significant glance and returned without comment to the living room. There they sat silent for so long that Mark got bored and went to his own room.

He was winding up a math assignment when he surfaced to an awareness of music—no, chanting. And a funny smell.

At the gate Dr. Weyland said wearily. "You might go and make certain they aren't burning the building down."

The living-room rugs were rolled up and the furniture had been moved back against the walls. Gray smoke curled from incense sticks thrust into the soft earth of the plant pots. All of the taller plants had been grouped in the center of the floor. The two women were prancing, stark naked, in a circle around this huddle of vegetation.

Under the plants lay a little heap of objects. Julie put down a peacock feather and took up a knife. Bearing it aloft in both hands she marched, with Bobbie behind her, first toward one corner of the room, then another.

Mark stood staring at their bodies. Bobbie was slim and tan all over, and Julie was white and chunky. She jiggled. He felt his face get all hot, and he was torn between intense embarrassment and panic. If Roger saw this . . .

"Casting out!" Julie cried. "Banishing the evil, blood-eating spirit by the power of Her dark phase." She held the stubby knife, a sort of mustard spreader with the handle wrapped in black electrician's tape, with the haft pointed at each corner of the room in succession. "By Her life-making loins." She dug a fistful of earth from under the avocado tree and sprinkled it on the floor. "By the power of Her shining face." A white ribbon fluttered through the smoky air.

Bobbie put down the platter she was holding and, hurrying over, whispered to Mark, "We'll be done pretty soon. I mean, I realize this is an imposition sort of, but I felt so bad about telling Alan about—him. Alan might not do anything, but you never can tell once he gets really involved and starts hearing spirits telling him to do things and all that. Alan is very powerful under certain planetary configurations.

"Julie has this different approach, you know, a warmer sort of attitude and these really glowing, positive vibrations."

Julie swayed alone in the middle of the room with her eyes shut, stroking the leaves of the plants.

"Make her stop," Mark pleaded, "and let's start cleaning up before Roger—"

Roger walked in.

The Land of Lost Content 193

Julie raised her arms. "By the power of my aiding spirits, I declare the caged man free, I cast the curse from him. I drive forth—"

"Jee-sus!" Roger burst into the living room, kicking at the magical objects and slapping down the incense sticks.

Julie spun around once in the middle of the floor. "So close our songs to the Mother!"

"Get your goddamn clothes on." Roger commanded, redder from his exertions than she was from hers. "There's a kid here, you slut!"

"We are skyclad," Julie retorted fiercely. She pulled on her caftan and started for the door, gathering her belongings and stuffing them into her knapsack. Bobbie, dressed and carrying her sandals, came after.

"Wait a minute," Roger said, grabbing at Bobbie's arm. "Damn it, Bobbie, what about all this mess you two have made here? I've got people coming over in a little while, serious Satanists."

Julie stood in the hallway holding her knapsack in both arms and glaring at him. "I'm sorry," she said icily, "but we're lousy at mundane tasks when our rites have been interrupted. All I can say is, if our work didn't help that poor man, it's your fault. Any fool but Alan could see in a minute that that person isn't a devil, not with a face like that, such a stern, beautiful mouth, so much gravity and wisdom in the eyes—and if it's Alan's friends you're expecting, they're just a bunch of—"

"Stuff it." Roger yanked open the front door and shoved her outside.

Bobbie gave a weak version of her sunny grin, murmured, "Sorry, Roger," and followed.

Roger slammed the door and snapped the locks. "Come on," he said angrily to Mark, "help me straighten up in here. I'm trying to work this into a real experience for Alan's people, and those two come and turn everything into a cheap, goofy side show! I thought Bobbie was bringing over some kind of exotic medium who'd give us some class, and this is what I get."

The visitors, a chic and chatty group, came soon afterward. To Mark's relief, Alan Reese was not among them. Roger, his good humor regained, told with relish the tale of how the vampire had been found and brought here. When he had them all fidgeting with anticipation, he led them down the hall to the cell.

Mark went, too. His mouth was dry. He didn't like the atmosphere these people brought with them. Roger didn't even seem to know them, he thought; they were like strangers you happen to be standing in line with for a movie.

A plump, nervous-looking woman went into the cell with Roger. When Dr. Weyland looked at her, she began to hang back.

"Come on, Anne," said the people at the gate. "You said you would. You told Alan you'd do it."

She smiled a scared smile and let Roger position her by the cot. He pressed her shoulder. She perched stiffly beside Dr. Weyland. Roger said softly to him, "Drink, vampire. The people are waiting to see you."

Dr. Weyland's glance moved from face to face. He looked very white. Sweat gleamed on his forehead. Mark felt sick, but he couldn't turn away.

"Come on inside where you can see," Roger told the spectators.

One of the women said, "It's good from here; we don't want to be piled up in each other's way. God, what a tiny room." She lit a cigarette.

"Start drinking," Roger said. "This is all you're going to get."

Dr. Weyland sat very still, looking at the floor now. Mark thought, Don't do it, don't do it in front of them.

"His hair's gray," a man said. "I thought they lived forever and never got old."

The man next to him answered, "Maybe when he drinks he gets younger right in front of us, like in the vampire movies."

"Or maybe something else happens to him that they're not allowed to show you in the movies." They all snickered.

Dr. Weyland reached over and took hold of Anne's arm.

"Ugh," she gasped as he began. "Jesus!" She sat straining as far from him on the cot as she could get, her face twisted with loathing and fright. The spectators pressed closer to the bars and whispered excitedly.

Mark couldn't see past them anymore. He was glad.

Afterward Anne came out crying and was led into the guest

bathroom. The others crowded down the hall to the living room, talking and exclaiming. Passing the bathroom, one woman tipped her head in the direction of the sobbing sounds from inside. "If she'd just relaxed and rolled with it, I bet she could have gotten off on that."

The one with the cigarette glanced back at Mark and shushed her, and they giggled together.

Dr. Weyland sat quietly on the cot, his big hands loose and heavy-looking in his lap, his craggy face still. His glance touched Mark remotely like the stare of a resting cat that watches any movement, out of habit: without intention, without desire, without recognition.

Mark went into his bedroom and closed the door.

A letter came for Mark in Roger's mail. It was from Mark's father, and there was money in it. He put the money into a drawer until he could take it down to the bank and add it to the savings account he kept especially for parental bribes. He had vowed never to make a withdrawal from that account. Someday he was going to give the money back to them and let them figure out what to do with it.

He went back to the cell.

"I got your glasses fixed," he said. This had been his own idea; he knew how a bad lens could give you headaches.

Dr. Weyland came to the gate. "That was very fast. I can't repay your expense."

"I told you, Roger's taking care of stuff like that." In fact, Roger would die before he would spend money on something like fixing the vampire's glasses. Mark had paid out of his own earnings. Later he would figure out how to get the money back from Roger. The amount was small. The glasses had turned out to be not prescription but simple magnifiers, the kind you could buy through a catalog to make reading easier on your eyes.

Mark settled down at his drawing table.

Dr. Weyland, still at the gate, said, "What is it that you do at that table for so many hours at a time?"

After that hatchet job on the paper for Carol Kelly, Mark was wary. But by the same token he knew he would get a straightforward response from Dr. Weyland. Nervously he handed over a Skytown drawing. Dr. Weyland spread the paper flat against the wall with a delicate touch of his long, clean hands. Now that he was stronger, he kept himself immaculate. Mark was uncomfortably aware of his own bitten nails and perpetually grubby knuckles.

"'Gravity plates,'" read Dr. Weyland. "Is this part of a space ship?"

"Space station, with two auxiliary vehicles and a squad of maintenance robots. It's set up for a single human operator."

"And this is a design for the library—how pleasantly old-fashioned, considering that so much information is already kept on microfilm and in computer memories rather than in print."

"Well, a library would be a kind of extra," Mark said.

"But well worth having," replied the vampire. "Electronic storage and retrieval systems are efficient, but efficiency is only one value among many. Books make fine tools and good friends—informative, discreet, controllable. Are there more of these plans?"

He looked at the Skytown drawings for a long time, and in the end he handed them back saying, with no trace of condescension, "I can see that your best thinking has gone into these. They're well worked out and handsomely drawn. You have a gift for visualization and an admirably steady hand."

Mark blushed with pleasure. Suddenly it was worth it to have endured the Great Housman Paper Massacre.

"This has been a much-needed relief from my current reading," Dr. Weyland added, indicating a stack of Roger's new books on the floor by the gate. They were all about magic and witchcraft and worshipping the Devil. On the top volume of this batch was stamped the word KABALLAH in gold. Dr. Weyland nudged the pile disdainfully with the toe of his slipper, exposing a book called *The Grimoire of Gudrun* and another, *Athames and Athanors*. The gaudy colors of the jackets made the white-walled cell seem bleaker than ever.

Mark said, "What's a 'grimoire'?"

Dr. Weyland corrected his pronunciation. "A grimoire is a witch's personal book of spells and procedures. 'Athame' or 'althame' is supposed to be the ancient name for the short-blad-ed, black-handled ceremonial knife a witch uses in her rituals, according to these texts. However, I seem to recall that this word was actually invented by an imaginative writer rather late in the nineteenth century."

"And 'athanor'?"

"I hope you've found your dictionary, because for the moment the meaning escapes me. At any rate, I'm done with these—I've read as much as I can bear to, and I can't quite bring myself to descend to the level of Gudrun's recipe book. You understand, I am obliged to you for providing these, but frankly they're scarce-ly readable—self-importantly conspirational, mind-numbing in their repetitions, abominably inaccurate, and foully edited."

"Roger mostly skims what he reads."

"Wise of him," Dr. Weyland said. "With books like these the choice is clearly sink or skim."

Mark clutched at his stomach and moaned appreciatively. He lifted the books out between the bars. "It's all made up, then? Magic and devils and all that stuff?"

"Primarily. I do think that there are gifted individuals who can accomplish supernormal feats, usually on an erratic and unpre-dictable basis and therefore to no great effect on the world at large."

"Can you? I mean, can you work magic?"

"I can behave in ways which while natural in me would be highly unnatural in you," said Dr. Weyland. "But magic—no."

Mark said impulsively, "You're very old, aren't you?"

"Yes."

Dr. Weyland would be all right, Mark decided, now that he had his strength back. Even up [Lawrence: couldn't read text]"

That night when Dr. Weyland reached for the young man Reese had sent, Roger commanded, "Not the arm. The neck. The people paid to see the real thing. Go for the neck."

For a moment the vampire looked out at them with an unfath-omable gaze. Then he took the young man by the shoulders and leaned in and up under his jawline. The watchers gasped. The victim caught ineffectually at Dr. Weyland's wrists and whim-pered.

Mark looked away. At the end the people applauded, and he hated them. They gathered in the living room and chattered: the vampire really was an attractive brute, even handsome in a harsh and distant way—that cold reserve, that eagle-stare. Didn't you get shivers watching him press against a person the way he did and suck on their neck like that? That was worth the money. Was it like sex for the vampire? Shh, where is Mark? Washing dishes, he can't hear us over the running water.

Somebody remembered reading that vampire bats sometimes drink so greedily from their prey that they get too heavy to fly and have to walk home. Ho, ha, that was a good one—waddling home at night along the roadside, burping all the way.

Mark finished up in the kitchen and went to bed. He put his pillow over his head to muffle the sound of their laughter.

May Eve was a week and a half away.

Dad called the next day. "Did you get what I sent you?" He often spoke as though he thought the phone line was tapped.

"Yes, Dad. It's in the bank."

"Mark, I've told you a hundred times, when I give you money it's for you to use. I could keep it in the bank myself. Look, I know your mother's given you some spiel about saving up in case I stop sending child support, but that's crap. You know you can depend on me."

"I know, Dad. When are we going to have dinner together?"

His father began to talk about a medical convention he was attending this week. Eminent heart surgeons one, two, and three; Dad was dropping names like crazy again. Mark held the phone between his cheek and shoulder, saying "Uh-huh" in the pauses. He was sitting on the sofa with his toes tucked cozily between the cushions, working on the game-room section of the Skytown plans.

Hearing his father's voice was nice, a reminder that the whole world didn't revolve around the cell down the hall. Maybe if Dad stayed on the phone long enough the time would go by, and then Mark would feed the vampire, and Roger would call too late to announce a live feeding. Then there would be a quiet evening, no sightseers leering into Dr. Weyland's cell.

". . . basketball game on Wednesday, all right? It means I'll have to pass up going to a talk on blah blah blah . . . Dr. Candleman, the transplant man . . . blah . . . We can have a bite first at that place right in the Garden, the steak house. You liked that last time." While they made arrangements Mark thought about what Dad would say if he remarked suddenly, "Hey, guess what, Dad; we've got this wounded vampire living here. Roger brings home victims so the vampire can drink their blood, and he charges admission for people to watch." A new spectator sport, hot dog. Dad would say a long silence, and then he'd say, Go see Dr. Stimme, I knew it was a mistake for you to stop talking to him, but your mother never liked him because he was too impartial.

Dad said, "How's Roger?"

"He's okay. Busy."

"Mark, don't let so much time go by again without a phone call, okay?"

Mark said good-bye and hung up. Then he put the Skytown plans aside and wandered down the hallway in his stocking feet to Dr. Weyland.

"Are you hungry?" he said.

"Shouldn't you wait with my food until you hear from Uncle Roger?"

Mark lingered. "I'm sorry," he said finally. "About Roger bringing people here."

Dr. Weyland regarded him, chin on hand. "As a performance, it has its unpleasant side; they stand at the gate staring like lions observing their appointed Christian. But fresh nourishment is welcome, and eating in public is common enough."

Mark should have been relieved to see him in this calm mood instead of panicky and full of wild or bitter talk. Yet he found himself resenting the detached tone. Nobody could be that cool about those degrading exhibitions.

"It isn't just eating to the ones who come here. They make it dirty."

"That, as people say nowadays, is their problem."

"I saw you the first time," Mark accused. "You didn't want to.

You knew it was rotten—those people staring . . ."

"Have you ever seen a mob at work?" asked Dr. Weyland. "You would be amazed to learn how many bits of a living body can be detached with the help of a knife, or even teeth and nails, so that people can carry away souvenirs of a memorable event. In these close quarters, five or six people comprise a mob, and I . . . was and remain outside the boundaries of morality. At first I was afraid of what they might do, seeing me at my food. But having you here helps. There are things they would like to do and see in addition to the central attraction, but they refrain from suggesting the worst of them before a child."

The vampire's thoughtful, heavy-lidded gaze at that moment made him seem impossibly ancient.

"At least," he added pensively, "we seem to be past the danger that Roger might simply turn me over to the Central Park Zoo."

"Would that be so bad?" Mark asked cautiously. "If there were somebody—maybe a scientist from the museum—instead of, well, Roger. And Alan Reese."

After a moment Dr. Weyland said softly, "Being forced to grow from a child's faith to an adult's realism so quickly must be painful for you. I appreciate your having given some thought to an alternative to May Eve. However, I must assure you that scientists would be no improvement, though they would be more systematic at first than Reese, who is steered by his lust for power. Men of science would soon learn the easy answers—that my name comes from a tombstone in a New England churchyard, the original bearer having died age seven; that the accomplishments of my career under that name can be sorted into those I achieved and those I fabricated in spite of the very great obstacles placed in my path by computerized record-keeping systems; also perhaps that I have in the past killed for food or to keep my nature secret, since those are recurrent necessities of my existence. All very thrilling, no doubt—unprecedented, marvelous, the makings of the best-seller Roger would like to write.

"But the inner secret, the secret of staying alive long after such curious men are dead dust, I can yield in only one way because I don't know that secret myself. Eventually they would lose patience and cut me apart to see whether they might find the answer in my body—in the brain, the heart, the gut, the bones. Science would be as cruel as the mob. The only kindness is freedom."

"Okay, no scientists," Mark said fiercely. "Forget I said anything. Just leave me alone. You said you wouldn't ask me for help again!"

"I ask," said Dr. Weyland in that same low voice, "because I am desperate."

Mark's heart stamped in his ribs. He looked at his watch. "It's four o'clock, time for your meal."

He was at the refrigerator when the phone rang. It was Roger: "Don't feed him."

Alan Reese came that night. He arrived late, when Roger's preliminary remarks "for our newcomers" were over and everyone had moved into the hallway outside Dr. Weyland's cell. Mark was watching uneasily from his doorway. He tried to shrink back out of sight so that Reese wouldn't notice him.

He hated, really hated, that round, self-satisfied face, those quick, calculating, greedy blue eyes. Without his briefcase of magical paraphernalia and dressed in a windbreaker, the man didn't look dangerous. The crowd parted deferentially to let him through to the front, and then people pressed closer behind him in anticipation of something special now that he had come. Roger, unlocking the gate, broke off in the midst of a comment that Mark couldn't hear.

Reese took command without raising his voice. He said in a stern, level tone, "Those of you who see in this cell only a freak do not belong here. You are all confronting a lesson in the depths that lie behind the surface of every 'reality' of your daily lives. Think about this: you look into this room and you see a creature of human appearance. He looks back—and sees you with the immense contempt and cruel appetite of an immortal who feeds his endless life on your tiny lives.

"Fortunately, there are those of us who are experienced and strong enough to render him tractable . . ."

Mark slipped out. He walked up and down Broadway, guilty at having abandoned the vampire to whatever games Reese had in mind for tonight, furious that Dr. Weyland had saddled him somehow with a feeling of responsibility. Wesley said the vampire was Roger's project, and he was right. Roger was responsible.

Anyway, Dr. Weyland wasn't even human, really, so how could he be sure what people were like, what they would or would not do to him?

When Mark returned a few people were hanging around outside talking, doubtless waiting for Reese, who was in the living room with Roger: ". . . from the Coast, influential contacts in the occult world. The arrangements for filming the special Sabbat on May Eve . . ."

Ducking down the hall and into his own bedroom, Mark listened for Reese's departure. When at last the front door shut and the locks turned, he let out a breath he seemed to have been holding for hours.

Roger looked in. "Hey, where'd you go? You should have stayed. Alan put on a great show. He's pretty pushy, likes to take over, but he does have this fantastic sense of drama. He's been building up the vampire, whetting people's appetites for the main event."

"I think Reese is a power freak," Mark mumbled. He sat on his bed hugging his knees, not meeting Roger's eyes. "He's like kids who like to cut up live little animals, you know? Only he calls it a 'rite.' He could do whatever he wanted and nobody could stop him. His hands could rip you up alive while he was explaining to you in all kinds of big words how your ghost needs its freedom so he's really doing you a favor."

"You read too much crappy fiction," Roger said sharply. "Nothing bad happened to the vampire tonight while you were gone; nothing awful is going to happen, either."

Across the hallway, Dr. Weyland avoided Mark's gaze. The vampire seemed indifferent, remote, but there were stains of fatigue under his eyes, and his shoulders were slumped as if after great tension.

"I think he's scared," Mark said.

"Nobody's scared but you," snapped Roger. "Everybody else knows—even the vampire himself, you can bet on it—everybody else knows it's all just great theater we're doing here, that's all." His voice softened. "Come on Markie, relax. Good night, now."

Mark lay huddled under his blankets thinking about Dr. Weyland. He knew how it felt to pretend composure and confidence in a situation where you were at the mercy of other people. It felt horrible.

◇◇◇

Roger brought home a ponytailed young man in ragged cut-offs and a Pakistani cotton shirt. Mark was in bed when they appeared in his doorway. Roger, behind the blond stranger, flicked on the light.

The blond started to turn to Roger, saying, "The kid keeps your stash for you?'

Roger grabbed him around the neck. The blond looked surprised and reached up, but then his eyes rolled back and he collapsed. Roger caught him and reeled against the doorjamb, swearing breathlessly. "Shit, ow, come on, Mark, give me a hand!"

Dazed and squinting, Mark got out of bed and went to help lower the unconscious stranger to the floor. Roger, squatting, began rolling up one sleeve of the Pakistani shirt.

"What did you do? What's the matter with him?" Mark said.

"I knocked him out a little, that's all. He's dinner for our guest. No audience tonight. This is a sort of a present." Roger lowered his voice. "Alan says no more feeding until May Eve."

"But, Roger, that's a week away!"

"Animals can live a month on just water. All you have to do is make sure he has plenty of water to drink. It's no big deal, you know, just a sort of fasting, purifying for the ceremony. Shit." Roger gave up and ripped the cotton to expose the blond's slack arm up to the shoulder. He began dragging him across the hallway, calling, "Feeding time! Come and get him before he gets cold."

He tucked the blond's flopping arm between the bars. Dr. Weyland got up and came over to the gate. He took hold of the bars with both hands and lowered himself over the offering. After a moment, Roger reached between the bars and pushed at the vampire's head so that the light fell on his lips, sealed to the tan skin of the stranger's inner elbow.

Mark whispered, "Don't, Roger."

"Why not? I can't see well enough. When you put on a show you never get a good look at it yourself, and tonight's—" Roger stopped short of saying "the last time." He laughed a little, shivering. "I'm almost tempted to give him a drink myself, it looks so—God, look at that. His eyes are open."

There was a pale glimmer under Dr. Weyland's lowered lids.

The blond man gave a sudden start and a breathy moan, and a sort of shudder ran along his limbs.

"Christ, he's waking up!" said Roger frantically, and he pressed beside the man's windpipe with his fingertips. The blond subsided once more into gape-mouthed slackness, his long hair spread like a halo around his head on the floor.

"What did you do to him?" Mark croaked.

"If you press right there, you can cut off the blood supply to the brain and put a person out. There's another place in the armpit. It's for handling drowning people so they don't drag you down with them; I learned it that summer in lifesaving class. They don't teach it anymore. It's too dangerous—You could turn a guy into a vegetable if you kept up the pressure too long." Roger tugged at the vampire's hair. "Greedy tonight, isn't he. Come on, that's enough—leave the kid some roses in his cheeks."

While Roger was out depositing the young man in the park, Mark heard gagging sounds form the vampire's cell. Dr. Weyland was in his bathroom being sick. Mark stood at the gate, scared to go in. Suppose it was a trick?

"What is it?" he called. "What's the matter?"

Dr. Weyland panted, "Something in the blood . . . bad blood . . ."

When Roger came back Mark hurried to tell him. Dr. Weyland was still in the bathroom. They could hear his hard, strained breathing.

"That guy must have been a pill-popper or something," Roger muttered. "He told me he was just looking for some good grass. Maybe he was really sick."

"What about Dr. Weyland?" Mark said. "That's all he's had to eat today, and he's throwing everything up."

"There's nothing I can do about it—I took the last package of blood from the fridge with me and dumped it; it was spoiled anyway. Listen, it won't kill him to start fasting a day early."

Next afternoon Roger called from one of the shops: "Mark. Listen. Alan just called. There's an item in the paper about a college student found dead this morning in Riverside Park . . . guess who. That greedy monster you're so worried about took too much. You might give that some thought. Alan wants me to come over—more complicated arrangements for May Eve. I'll see you later."

Mark took his work and a camp chair out into the yard. He couldn't concentrate. Inevitably, he went down the hall.

The vampire sat on the cot with his back against the wall, doing nothing.

"That guy died," Mark said.

He got no reply. Dr. Weyland's shirt looked rumpled. It was buttoned wrong so that the collar stuck up on one side. His gaze was flat and unfocused. A vein stood in his temple like a smear of ink.

"You're like a wild animal," Mark continued. "You hear like a fox, don't you—everything we say around here. You heard Roger say Alan doesn't want him to bring any more people for you, so you tanked up while you had the chance."

"Yes," Dr. Weyland said, "against hunger. I drank what I could while I could, even though I tasted some impurity. I had to eat, I had to try. I protect myself as best I can, as might also be said of you."

His sudden glance seemed to pierce right through Mark. "But I had no profit of it, and I am hungry now; truly hungry, bitterly hungry, with a hunger you know nothing about and never can. Reese, who has his own appetite, guesses. He means to use my hunger to break me to my role in his performance.

"Your uncle was right, you should have stayed the other night to see Reese display the antagonist he means to subdue. In reality I can give Reese nothing—but he can take from me. He 'builds me up,' as Roger put it, in order to stand higher himself when he has cast me down. He presents me as some mystical and powerful being which he alone, the leader, the master, can conquer and destroy." His knuckles whitened where he gripped the side of the cot. "Do you hear, do you understand? Let me out or Reese and his people will kill me."

"Stop saying that! Roger—"

"Stop dodging, face the truth! Roger can't help now even if he wants to. He consoles himself for his loss of control with thoughts of how rich he'll become from Reese's enterprise. Against that the slaughter of a mere animal, an investment made on a whim, weighs very little. Have you noticed, Roger never refers to or addresses me by name? He is preparing himself to be indifferent to my death."

Mark struck the bars with his fist. "Shut up. Roger's not a coward, he'd never let anybody get killed! You're the killer, and you're a dirty liar, you'd say anything to turn me against Roger so I'd let you go! You'd do anything, you freak, you murderer!"

"And you," replied the vampire with weary bitterness, "are clearly Roger's kin. He makes his preparations and you make yours. At the level of name-calling there's nothing can be said or done. Go tend to your school work." He closed his eyes.

Mark turned away. "Old liar," he whispered furiously to himself. "Murdering old lying freak!"

⟨⟨⟩⟩

The weather turned warmer. Mark spent as much time away from Roger's as he could, sitting through foolish movies, wandering blankly down quiet museum halls. Neither his school assignments nor Skytown could hold his attention even when he took all his papers to the library and tried to work there. Once he fell asleep on the carpeting in the muted glow of the gem exhibit at the museum. A noisy class of children came in and woke him. He left and found himself walking uptown toward his mother's: running away.

He could no longer remember the college student's face. The young man's death seemed to him now like . . . like a kid getting his arm pulled off by a bear at the zoo, except of course he hadn't stuck his own arm through the bars to the bear. Roger had done that for the man, literally. Alan Reese had sort of done it, too, through Roger. Sometimes Mark scarcely believed it had really happened. He hadn't seen the student die; maybe it was a mistake, maybe the newspapers had gotten the facts wrong or exaggerated for some reason, or maybe Reese had lied to Roger.

All that was taking Mark's mind off what mattered now; the possibilities of Reese's Great Sabbat on May Eve.

His thoughts veered away in a panic. What was he supposed to do, go to the police station and bring the cops back to Roger's? That might stop Reese, but it would get Roger into a lot of trouble, and Dr. Weyland too once people knew what he was. Or should he stay around in case Dr. Weyland was right about a kid's presence being a restraint? Suppose being there didn't help, how was Mark supposed to stand it, watching Reese do . . . whatever he was going to do? Or should he let the vampire loose on the city to save him from Alan Reese?

Mark was only a kid, how could he take it on himself to do those things? He told himself that none of this craziness was his own fault. Remember what the school psychologist had said about the divorce: Not everything is about you, grown-up people are responsible for their own lives. And Dr. Stimme had said, You are not in charge of things that you have no power to change. Though sometimes you can be a good influence . . .

Mark turned and trudged back toward Roger's.

Roger was away all day and for several evenings, saying that he had to consult with some people about maybe opening a new store on the East Side, or complaining that with May Eve coming up he had to be at Reese's beck and call all the time over the details. Mark thought Roger was just not comfortable around the apartment these days.

So it was Mark, not Roger, who watched the vampire starve. Dr. Weyland spent his days huddled over, hugging his hunger, each breath a shaking, exhausted hiss of pain. It was Mark, not Roger, who came home Tuesday to find the water pitcher knocked over. He couldn't tell whether Dr. Weyland had drunk first and dropped the pitcher afterward, or dropped it first and had to lap up the spilled water like a dog. After Tuesday, Mark laid out a row of filled plastic cups each morning so that the weakened vampire wouldn't have to lift and pour from the heavy pitcher.

It's an act, he told himself. He fakes being so hungry just to get to me.

But he didn't believe it. The vampire seemed curled around his suffering, holding it private to himself—as private as anything could be, when anyone might come and look through the bars into his tiny cell.

◇◇◇

On Wednesday evening Mark went to the ball game with his father. He longed for a shared pleasure that would bring him close enough to his dad to—maybe—share the nightmare that waited back at Roger's

The sharing didn't happen. He wasn't allowed to like the game itself for the speed and grace of the players, the wonderful way they leaped up with everything they had. What his father savored was the violence.

He shouted and sweated, and he pounded on Mark's shoulder to drive home to him every ecstatic moment of impact. Mark felt those heavy hands trying to pummel him into some kind of fellowship of force. It was Dad's idea of closeness to a teenage son.

Dad couldn't help it; he had hitter's hands, hands like Alan Reese's.

On the way back to Roger's his father said, "Is there anything you need, Mark? Anything I can do for you? Just say the word."

Sure. "Everything's cool, Dad."

Roger was out, as usual now. When Mark let himself in, he found that the vampire had worked free one of the legs of the cot. The length of pale wood lay by the gate, battered and splintered from his efforts to beat open the gate lock with it.

Dr. Weyland himself sat cramped against the wall, gasping. One of his slippers had been kicked off across the room.

Mark said, "Drink some water, maybe you'll feel better." He got no response.

An hour later Dr. Weyland had not moved, and Roger was still not back.

Mark dialed Wesley's number. Since the blood deliveries had ended, Wesley hadn't come around.

"Wesley, please come over. You've got to help." To his horror he heard a catch in his voice and stopped to gulp down a big breath and steady himself. "It's hurting him really badly, Wesley. Please bring some blood. I'll pay for it myself. Roger won't ever know."

There was a pause. Then Wesley said, "He'd find out. And I don't want to get mixed up with Alan Reese. The vampire's just putting you on, anyhow, trying to soften you up so you'll spring him. You watch out for him."

"I think he's dying, Wesley."

"Look, he's Roger's baby, I told you. Go home, walk out of it. Don't let this thing get to you, Markie. Go on back to your mother's."

"Can you give me Bobbie's phone number?" Carol Kelly had paid for the Housman paper. Mark thought maybe he could bribe Bobbie to help.

Bobbie was home. In a sleepy voice she said Alan Reese was mad about her getting Julie into the vampire deal. He'd put a heavy curse on her so that she was sick. Julie? Julie was smart, she'd taken off for California, out of range of Alan's bad magic. It was too bad about the vampire—if she wasn't so sick, Bobbie said kindly, she would come over and let him do it, you know; you could really groove on that, it was like some dreamy kind of kiss . . . Had Mark tried talking to Wesley?

He sat by the phone and gnawed at his nails. Tomorrow night was May Eve. He mixed a batch of sweet lemonade and put it in the cups for the vampire. It was all he could think of to do.

◊◊◊

On the morning of the last day Mark was too nervous to eat his cereal. He stared at Roger across the kitchen table, hoping he would see some kind of good sign in Roger's face, some promise that tonight things would go all right. Maybe Dr. Weyland was wrong about Roger.

"You'll be late for school," Roger said, poking at the runny yellow of his breakfast egg with his fork.

"I don't want to go today."

Roger smiled brilliantly. "Big night tonight, right. Okay, don't worry, I'll se that you're all squared away with the school for today."

"I think he's dying, Roger," Mark said. "I'm scared he'll die if we don't feed him something."

"What, feed him and ruin all his conditioning?" Roger got up, dabbing at his chin with his napkin. "Forget it, Markie. Reese said absolutely do not feed the animal, and we're going along with his arrangements. He has the whole thing under control. The man may be an egomaniac, but he does see that things get done right, and this is a show that has to be done right.

"Did I tell you? Alan's invited some hotshots from out of town for tonight. He's so pleased with himself over it that he's picking them up himself at the airport. Then he wants to make the preparations with everybody at his place. I'll be coming back ahead of the others to set up some things he hasn't even told me yet. The performance isn't really due to begin here before nine o'clock. So find yourself something to keep you busy till after dinner, and leave the vampire show to Reese."

Roger himself spent the morning padding about the apartment in his bathrobe neatening up, in a state of jittery cheerfulness that Mark couldn't bear. Near noon there were phone calls from two of the shops and Roger had to go out.

The apartment was no more tolerable with Roger gone than it had been before. It seemed to be empty of all but Dr. Weyland's merciless appetite and the almost palpable agony of Dr. Weyland's fear. Overhearing the breakfast conversation as he overheard everything Dr. Weyland would know the schedule now, which must make the waiting more terrible, the hunger more keen.

Mark couldn't go down the hall. He felt like an intruder in the apartment. He walked slowly to the public library and sat staring into space a long time, a book uselessly open on the table in front of him. He wandered in the park. Around midafternoon he returned to Roger's.

Dr. Weyland did not seem to have moved at all since morning. He lay silent as death on the collapsed cot, his long body bent in sharp angles like a snapped stick, knees and forehead pressed to the wall.

Mark sat down wearily in his own bedroom, trying not to think ahead to the night.

The Land of Lost Content   211

A sound woke him in his chair, a horn blaring outside. Even without looking at his watch he could tell that hours had passed. The light had changed, dusk was coming on.

Dr. Weyland had moved at last. He sat huddled in a corner of his room, knees raised, head down and buried in his folded arms. Mark could see a tremor in his shoulders and in the taut line of his neck. His left sleeve was torn, pulled back to hang from the thin bicep, above the crook of the elbow where he had his face pressed, where his mouth was tight against the tender inside of the arm with the raised blue veins—from which he was sucking—drinking—

"Don't, don't do that!" the boy shrilled. Into his mind flashed the image of a trapped coyote in the museum film, chewing off its own foot to escape the steel jaws and death by thirst. He saw the mangled limb, clotted blood and bone—

He flew down the hallway for the key, rushed back, fumbled it into the lock with sweaty, shaking fingers. He lunged at Weyland, weeping, and with frantic strength beat his arms down.

There was a dew of blood on Weyland's lips, a red smear on one seamed cheek. His eyes were blank slits in dark sockets. Mark swallowed nausea and, kneeling, pressed his own arm against the bloody mouth. Warm breath flared onto his shrinking skin.

All in one motion, like being hurled down by an ocean tide, he was seized and pinned breathless to the floor. There came a faint sting and a surging sensation in his arm, and then a growing lightness in all his limbs.

Eyes tight shut, he cried, "Don't kill me, please don't kill me, oh please don't, please!" He was borne under, his head full of the wet sound of the vampire swallowing. On a rush of terror he screamed, "Oh, Mom help!" and beat wildly at Weyland with his free hand. Dark spots spattered his vision.

Silence. With great effort he opened his eyes. He lay alone on the floor of the cell. The gate was open.

After a long, blank time he noticed sounds of locks clicking. Roger called him. He could find no strength to answer. Roger started down the hall, still calling. Then his voice ceased uncertainly, his footsteps paused, retreated, returned more softly. Turning his head, Mark could see Roger hovering outside the gate, carrying the length of lead pipe in his hand.

"Look out," Mark said. Only no sound came out of him.

"Mark?" Roger whispered. "Oh, my God—"

A shadow glided from the doorway of Mark's bedroom and a hand reached out and closed on Roger's throat. The lead pipe thumped to the floor. As Roger folded the vampire caught him, swayed, slid down against the wall, holding him.

Mark struggled to sit up.

In the hallway Weyland sat cross-legged. He had pulled Roger's upper body into his lap and wrapped the lean arms around Roger so that Roger's arms were caught to his sides. The striped blue shirt that Roger wore was torn open down the front. Roger's head hung back nearly to the floor.

Weyland leaned deeply over him, chest to chest, mouth pressed up under Roger's jaw, lips fastened to Roger's throat. He was drinking not in some blissful dream but fiercely, ravenously, breathing in long, grateful gasps between swallows.

Roger's eyelids fluttered. Roger emitted one faint cry and turned his head painfully, flinching from the vampire's grip. The heels of Roger's shoes scratched feebly at the floor.

Weyland pressed closer, working his jaw to shift and improve his hold, and he drank and drank. Now Roger's legs sagged limp as ropes. Paralyzed with weakness and horror, Mark kept thinking, This is Roger this is happening to, my Uncle Roger, this is Roger.

At last the vampire raised his head and met Mark's gaze. In Weyland's haggard face the eyes glittered keen as stars. He got up abruptly, dumping Roger out of his lap like a brightly wrapped parcel from which the gift has been removed.

"You killed him," Mark moaned.

"Not yet." Weyland had the lead pipe in his hands. As Mark lurched to all fours, trying to rise, he saw Weyland cock the pipe like a golfer prepared to swing.

"No!" he cried.

"Why not?" The vampire paused, looking at Mark.

Seconds seemed to spin out endlessly. Weyland had not moved. Now he straightened and said, "Very well. You've bought the right. It was as good as paying money." He put aside the pipe and stepped over Roger and into the tiny room. His long hands descended and gripped Mark's shoulders. Mark tried to twist free, panic rising. He had no strength, and the vampire was astonishingly, appallingly strong.

"Please," Mark wailed.

"Get up." The lean fingers dragged him to his feet. "Where does that bedding go? The cot? Put the pillows and blanket away." Mark moved sluggishly to obey, feeling dazed and drowned. Weyland set about gathering up the cot and brought it out to be stowed at the back of the hall closet. "Broom and dustpan," he said. "Shopping bag. Paper towels."

They cleaned up. In the cramped bathroom every surface was wiped down. Toilet articles, used paper towels and Weyland's dirty laundry went into the shopping bag. Weyland swept. He carried out the dustpan, stepping over Roger's inert form as if over a log of wood.

Stumbling in his wake, Mark stopped there, staring at Roger, who lay sprawled face down on the floor.

Weyland said, "No need to worry about your excitable uncle. He'll live." He pulled the gate shut behind him, and the lock clicked on the empty room.

Mark trailed after Weyland up the hall and through the dark living room. In the brightness of Roger's bedroom, the vampire flung open the wall-length closets. Mark sat slumped on the bed while Weyland chose a short-sleeved shirt of cream white polyester. The rest were clearly impossible: Roger's clothes were sized to a smaller frame.

Weyland glanced at the bedside clock and said. "Wait."

Blearily Mark saw that the hands showed eight o'clock. Weyland had time to freshen up.

After a while he emerged from the bathroom looking very much the man of his book-jacket photograph. Shaven, washed, brushed, the rumpled slacks neatened by one of Roger's belts, he was imposing enough so that the bedroom slippers on his feet were scarcely noticeable.

"My things," he said. "Fetch them."

Mark got the paper bag and gave back the knife. Cards, pencils, even paper clips, Dr. Weyland slipped it all into his trouser pockets. "That seems to be everything I came with, minus a few coins." Then he said, "Roger keeps money in the house."

Mark was only distantly sorry for Roger now. He was absorbed in getting his exhausted body to move. He went into the kitchen, opened the oven door, and pulled out the money box.

Dr. Weyland took all the bills and change without counting. "Put the box back. If there's anything that you want from your room, go and get it."

Mark thought of the plans for Skytown, the shelves of books, the comfortable messiness, all empty of comfort now. He thought of Roger lying in the hall, and he had an impulse to go and help, to do something—but what he could do for Roger was already done. Anything more would be up to somebody else.

He shook his head.

"Come, then. Quickly."

It was cool outside. Dr. Weyland was slightly unsteady in mounting the steps of the areaway. On the sidewalk he stopped. "God damn it. My eyeglasses."

Mark sat on the steps with the shopping bag and waited for him. Trying to run away would be stupid: he could barely walk.

The long shadow fell across him. "Ah," Dr. Weyland breathed, head up, tasting the breeze from the west. "The river."

They walked toward Riverside Drive. Dr. Weyland's hand rested firmly on Mark's shoulder.

"You were only pretending," Mark said.

"Not at all," snapped Dr. Weyland. "I pretended nothing; no stoicism, no defiance, nothing." Broodingly he added, "I left the truth of my condition open to you, in hopes of saving my life—but I was sure I had lost, because of that one who died. I was sure. You would budge only so far, and I needed to push you so much further."

They started over the damp grass toward the promenade beside the water. River-smell enveloped them.

"I thought you were dying," Mark whispered.

"I was," came the low reply.

"That was real, when you drank—your own—" Mark shuddered.

"Oh yes, that was real. The great temptation has always been just that. It tasted good; you can't know how good it was." The hand on Mark's shoulder tightened for an instant. "If you hadn't stopped me . . . I was so hungry . . ."

They crossed the pavement and stopped at the rail. There was a rustle of rats on the wet rocks below. Dr. Weyland turned to watch a trio of evening joggers patter past.

He said, "Your young blood restored me. Even so, I could only manage Roger because of his excellent lesson in producing unconsciousness with the pressure of a finger. There's always something new to learn. Needless to say, I never studied lifesaving."

Mark looked across at Jersey, spangles of light above the black, oily water. Tears welled in his eyes, and his breath broke into sobs.

"Stop snuffling," Dr. Weyland said irritably. "You'll attract attention. There's nothing the matter with you. As Roger correctly deduced, I am not contagious. I did you no serious damage and Roger will recover, thanks to you. You saved his life even before you spoke up for him, just by dulling the edge of my need."

All Mark's control was gone. His whole body shook with the force of his crying.

The vampire added sharply, "I told you to stop that. You have work to do. You must use your fertile imagination to design a story for your mother, something to explain your sudden return from Roger's and whatever else may come out of all this. You did Skytown; you can do this."

"You're lying," Mark blubbered. "You're just going to throw me in the river anyway, so I can't tell."

There was a brief, considering pause. "No," said Dr. Weyland at last. "Corpses lead to questions. Besides, killing you would make no difference. Many people know about me now, although without my physical presence the authorities are unlikely to believe any gossip they may hear.

"You must simply go back to your parents, play the innocent, let them think Roger tried to turn you on or whatever other fiction will serve. You live in a culture that treats childhood as a disadvantage; make a strength of that weakness. Sulk, whine, run away a few times if they press you. You won't be so foolish as to speak of me at all, unless you wish to spend the remainder of your adolescence in analysis."

Two women came by, walking their dogs. One of the women gave Dr. Weyland a tiny smile in passing. Mark looked up at him, saw the predatory profile in the lamplight, the intent eyes thoughtfully following the women. He felt tired, chilly, abandoned. Furtively, he wiped his nose on the front of this shirt.

His arm ached faintly where the vampire had drunk. To have someone spring on you like a tiger and suck you blood with savage and single-minded intensity—how could anybody imagine that was sexy? He would never forget that moment's blinding fear. If sex was like that, they could keep it.

The two of them were alone for the moment. Dr. Weyland turned and slung the shopping bag into the river. It bobbed, swirled round slowly twice, and sank.

Mark said, "Are you going to go after Alan Reese?"

"No. When he is dead, I will still be alive. That suffices."

"What are you going to do?"

"Begin again," Dr. Weyland said grimly. "Unless I can invent some tale to keep my present identity alive and useful. I have my own imagining to do, and then work, a great deal of work. How do you get back to your mother's from here?"

There came no inner recoil. The terrors of home were gone, burned away by the touch of something ancient and wild beyond the concerns of this city. "I take the subway," Mark said.

"Have you money?"

He felt in his jeans pocket. He had Carol Kelly's payment. "Yes."

"Of course—the school scribe has his earnings, and a good thing; I need all that I have. My God, even this rank, filthy river smells wonderful after that foul cupboard of a room!"

He was looking past Mark up the river, turning to sweep his gaze along the bridge to the north and down the lamplit mouths of the streets along the Drive. There was an eagerness to the lift of his head that made Mark think he might simply stride off without another word, so clear was Dr. Weyland's impatience to be away, once more free and secret among men.

Mark shivered, flooded with relief and desolation.

Dr. Weyland looked down at him, frowning slightly as if his

thoughts had already left Mark behind. "Come on," he said.
  They started back across the narrow park.
  "Where are we going?"
  "I am walking you to the subway," the vampire said.

Suzy McKee Charnas is the author of *The Vampire Tapestry, Motherlines, Walk to the End of the World, Dorothea Dreams,* and *The Furies.* She has also written four novels for young adults: *The Golden Thread, The Silver Glove, The Bronze King,* and *The Kingdom of Kevin Malone.*

A young girl may yearn for the romantic vampire—
and never recognize him when he's at her side!

Seat Partner

BY CHELSEA QUINN YARBRO

illian had lucked out. TWA had too many passengers in coach, and so she—she almost giggled as she came down the aisle of the huge plane—had to ride in first class, jeans, muslin shirt and all. She found her seat by the window and shoved her camera bag that doubled as a purse under the seat, then dropped gratefully into the wide, padded chair. This was great, she thought as she fastened her seat belt, and reached down to pull a couple of paperback books out of her bag, then settled back to read.

She had just got into the story when a voice spoke beside her. "Excuse me."

Marking her place with her finger, she looked up and smiled a little at what she saw. The man was short, dark-haired, and dark-eyed, with the look of early middle age about him. His clothes were very simple and obviously expensive. His black three-piece suit was a wool and silk blend, superbly tailored to his trim but stocky figure. His shirt was lustrous white silk against a black silk tie, just the right width, and secured with an unadorned ruby stickpin. Jillian noticed with amusement that his shoes were thick-soled and slightly heeled. "Excuse me," he said again in his pleasant, melodic voice. "I believe that is my seat."

Jillian's face sank. This couldn't happen, not after she had been so lucky. She fumbled in her pockets for her boarding pass. "This is the pass they gave me," she said, holding it out to him.

A stewardess, attracted by the confusion, approached them. "Good morning. Is there some trouble?"

The man turned an attractive, wry smile on the woman. "A minor confusion. Your excellent computer seems to have assigned us the same seat."

The stewardess reached for boarding passes, frowning as she read them. "Just a moment. I'm sure we can correct this." She turned away as she spoke and went toward the galley.

"I'm sorry," Jillian said apologetically. Now that she had had a moment to watch the man, she found him quite awesome.

"No, no. Don't be foolish. Machines are far from perfect, after all. And first class is not wholly filled. We will be accommodated easily." He looked down at her with steady, compelling eyes. "I have no wish to impose on you."

Jillian waved her hands to show that there was no imposition and almost lost the book she was holding. She blushed and felt abashed—here she was, almost twenty-two, and *blushing* for chrissake. A swift glance upward through her fair lashes showed her that the stranger was amused. She wanted to give him a sharp, sophisticated retort, but there was something daunting in his expression, and she kept quiet.

A moment later the stewardess. "I'm sorry, sir," she said to the man. "Apparently there was some difficulty with the print-out on the card. Yours is seat B, on the aisle. If this is inconvenient . . ."

"No, not in the least. He took the boarding passes from her and handed one to Jillian. "I thank you for your trouble. You were most kind." Again the smile flashed and he bent to put his slim black leather case under the seat, saying to Jillian, "I am, in a way, grateful you have the window."

"Oh," Jillian said, surprised, "don't you like the window?"

"I'm afraid that I am not comfortable flying. It is difficult to be so far from the ground." He seated himself and fastened the seat belt.

Jillian started to open her book again, but said, "I think flying's exciting."

"Have you flown often?" the man asked somewhat absent-mindedly.

"Well, not very often," she confided. "Never this far before. I flew to Denver a couple of times to visit my father, and once to Florida, but I haven't been to Europe before."

"And you've spent the summer in Italy? What did you think of it?" He seemed to enjoy her excitement.

"Oh, Italy's okay, but I did a lot of traveling. I decided to fly in and out of Milan because it seemed a good place to start from." She folded down the corner of her page and set the book aside for the moment. "I liked Florence a lot. You've been there, I guess."

"Not for some time. But I had friends there, once." He folded small, beautiful hands over the seat belt. "What else did you see? Paris? Vienna? Rome?"

"Not Paris or Rome. I went to Vienna, though, and Prague and Budapest and Belgrade and Bucharest and Sofia, Sarajevo, Zagreb, Trieste, and Venice." She recited the major cities of her itinerary with a glow of enthusiasm. It had been such a wonderful summer, going through those ancient, ancient countries.

The man's fine brows lifted. "Not the usual student trek, is it? Hungary, Rumania, Bulgaria, Yugoslavia . . . hardly countries one associates with American students."

On the loudspeaker, the stewardess said in three languages that cigarettes must be extinguished and seat belts fastened in preparation for take-off.

Jillian frowned. "Is my being an American student that obvious?"

"Certainly," he said kindly. "Students everywhere have a kind of uniform. Jeans and loose shirts and long, straight blonde hair—oh, most surely, an American, and from the way you pronounce your r's, I would say from the Midwest."

Grudgingly, Jillian said, "Des Moines."

"That is in Iowa, is it not?"

Their conversation was interrupted by the sound of engines roaring as the jet started to move away from the terminal.

The stewardess reappeared and gave the customary speech about oxygen masks, flotation pads, and exits in English, French, and Italian. Jillian listened to the talk, trying to appear nonchalant and still feeling the stir of pleasure in flying. The man in the seat beside her closed his eyes.

For five minutes or so they taxied, jockeying for a position on the runway, one of three jets preparing for takeoff. Then there was the fierce, lunging roll as the plane raced into the air. The ground dropped away below them, there was the ear-popping climb and the hideous sound of landing gear retracting, and then the stewardess reminded the passengers that smoking was permitted in specified sections only, that they were free to move about the cabin, and that headsets for the movie would be available shortly, before lunch was served.

Jillian looked out the window and saw Milan growing distant and small. Without being aware of it, she sighed.

"You are sad?" asked the man beside her.

"In a way. I'm glad to be going home, but it was such a wonderful summer."

"And what will you do when you get home?" was his next question.

"Oh, teach, I guess. I've got a job at the junior high school. It's my first . . ." She looked out the window again.

"You don't seem much pleased with your job." There was no criticism in his tone. "If it is not what you wish to do, why do you do it?"

"Well," Jillian said in what she hoped was her most reasonable tone, "I have to do something. I'm not planning to get married or anything . . ." She broke off, thinking of how disappointed her mother had been when she had changed her mind about Harold. But it wouldn't have worked, she said to herself, as she had almost every day since the tenth of April when she had returned his ring.

"I'm intruding," said the man compassionately. "Forgive me."

"It's nothing," Jillian responded, wanting to make light of it. "I was just thinking how high up we are."

"Were you." His dark, enigmatic eyes rested on her a moment. "Perhaps you would like to tell me of some of the things you saw in eastern Europe."

"Well," she said, glad to have something to occupy her thoughts other than Harold. "I wanted to see all those strange places. They were really interesting. I was really amazed at how different everything is."

"Different? How?"

"It's not just the way they look, and everything being old," Jillian said with sudden intensity. "It *feels* different here, like all the things they pooh-pooh in schools are real. When I went to Castle Bran, I mean, I really understood how there could be legends about the place. It made sense that people would believe them."

The man's interest increased. "Castle Bran?"

"Yes, you know, it's very famous. It's the castle that Bram Stoker used as a model for Castle Dracula, at least that's what most of the experts are saying now. I wanted to go to the ruins of the real Castle Dracula, but the weather was bad, so I didn't."

"Strange. But why are you interested in such places? Surely the resistance to the Turkish invasions is not your area of study."

"Oh, no," she laughed a little embarrassed. "I like vampires. Books, movies, anything."

"Indeed." There was an ironic note in his voice now.

"Well, they might not be great art, but they're wonderful to . . ."

"Fantasize about?" he suggested gently.

Jillian felt herself flush and wished that she hadn't mentioned the subject. "Sometimes." She tilted her chin up. "Lugosi, Lee, all of them, they're just great. I think they're sexy."

The man very nearly chuckled, but managed to preserve a certain gravity that almost infuriated Jillian. "A novel idea," he said after a moment.

"It isn't," she insisted. "I know lots of people who think vampires are sexy."

"American irreverence, do you think?" He shook his head. "There was a time, not so very long ago, when such an avowal would be absolutely heretical."

"That's silly," she said, a little less sure of herself. In her travels, she had come to realize that heresy was not just an obsolete prejudice.

"Hardly silly," the man said in a somber tone. "Men and women and even children died in agony for believing such things. And there are those who think that the practice should be reinstated."

"But it's just superstition," Jillian burst out, inwardly shocked at her reaction. "Nobody today could possibly believe that vampires really exist . . ."

"Are you so certain they do not?" he inquired mildly.

"Well, how could they?" she retorted. "It's absurd."

He favored her with a nod that was more of a bow. "Of course."

Jillian felt the need to pursue the matter a little more. "If there were such things, they would have been found out by now. There'd be good, solid proof."

"Proof? But how could such a thing be proved? As you said yourself, the idea is absurd."

"There ought to be ways to do it." She hadn't considered the matter before, but she felt challenged by the stranger in the seat beside her. "It wouldn't be the premature burial concerns, because that's a different matter entirely."

"Certainly," he agreed. "If legends are right, burial of a vampire is hardly premature."

She decided to overlook his remark. "The trouble is," she said seriously, "the best way would be to get volunteers, and I don't suppose it would be easy to convince any real vampire that he ought to submit himself to scientific study."

"It would be impossible, I should think," her seat partner interjected.

"And how could it be proven, I mean, without destroying the volunteer? I don't suppose there are any real proofs short of putting a stake through their hearts or severing their heads."

"Burning is also a good method," the man said.

"No one, not even a vampire, is going to agree to that. And it wouldn't demonstrate anything at all. Anyone would die of it, whether or not they were vampires." Suddenly she giggled. "Christ, this is weird, sitting up here talking about experimenting on vampires." Actually, she was becoming uncomfortable with the subject and was anxious to speak of something else.

The man seemed to read her thoughts, for he said, "Hardly what one would call profitable speculation."

Jillian had the odd feeling that she should be polite and decided to ask him a few questions. "Is this your first trip to America? You speak wonderful English, but . . ."

"But you know I am a foreigner. Naturally." He paused. "I have been to America, but that was some time ago, and then it was to the capital of Mexico. A strange place, that city built on swamps."

His description of Mexico City startled Jillian a little, because though it was true enough that the city had been built on swamps long ago, it seemed an odd aspect of its history to mention. "Yes," she said, to indicate she was listening.

"This is my first visit to your country. It is disquieting to go to so vast a land, and be so far from home."

The stewardess appeared at his elbow. "Pardon me, Count. We're about to serve cocktails, and if you'd like one . . . ?"

"No, thank you, but perhaps"—he turned to Jillian—"you would do me the honor of letting me buy one for you."

Jillian was torn between her delight at the invitation and the strictures of her youth that had warned against such temptations. Pleasure won. "Oh, please; I'd like a gin and tonic. Tanqueray gin, of you have it."

"Tanqueray and tonic," the stewardess repeated, then turned to the man again. "If you don't want a cocktail, we have an excellent selection of wines . . ."

"Thank you, no. I do not drink wine." With a slight, imperious nod, he dismissed the stewardess.

"She called you Count," Jillian accused him, a delicious thrill running through her. This charming man in black was an aristocrat! She was really looking forward to telling her friends about the flight when she got home. It would be wonderful to say, as casually as she could, "Oh, yes, on the way back, I had this lovely conversation with a European count," and then watch them stare at her.

"A courtesy title, these days," the man said diffidently. "Things have changed much from the time I was born, and now there are few who would respect my claims."

Jillian knew something of the history of Europe and nodded sympathetically. "How unfortunate for you. Does it make you sad to see the changes in your country?" She realized she didn't know which country he was from and wondered how she could ask without seeming rude.

"It is true that my blood is very old, and I have strong ties to my native soil. But there are always changes, and in time, one grows accustomed, one adapts. The alternative is to die."

Never before had Jillian felt the plight of the exiled as she did looking into that civilized, intelligent face. "How terrible! You must get very lonely."

"Occasionally, very lonely," he said in a distant way.

"But surely, you have family . . ." She bit the words off. She had read of some of the bloodier revolutions, where almost every noble house was wiped out. If his was one of them, the mention of it might be inexcusable.

"Oh, yes. I have blood relatives throughout Europe. There are not so many of us as there once were, but a few of us survive." He looked up as the stewardess approached with a small tray with one glass on it. "Ah, your cocktail, I believe." He leaned back as the stewardess handed the drink to Jillian. "Which currency would you prefer?" he asked.

"How would you prefer to pay, sir?" the stewardess responded with a blinding smile.

"Dollars, pounds, or francs. Choose." He pulled a large black wallet from his inner coat pocket.

"Dollars, then. It's one-fifty." She held out her hand for the bill, and thanked him as she took it away to make change.

Jillian lifted the glass, which was slightly frosted, and looked at the clear liquid that had a faint touch of blue in its color. "Well, thanks. To you." She sipped at the cold, surprisingly strong drink.

"You're very kind," he said, an automatic response. "Tell me, he said in another, lighter tone, "what is it you will teach to your junior high school students?"

"English," she said, and almost added, "of course."

"As a language?" the Count asked, plainly startled.

"Not really. We do some grammar, some literature, some creative writing, a lot of reading." As she said it, it sounded so dull, and a little gloom touched her.

"But surely you don't want to spend your life teaching some grammar, some literature, some creative writing, and a lot of reading to disinterested children." He said this gently, kindly, and watched Jillian very closely as she answered.

226

"Sometimes I think I don't know what I want," she said and felt alarmed at her own candor.

"I feel you would rather explore castles in Europe than teach English in Des Moines." He regarded her evenly. "Am I correct?"

"I suppose so," she said slowly and took another sip of her cocktail.

"Then why don't you?"

It was a question she had not dared to ask herself and she was angry at him for asking. He had no right, this unnamed former count in elegant black who watched her with such penetrating dark eyes. He had no right to ask such things of her. She was about to tell him so when he said, "A woman I have long loved very dearly used to think she would not be able to learn everything she wanted to during her life. You must understand, European society has been quite rigid at times. She comes from a distinguished French family, and when I met her, she was nineteen and terrified that she would be forced into the life other women had before she had opportunities to study. Now," he said with a faint, affectionate smile, "she is on a dig, I think it's called, in Iran. She is an accomplished archeologist. You see, she did not allow herself to be limited by the expectations of others."

Jillian listened, ready to fling back sharp answers if he insisted that she turn away from the life she had determined upon. "You changed her mind, I suppose?" She knew she sounded petulant, but she wanted him to know she was displeased.

"Changed her mind, no. It could be said that she changed mine." His eyes glinted with reminiscence. "She is a remarkable woman, my Madelaine." He turned his attention to Jillian once more. "Forgive me. Occasionally I am reminded of . . . our attachment. I did not mean to be rude. Perhaps I meant to suggest that you, like her, should not permit those around you to make decisions for you that are not what you want."

The stewardess returned with headphones for the movie. It was, she explained, a long feature, a French and English venture, shot predominantly in Spain with an international cast. She held out the headsets to Jillian and to the man beside her.

Though Jillian knew it was unmannerly of her to do so, she accepted the headset with a wide smile and said to her seat partner, "I hate to do this, but I've wanted to see this flick all summer long, and I don't know when I'll have the chance again."

She knew by the sardonic light to his smile that he was not fooled, but he said to her, "By all means. I understand that it is most entertaining."

"Headphones for you, Count?" the stewardess asked solicitously.

"I think not, but thank you." He looked toward Jillian. "If you decide that it is truly worthwhile, tell me, and I will call for headsets."

The stewardess nodded and moved away to the next pair of seats.

"You don't mind, do you?" Jillian asked, suddenly conscience-stricken. The Count had bought her a drink and was being very courteous, she thought, but then again, she did not want him to think that she was interested in him.

"No, I don't mind." He glanced down at his leather case under the seat. "Would it disturb you if I do a little work while the film is running?"

Jillian shook her head and put the thin blue plastic leads to the socket on the arm of her seat. "Go ahead."

He had already pulled the case from under the seat and opened it on his lap. There were three thick, leather-bound notebooks in the case, and he pulled the largest of these out, closed the case, and replaced it. He took a pen from one of his coat pockets and pulled down the table from the seat ahead. He gave Jillian a swift, disturbing smile, then bent his head to his work.

Before the film was half over, Jillian was bored. The plot, which she had thought would be exciting, was tedious, and the filming was unimaginative. Most of the actors looked uncomfortable in their nineteenth-century costumes, and the dialogue was so trite that Jillian could not blame the actors for their poor delivery. She longed to be able to take off the headset and get back to reading, but she was afraid that the Count would engage her in conversation again, and for some reason, this prospect unnerved her. He had a knack for drawing her out. Another half-hour and she would have been telling him about Harold and how he had laughed when she said she wanted to get her master's before they married.

Already he had got her to talk about vampires, and she had never done that before, not with a stranger. So she kept her eyes on the little screen and tried to concentrate on the dull extravaganza. Once she caught the count looking at her, amusement in his dark eyes, but then he turned back to the notebook, and she could not be certain whether or not he had sensed her dilemma.

When at last the film ground to a messy, predictable finish, Jillian was anxious to take off the headset. She made a point of reaching for a book before handing the plastic tubing to the stewardess, and shot a quick look at her seat partner.

"If you do not wish to speak to me," he said without turning his attention from the page on which he wrote, "please say so. I will not be offended."

Jillian was grateful and annoyed at once. "I'm just tired. I think I want to read a while."

He nodded and said nothing more.

It was not until they were nearing Kennedy Airport that Jillian dared to talk to her seat partner. She had been reading the same paragraph for almost twenty minutes, and it made no more sense now than the first time she had looked at it. With a sigh she closed the book and bent to put it in her bag.

"We're nearing New York," the Count said. He had put his notebook away some minutes before and had sat back in his seat, gazing at nothing in particular.

"Yes," she said, not certain now if she was glad to be coming home.

"I suppose you'll be flying on to Des Moines."

"In the morning," she said, thinking for the first time that she would have to ask about motels near the airport, because she knew she could not go into Manhattan for the night. Between the taxi fare and the hotel bill, she could not afford that one last splurge.

"But it is only . . ."—he consulted his watch and paused to calculate the difference in time—"six-thirty. You can't mean that you want to sit in a sterile little room with a poor television for company all this evening."

That was, in fact, precisely what she had intended to do, but his description made the prospect sound more gloomy than she had thought it could be. "I guess so."

"Would you be offended if I asked you to let me buy you dinner? This is my first time in this city, in this country, and it will feel less strange to me if you'd be kind enough to give me the pleasure of your company."

If this was a line, Jillian thought, it was one of the very smoothest she had ever heard. And she did want to go into Manhattan, and she very much wanted to spend the evening at a nice restaurant. A man like the Count, she thought, wouldn't be the sort to skimp on a night out. He might, of course, impose conditions later.

"I have no designs on your virginity," he said, with that uncanny insight that had bothered her earlier.

"I'm not a virgin," Jillian snapped, without meaning to.

The seatbelt sign and no smoking signs flashed on, one after another, and the stewardess announced that they had begun their descent for landing.

The Count smiled, the whole force of his dark eyes on her. "Shall we say your virtue, then? I will allow that you are a very desirable, very young woman, and it would delight me to have you as my guest for the evening. Well?"

"You don't even know my name," she said with a smile, her mind already made up.

"It's Jillian Walker," he answered promptly, and added as she stared at him, "It was on the envelope your boarding pass is in."

For a moment, Jillian had been filled with a certain awe, almost a dread, but at this simple explanation, she smiled. A niggling image had risen in her mind, an image developed from her reading and the films she loved. A foreign exiled Count, in black, of aristocratic, almost regal bearing, who had refused wine . . . It was an effort not to laugh. "You know my name, but I don't know yours."

"You may call me Franz, if you like. I am Franz Josef Ragoczy, onetime Count, among other things."

"What's that name again?" something about it was familiar, but she couldn't place it.

"Ragoczy. *Rah*-go-schkee," he repeated. "It's the German version of the Hungarian variant of the name. As I told you, I come from an ancient line." His expression had softened. "It is agreed, then?"

STREETS OF BLOOD

The plane was descending rapidly, and there was that wrenching clunk as the landing gear was lowered. Ahead the sprawl of Kennedy Airport rose up to meet them.

Whatever reservations that were left in Jillian's mind were banished by the warmth in his eyes. If he wanted more than her company, she decided, she would deal with that as it happened. As the plane jounced onto the runway, she grinned at him. "Count, I'd love to have dinner with you."

He took her hand in his and carried it gallantly, ironically, to his lips. "Dinner with me," he echoed her, "dinner with me." There was a secret meaning in the soft words that followed, almost lost in the shrieking of the engines. " I will hold you to that, Jillian Walker. Believe this."

Chelsea Quinn Yarbro is the author of more than fifty novels, including the historical novels The Chronicles of Saint-Germain, which are among the most popular vampire series.